Lord Darcy looked at Chief Jaque.

"Could he have jumped, Chief?"

"Could have. Doesn't make sense, though. Man doesn't commit suicide by jumping through a closed window. Doesn't make sense. A suicide who decides to jump opens the window first. Doesn't just take a flying leap through a pane of glass."

"That's not the point I had in mind," said Dr. Pateley, replacing his glasses carefully. "What if he were trying to get away from something?"

Chief Jaque's eyes widened. "I knew it! Demons!"

To the inheritors of the great Anglo-French Empire Great King Richard the Lionheart created after his miraculous escape at Chaluz seven hundred years ago, magic is as much a tool of everyday life as the steamship or the railroad. But brilliant deductive skills like Lord Darcy's are as rare as ever, and just as vital to the defense of Crown and Country when faced with the myriad threats that —

LORD DARCY INVESTIGATES

№ 2 0 0 0 0 1 2 1 0

Other titles in the *Lord Darcy* series by Randall Garrett
available from Ace Science Fiction & Fantasy:

- MURDER AND MAGIC
- TOO MANY MAGICIANS

Lord Darcy Investigates

RANDALL GARRETT

SF
ace books
A Division of Charter Communications Inc.
A GROSSET & DUNLAP COMPANY
51 Madison Avenue
New York, New York 10010

Table of Contents

DEDICATION

To Jerry Pournelle and James Baen,
who made it possible

A Matter of Gravity

The death of My Lord Jillbert, Count de la Vexin was nothing if not spectacular.

His lordship lived and worked in Castle Gisors, which towers over the town of the same name, the capital of the County of the Vexin in the eastern part of the Duchy of Normandy. The basic structure of the ancient fortress has been there since the Eleventh Century although it has been added to and partly rebuilt since.

De la Vexin had succeeded to the County Seat in 1951, and had governed the Vexin wisely and well. He had a son, a daughter, and a hobby.

It was a combination of all these that killed him.

On the night of April 11, 1974, after attending the Mass of Holy Thursday, My Lord of the Vexin ascended the helical stairway that wound itself around the inside of the Red Tower, followed by two trusted sergeants of the Count's Own Guard—who were, in turn, followed by a four-man squad of ordinary guardsmen.

This was My Lord Count's regular procedure when he went to his *sanctum sanctorum* on the top floor of the Red Tower. When he went up there, eighty feet above the flagstoned courtyard, he wanted no interruptions while he attended to his avocation.

At one minute of ten, he entered his private rooms, leaving his guardsmen outside. No one but himself had been authorized to enter the uppermost room of the Red

Tower in twenty years.

He dropped the heavy bar after locking the door, completely sealing the room.

Only two people saw him alive again, and then only for a matter of seconds.

Across the wide, flagstoned courtyard from the Red Tower stood St. Martin's Hall, a new addition built in the early Sixteenth Century, as its Ricardian style attested. Its great mullioned windows cast a warm, yellowed light on the courtyard outside; the hall was brightly illuminated from within, and would remain so all night, for there was a vigil at the Altar of Repose in the Lady Chapel.

Inside, a small fire crackled in the enormous fireplace —just enough blaze to take the slight chill from the air of a pleasant spring evening. On the mantelpiece, a large clock swung its pendulum as the minute hand moved inexorably upward to mark the hour of ten.

Lord Gisors, the only son of de la Vexin, poured himself another glass of Xerez. Of average height, his blocky, not unhandsome face was almost a younger replica of his father's, except that he had his mother's near-black hair and dark brown eyes instead of the brown-and-blue combination of his father. He turned from the sideboard, still holding the unstoppered decanter. "Care for another, my dear?"

The girl seated in the big easy chair in front of the fireplace smiled. "Please." With her right hand, she held out her glass, while her left brushed the long fair hair back from her brow. *She looks beautiful,* his lordship thought.

Lord Gisors poured, then walked back to the sideboard with the decanter. As he put the glass stopple back in, he began: "You mustn't think badly of My Lord father, Madelaine, even though he is a bit testy at times. He—"

"I know," she interrupted. "I know. He thinks only of

the County. Never of individuals."

Frowning slightly, his lordship came back with his glass and sat down in another easy chair near her. "But he does think of individuals, my love. He must think of every individual in the Vexin—as *I* must when I succeed to the County Seat. He has to take the long view and the broad view, naturally, but he *is* concerned about individuals."

She sipped at her glass of wine, then looked up at him with solemn gray eyes. "Does his concern for individuals include you? Or me? He knows we love each other, but he forbids our marriage, and insists that you marry Lady Evelynne de Saint-Brieuc—in spite of the fact that you do not love her nor she you. Is that concern for the individual or simply the desire to make an advantageous political marriage for you?"

Lord Gisors closed his eyes and held his tongue for a moment. The two of them had been over and over this ground many times; there was nothing new here. He had explained many times that, whereas My Lord the Count could forbid a marriage, he could not force one. Gisors had even reiterated time and again that he could appeal his case for marriage to His Royal Highness of Normandy, and, if that failed, to His Imperial Majesty—but that he would not do so out of deference to his father. His head seemed to ache at the monotony of "time and again."

He had not, of course, mentioned his own plans for marrying Madelaine without all the rigamarole. She might very likely rebel at the notion.

He opened his eyes again. "Be patient, my darling. I can assure you that he will—"

"—Come round to your way of thinking?" she cut in. "Never! The only time the Count de la Vexin will give his consent to our marriage will be when *you* are Count de la Vexin! Your father—"

"*Quiet!*" Lord Gisors said in an imperative undertone. "*My sister.*"

At the far end of the hall, the door to the Lady Chapel had opened and closed. The woman walking toward them with a rather solemn smile on her face was carefully removing her chapel veil as she came down the wide carpeting to the fireplace. She nodded silently to each of them, then said: "Your watch, My Lord brother. Ten to eleven, remember?"

Lord Gisors finished his wine and stood up with a smile. "Of course, My Lady Beverly. '*Can you not spend one hour with me?*' The Gospel according to Matthew." Tomorrow would be the Friday of the Crucifixion; this, the night before, would be symbolically spent in the Garden of Gethsemane with Our Lord. Gisors looked at the clock. It was the last second before ten.

" '*Father, my hour has come,*' St. John—" Gisors began.

The pendulum swung down.

The clock struck the first note.

"*What the devil was that?*" Lord Gisors yelled.

Outside, there had been a horrendous scream.

In the courtyard itself, a minute or so earlier, two militiamen of the Count's Own had been standing near the wall of St. Martin's Hall. One was the man at post, the other the Sergeant-of-the Guard, who was making his evening rounds. They exchanged the usual military courtesies. The guardsman reported the state of his post as being quiet; the sergeant thanked him in the proper military manner. Then he said, with a grin: "It's better doing night duty in April than in March, eh, Jaime?"

Guardsman Jaime grinned back. "At least I'm not freezing my nose off, Sergeant Andray." His eyes shifted upward as he saw a gleam of light from the corner of his eye. "Here comes My Lord Count."

Sergeant Andray turned his head to follow Jaime's gaze. He knew that Jaime did not mean that My Lord the Count was actually approaching the post, merely that his lordship was going into his private room at the top of the Red Tower. It was an occurrence both of them were used to. The Count was irregular in his visits to his private workshop, but his behavior each time was predictable. He made his presence known to those in the courtyard below by the light of his flickering torch showing through the lozenged window as he approached it from the door of his laboratory.

Then, as he stood on the desk in front of the window to light the gas jet just above the lintel, the flame of the torch rose, lifting out of sight above the window, leaving only a half-halo of light beneath.

Then the routine changed drastically.

Instead of the warm glow of the gaslight, there was an odd, moving flare of white light that seemed to chase itself around the room for a second or two.

Then, suddenly and violently, the leaded, lozenged window burst asunder, splattering glass through the air. Through that shattered window came the twisting figure of My Lord de la Vexin, a scream tearing from his throat as he somersaulted eighty feet to the stone pavement below, his small torch still in his hand, trailing a comet's tail of flame and sparks.

The Count and the courtyard met with fatal violence, and the sudden silence was punctuated only by the tinkling rain of shards of glass still falling from the ruined window above.

At 12:44 that evening, Jaque Toile, Chief Master-at-Arms for the city of Gisors, was waiting at the railroad station with two Sergeants-at-Arms as the train from Rouen pulled into the station.

Chief Jaque's hard eyes scanned the late-night passengers as they alighted from the first-class coaches. There were few of them, and the Chief quickly spotted the trio he was looking for. "Let's go," he said to the sergeants. "that's them."

The three Officers of the King's Peace moved in.

The three men who were their target stepped out of

the coach and waited. The first was a tall, brown-haired, handsome man with lean features, wearing the evening dress of an aristocrat; the second was shorter and muscularly tubby wearing the working dress of a sorcerer; the third was a rather elderly, dried-up-looking fellow with gray hair, who wore pince-nez and the evening dress of a gentleman. On the shoulders of the latter two was embroidered the badge of the Duke of Normandy.

Chief Jaque walked up to the aristocratic-looking gentleman. "My Lord Darcy?"

Lord Darcy, Chief Investigator for His Royal Highness the Duke of Normandy, nodded. "I am. Chief Jaque Toile, I believe?"

"Yes, m'lord."

"My colleagues," said Lord Darcy by way of introduction, "Sean O Lochlainn, Master Sorcerer, Chief Forensic Sorcerer for His Royal Highness; Doctor James Pateley, Chief Forensic Chirurgeon."

The Chief Master-at-Arms acknowledged the introductions, then: "Sergeants Paul and Bertram, m'lord. We have an official carriage waiting, m'lord."

Four minutes later, the carriage was rolling toward Castle Gisors, its coil spring suspension and pneumatic tires making the ride comfortable in spite of the cobblestone streets. After what seemed a long silence, Lord Darcy's voice came smoothly.

"You seem pensive, my dear Chief."

"What? Oh. Yes. Sorry, m'lord. Just thinking."

"That was painfully apparent. May I inquire as to the subject of your thoughts?"

"Don't like cases like this," said Chief Jaque. "Not equipped for 'em. Ghosts, demons, black magic, that sort of thing. I'm not a scientist; I'm a peace officer."

Master Sean's blue eyes lit up with interest. "Ghosts? Demons? Black magic?"

"One moment," Lord Darcy said. "Let us be systematic. The only information we received at Rouen was that de la Vexin has fallen to his death. No details were given us via teleson. Just what did happen, Chief Jaque?"

The Chief Master-at-Arms explained what had happened as pieced together from the reports of the guardsmen on duty, just prior to My Lord de la Vexin's death.

"No question he was dead," the Chief said. "Skull smashed. Neck broken. Guard Sergeant Andray called for an extension fire ladder. Only way to get up into that room. Sent the guard from the courtyard up the stairs to notify the two men on duty at his lordship's door."

"They hadn't known?" Lord Darcy asked.

Chief Jaque shook his head. "Door's too thick. Too thick to break down in a short time, even. Need an ax. That's why Andray went up the ladder. Climbed in the window and went over to unbar the door. By that time, the door guards were alerted. That's where the funny part comes in."

"Indeed?" murmured Lord Darcy. "Funny in what way?"

"Nobody in the room. Doesn't make sense."

Master Sean thumbed his chin thoughtfully. "If that's the case, Chief Jaque, then he wasn't pushed, eh? Might it be that it was purely an accident? That when he got up on that desk to light the gaslamp, something slipped and he fell accidentally through the window and to his death?"

The Chief Master-at-Arms shook his head. "Not very likely, Master Sorcerer; body was eighteen feet from the wall. Glass spattered even farther." He shook his head again. "Didn't just fall. Not possible. He was pushed."

Dr. Pateley took his pince-nez from his thin nose and looked at them as he polished them with a fine linen handkerchief. "Or *jumped*, perhaps?" he asked in his diffident voice.

The chief glanced at him sharply. "*Jumped?* You mean suicide?"

"Not necessarily," said the chirurgeon. He glanced up at Lord Darcy. "There are many reasons why a man might jump—eh, my lord?"

Lord Darcy held back a smile. "Indeed, Doctor. Most astute of you." He looked at Chief Jaque. "Could he have jumped, Chief?"

"Could have. Doesn't make sense, though. Man doesn't commit suicide by jumping through a closed window. Doesn't make sense. A suicide who decides to jump opens the window first. Doesn't just take a flying leap through a pane of glass."

"That's not the point I had in mind," said Dr. Pateley, replacing his glasses carefully. "What if he were trying to get away from something?"

Chief Jaque's eyes widened. "I knew it! Demons!"

Twenty-five minutes later, Master Sean was saying: "Well, me lord, whatever it was that killed My Lord de la Vexin, it was certainly none of Chief Jaque's 'demons,' nor any other form of projected psychic elemental."

Dr. Pateley frowned. "A what?"

"Elemental, my dear Doctor. A projected psychic manifestation symbolized by the four elementary states of matter: solid, liquid, gas, and plasma. Or earth, water, air, and fire, as they used to call them."

Along with Lord Darcy, Master Sean and the chirurgeon were standing in the room in the Red Tower from which the late Count had been ejected so forcibly. Master Sean had prowled round the room with his eyes half closed, his golden *crux ansata* in his right hand, probing everywhere. The others had stood by silently; it is unwise to disturb a magician at work. Then the round little Irish sorcerer had made his pronouncement.

Lord Darcy had not wasted his time in watching Master Sean; he had seen that process too many times to be interested in it. Instead, his keen gray eyes had been carefully surveying the room.

It was a fairly large room, covering the entire top floor of the Fourteenth Century tower except for the small landing at the head of the stairs. The landing was closed off by a heavy, padded walnut door.

Having noted that, Lord Darcy looked at the rest of the large room.

It was square, some twenty by twenty feet, the tower having been built in the old Norman style. There was only the one window in the room; the rest of the walls were covered with shelving and cabinets. Along the length of the west wall ran a shelf some thirty-two inches deep and three feet from the floor: it was obviously used as a worktable, for it was littered with various kinds of glassware, oddly-shaped pieces of wood and metal, a couple of balances and other paraphernalia. The shelves above it contained rows of bottles and jars, each neatly labeled, containing liquids, powders, and crystals of various kinds.

On the south wall, flanking the shattered window, were two sections of shelving full of books. Half the east wall was filled with books, the other half with cabinets. There were more shelves and cabinets flanking the door of the north wall.

Because of the slight breeze that came in chillingly through the broken window, the gas flame in the sconce above it flickered and danced, casting weird shadows over the room and making glittering highlights on the glassware.

The Count's writing desk was set directly beneath the big window, its top flush with the sill. Lord Darcy walked over to the desk, leaned over it and looked down through the smashed window. There had been no unusual evidence there. My Lord the Count had, from all indications, died of a broken neck and a crushed skull although the autopsy might tell more. A search of the body had revealed nothing of any consequence—but Lord Darcy now carried the key to the late Count's ultraprivate chamber in his pocket.

Below Chief Jaque and his men were carefully lifting the body from a glittering field of broken glass and putting it into the special carriage of the local chirurgeon. The autopsy would be performed in the morning by Master Sean and Dr. Pateley.

Lord Darcy leaned back and looked up at the gas flame above the window. The Count de la Vexin had come in with his torch, as usual. Climbed up on his desk as usual. Turned on the gas, as usual. Lit the gas with his torch, as usual. Then—

What?

"Spooky-looking place, eh, me lord?" Master Sean said.

His lordship turned round, putting his back to the window.

"Gloomy, at any rate, my dear Sean. Are there no other gas jets in this room? Ah, yes; I see them. Two on each of the other walls. Evidently the pipes were lengthened when the shelving was put in." He took out his pipe lighter. "Let's see if we can't shed a little more light on the subject." He went around the room carefully and lit the other six lamps. Even inside their glass chimneys, they tended to flicker; the room was better illuminated, but the shadows still danced.

"Ah! And an old-fashioned oil chandelier," Lord Darcy said, looking up. It was a brass globe some fifteen inches in diameter with a ring at the bottom and a wick with a glass chimney on top, suspended by a web of chains and a pulley system that allowed it to be pulled down for refueling and lighting. Even standing on tiptoe, Lord Darcy couldn't reach the ring.

He looked around quickly then went to the door and opened it.

"Corporal, is there a hook to lower that oil lamp?"

"Blessed if I know, my lord," said the Corporal of the Guard. "His lordship never used it, the lamp, I mean. Hasn't been used as long as I know. Doubt if it has any oil in it, even, my lord."

"I see. Thank you." He closed the door again. "Well, so much for additional illumination. Hm-m-m. Dr. Pateley, you measured the body; how tall was My Lord Count?

"Five feet six, my lord."

"That accounts for it, then."

"Accounts for what, my lord?"

"There are seven gas jets in this room. Six of them are some seven and a half feet from the floor; the seventh, over the window, is nine feet from the floor. Why did he habitually light that one first? Because it is only six and a half feet from the desk top, and he could reach it."

"Then how did he reach the others if he needed more light?" Dr. Pateley asked, adjusting his pince-nez.

Master Sean grinned, but said nothing.

Lord Darcy sighed. "My dear chirurgeon, I honestly think you never look at anything but human bodies, ill, dying, or dead. What do you see over there?" He pointed to the northeast corner of the room.

Dr. Pateley turned. "Oh. A ladder." He looked rather embarrassed. "Certainly. Of course."

"Had it not been here," Lord Darcy said, "I would be quite astonished. How else would he get to his books and . . ."

His voice trailed off. His eyes were still on the ladder. "Hm-m-m. Interesting." He went over to the ladder, tested it, then climbed up it to the ceiling. He bent his head back to look at the ceiling carefully. "Aha. This was the old watchtower." He pushed up with one hand, then with both. Overhead, a two-and-a-half foot panel swung back on protesting hinges. Lord Darcy climbed on up and hoisted himself through the opening.

He looked around the roof of the tower, which was surrounded by crenellated walls. Then he came back down, closing the panel.

"Nothing up there, apparently, but I'll have to come back by daylight to check again, more thoroughly."

Then, without another word, he moved silently

around the room, looking intently at everything but touching nothing. He looked up at the ceiling. "Heavy brass hooks," he murmured. "Why? Oh, of course. To suspend various pieces of his apparatus. Very good."

He had covered almost all the room before he finally came across something the really piqued his interest. He was standing near the door, his eyes searching the floor, when he said: "Aha! And what might this be?"

He knelt down, looked down at the object carefully, then picked it up between thumb and forefinger.

"It looks," said Master Sean, "like a four-inch piece of half-inch cotton rope, me lord. Very dirty, too."

His Lordship smiled dryly. "That appears to be exactly what it is , my good Sean. Interesting." He examined it closely.

"I would be obliged, my lord," said Master Sean in a semi-formal manner, "if you would explain why it is so interesting."

Dr. Pateley merely blinked behind his pince-nez and said nothing.

"You have noticed, my dear Sean," Lord Darcy said, "how immaculately clean this laboratory is. It is well dusted, well cleaned. Everything seems to be in its place. There are no papers scattered about. There are no messy areas. The place is as neat and as well-kept as a cavalry officer's sabre." He made a sweeping gesture to take in the whole room.

"It is, me lord, but—" Master Sean began.

"Then what, may I ask," His Lordship continued, "is a short piece of dirty rope doing on the floor?"

"I don't know, me lord." Master Sean was honestly puzzled. "What is its significance?"

Lord Darcy's smile broadened. "I haven't the foggiest notion in the world, Master Sean. But I have no doubt that there is *some* significance. What it is will await upon further information."

Another dozen minutes of inspection revealed nothing further to Lord Darcy's scrutiny. "Very well," he said, "we'll leave the rest of this until the morrow, when the light's better. Now let us go down and discuss this affair with those concerned. We'll get little sleep tonight, I fear."

Master Sean cleared his throat apologetically. "My lord, the good chirurgeon and I, not being qualified for interrogating witnesses, had best occupy our time with the autopsy. Eh?"

"Eh?" Oh, certainly, if you wish. Yes, of course." This, Lord Darcy thought, is what comes of assuming that others, even one's closest associates, have the same interests as oneself.

Within St. Martin's Hall, the clock on the mantelpiece solemnly struck the quarter-hour. It was fifteen minutes after two on the morning of Good Friday, 12 April 1974.

The Reverend Father Villiers stood near the fireplace, looking up at Lord Darcy. He was not tall—five-six or so—but his lean, compact body had an aura of physical strength about it. He was quick and accurate in his movements, but never seemed jerky or nervous. There was a calm awareness in him that showed spiritual strength as well. He was, Lord Darcy judged, in his forties, with only a faint touch of gray in his hair and mustache. The fine character lines in his handsome face showed strength, kindliness, and a sense of humor. But at the moment he was not smiling: there was a feeling of tragedy in his eyes.

"They are all in the Chapel, my lord," he was saying in his brisk, pleasant, low tenor. "Lord Gisors, Lady Beverly, the Demoselle Madelaine, and Sir Roderique MacKenzie."

"Who are the latter pair. Reverend Sir?" Lord Darcy asked.

"Sir Roderique is Captain of the Count's Own Guard. The Demoselle Madelaine is his daughter."

"I shall not disturb them. Reverend Father." Lord Darcy said. "To seek solace before our Sacramental Lord on His Altar of Repose on this night is the sacrosanct right of every Christian, and should not be abrogated save in dire emergency."

"You don't consider murder an emergency?"

"Before its commission, yes. Not after. What makes you think it was murder, Reverend Father?"

The priest smiled a little. "It wasn't suicide. I spoke to him shortly before he went over to the Red Tower: as a Sensitive, I'd have picked up any suicidal emotions easily. And it could hardly have been an accident; if he'd merely lost his balance and fallen, he'd have landed at the foot of the wall, not eighteen or twenty feet away."

"Eighteen," murmured Lord Darcy.

"*Ergo*—murder." Father Villiers said.

"I agree, Reverend Father," Lord Darcy said. "The theory has been advanced that My Lord Count saw some sort of apparition which so frightened him that he leaped to his death through a closed window rather than face it. What is your opinion?"

"That would be Chief Jaque." The priest shook his head. "Hardly. His late lordship would not even have sensed the presence of a true psychic apparition, and a phony—a piece of trickery—would have neither fooled nor frightened him."

"He couldn't have perceived a true psychic apparition?"

Father Villiers shook his head once more. "He was an example of that truly rare case, the psychically blind."

Ever since St. Hilary of Walsingham had formulated his analog equations on the Laws of Magic in the late Thirteenth Century, scientific sorcerers had realized that those laws could not be used by everyone. Some had the Talent and some did not. It was no more to be expected that everyone could be a sorcerer or healer or sensitive than to expect everyone to be a musician, a sculptor, or a chirurgeon.

But the inability to play a violin does not mean an inability to enjoy—or *not* enjoy—someone else's playing. One does not have to be a musician to perceive that music exists.

Unless one is tone-deaf.

To use another analogy: There are a few—very few—men and women who are *totally* color-blind. They are not just slightly crippled, like those who cannot distinguish between red and green; they see all things in shades of gray. To them, the world is colorless. It is difficult for such a person to understand why or how three identical objects, all the same shade of gray, can be identified by someone else as "red," "blue," and "green." To the totally color-blind, those words are without referents and are meaningless.

"His late lordship," the priest said, "had an early desire to go into the priesthood, to forgo his right to the County Seat in favor of his younger brother. He could not do so, of course. An un-Talented, psychically blind man would be as useless to the Church as a color-blind man would be to the Artists' Guild."

Naturally, Lord Darcy thought, that would not exclude the late de la Vexin from an executive position in His Imperial Majesty's Government. One doesn't need magical Talent to run a County effectively.

For over eight centuries, since the time of Henry II, the Anglo-French Empire had held its own and expanded. Henry's son, Richard, after narrowly escaping death from a crossbow bolt in 1199, had taken firm control of his kingdom and expanded it. At his death in 1219, his nephew Arthur had increased the kingdom's strength even more. The Great Reform, during the reign of Richard the Great, in the late Fifteenth Century, had put the Empire on a solid working basis, using psychic science to establish a society that had been both stable and progressive for nearly half a millennium.

"Where is My Lord the late Count's younger brother?" Lord Darcy asked.

"Captain Lord Louis is with the New England Fleet," Father Villiers said. "At present, I believe, stationed at Port Holy Cross on the coast of Mechicoe."

Well, that eliminates him *as a suspect,* Lord Darcy told himself. "Tell me, Reverend Father," he said aloud, "do you know anything about the laboratory his late lordship maintained on the top floor of the Red Tower?"

"A laboratory? Is that what it is? No, I didn't know. He went up there regularly, but I have no idea what he did up there. I assumed it was some harmless hobby. Wasn't it?"

"It may have been," Lord Darcy admitted. "I have no reason to believe otherwise. Have you ever been in that room?"

"No; never. Nor, to my knowledge, has anyone else but the Count. Why?"

"Because," Lord Darcy said thoughtfully, "it is a very odd laboratory. And yet there is no doubt that it *is* some kind of laboratory for scientific research."

Father Villiers touched the cross at his breast. "Odd? How?" Then he dropped his hand and chuckled. "No. Not Black Magic, of course. He didn't believe in magic at all—black, white, purple, green, red, or rainbow. He was a Materialist."

"Oh?"

"An outgrowth of his psychic blindness, you see," the priest explained. "He wanted to be a priest. He was refused. Therefore, he rejected the basis for his refusal. He refused to believe that anything which he could not detect with his own senses existed. He set out to prove the basic tenet of Materialism: 'All phenomena in the Universe can be explained as a result of nonliving forces reacting with nonliving matter.' "

"Yes," said Lord Darcy. "A philosophy which I, as a living being, find difficult to understand, to say nothing of accepting. So that is the purpose of his laboratory—

to bring the scientific method to bear on the Theory of Materialism."

"So it would appear, my lord," said Father Villiers. "Of course, I have not seen his late lordship's laboratory, but—"

"Who has?" Lord Darcy asked.

The priest shook his head. "No one that I know of. No one."

Lord Darcy glanced at his watch. "Is there anyone else in the Chapel besides the family, Reverend Sir?"

"Several. There is an outer door through which the occupants within the walls can come in directly from the courtyard. And there are four of the Sisters from the convent.

"Then I could slip in unnoticed for an hour of devotion before the Blessed Sacrament at the Altar of Repose?"

"Most assuredly, my lord; there are people coming and going all the time. But I suggest you use the public entrance; if you use the family entrance, someone is sure to notice."

"Thank you, Reverend Father. At what hour will you celebrate the Mass of the Presanctified?"

"The service begins at eight o'clock."

"And how do I get to this outside door? Through that door and turn to my left, I believe?"

"Exactly, my lord."

Three minutes later, Lord Darcy was kneeling in the back of the Chapel, facing the magnificently flowered Altar of Repose, his eyes on the veiled ciborium that stood at its center.

An hour and a quarter after that, he was sound asleep in the room which had been assigned him by the seneschal.

After the abrupt liturgical finale of the Mass of the Presanctified at a little past ten on Good Friday morning, Lord Darcy and Master Sean stood waiting outside the family entrance of the Chapel. Dr. Pateley had excused himself immediately; he had volunteered to help one of the local men to prepare the late Count's body for the funeral. "Put things back the way we found 'em, my lord," was the way he worded it.

Darcy and the stout little Irish sorcerer had placed themselves at the back of the congregation and had come out ahead of the family who were in their reserved pew at the front.

"I trust," murmured his lordship very softly, "that Almighty God has reserved a special place of punishment for people who commit murder during Holy Week."

"Aye, me lord; I know what you mean," Master Sean whispered. "Meself, I enjoy the Three Hours of Sermon on Good Friday—especially by a really good preacher, which Father Villiers is reputed to be. But—'business before pleasure.' " He paused, then went on in the same low tone. "D'you expect to clear up the case soon?"

"Before the day is out, I think."

Master Sean looked startled. "You know who did it then?" He kept his voice down.

"*Who?* Of course. That should be plain. But I need more data on *how* and *why.*"

Master Sean blinked. "But you haven't even questioned anyone yet, my lord."

"No need to for that. But my case is as yet incomplete."

Master Sean shook his head and chuckled. "Your touch of the Talent, me lord."

"You know, my dear Sean, you have almost convinced me that I *do* have a touch of the Talent. How did you put it?"

"Like all great detectives, my lord, you have the ability to leap from an unjustified assumption to a foregone conclusion without passing through the distance between. Then you back up and fill in." He paused again.

"Well, then, who—"

"*Ssst!* Here they come."

Three people had come out of the Chapel: Lord Gisors, Lady Beverly, and the Demoselle Madelaine MacKenzie.

Master Sean's lips barely moved and his voice was barely audible as he said: "Wonder where the rest of the Clan MacKenzie went, me lord?"

"We'll ask." Both of them knew that Captain Sir Roderique MacKenzie and his son, Sergeant Andray, had been sitting in the family pew with the others.

The three came up the hallway toward the big fireplace in St. Martin's Hall, where Lord Darcy and Master Sean were waiting.

Lord Darcy stepped forward and bowed. "My Lord de la Vexin."

The young man looked startled. "No. My fa—" He stopped. It was the first time anyone had ever addressed him as "Lord de la Vexin." Of course it was only a courtesy title; he would not be the Count of the Vexin until his title had been validated by the King.

Lord Darcy, seeing the young man's confusion, went on: "I am Lord Darcy, my lord. This is Master Sean. We appreciate the invitation to breakfast that was conveyed to us by your seneschal."

The new Lord de la Vexin had recovered his composure. "Ah, yes, I am pleased to meet you, my lord. This is my sister, Lady Beverly, and the Demoselle Madelaine. Come; breakfast should be ready for us immediately." He led the way.

The breakfast was delicious, not sumptuous: small, exquisitely poached *quinelles de poisson;* portions of eggs Boucher; hot cross buns; milk and caffe.

Captain Roderique and Sergeant Andray made their appearance a few minutes before the meal began, followed almost immediately by Father Villiers.

Conversation during breakfast consisted only of small

talk, allowing Lord Darcy to observe the others of the party without being obtrusive about it.

De la Vexin still seemed dazed, as though his mind were somewhere else, only partly pulled back by conversation. The Demoselle Madelaine, blond and beautiful, behaved with decorum, but there was a bright, anticipatory gleam in her eyes that Lord Darcy did not care for. Lady Beverly, some ten years older than her brother, her dark hair faintly tinged with gray at the temples, looked as though she had been born a widow— or a cloistered nun; she was quiet, soft-spoken, and self-effacing, but underneath Lord Darcy detected a firmness and intelligence kept in abeyance. Captain Sir Roderique MacKenzie was perhaps an inch taller than Lord Darcy—lean, with an upright, square-shouldered posture, a thick light-brown mustache and beard, and a taciturn manner typical of the Franco-Scot. His son was a great deal like him, except that he was smooth-shaven and his hair was lighter, though not as blond as that of his sister Madelaine. Both had an air about them that was not quite either that of the military or that of the Keepers of the King's Peace, but partook of both. They were Guardsmen and showed it.

Father Villiers seemed preoccupied, and Lord Darcy could understand why. The symbolic death of the Lord Jesus and the actual death of the Lord de la Vexin were too closely juxtaposed for the good Father's own spiritual comfort. Being a priest is not an easy life-game to play.

After breakfast, a fruit compote of Spanish oranges was served, followed by more caffe.

The late Count's son cleared his throat. "My lords, ladies, gentlemen," he began. He paused for a moment and swallowed. "Several of you have addressed me as 'de la Vexin.' I would prefer, until this matter is cleared up, to retain my title of Gisors. Uh—if you please." Another pause. He looked at Lord Darcy. "You came here to question us, my lord?"

Lord Darcy looked utterly guileless. "Not really, Lord Gisors. However, if you should care to discuss the death of his lordship, it might clear up some of the mysterious circumstances surrounding it. I know that none of you were in that room at the time of the—ah—incident. I am not looking for alibis. But have any of you any conjectures? How did the late Count de la Vexin die?"

Silence fell like a psychic fog, heavy and damp.

Each looked at the others to speak first, and nobody spoke.

"Well," Lord Darcy said after a time, "let's attack it from another direction. Sergeant Andray, of all the people here, you were apparently the only eyewitness. What was your impression of what happened?"

The sergeant blinked, sat up a little straighter, and cleared his throat nervously. "Well, your lordship, at a few minutes before ten o'clock, Guardsman Jaime and I were—"

"No, no, Sergeant," Lord Darcy interrupted gently. "Having read the deposition you and Jaime gave to Chief Jaque, I am fully conversant with what you *saw*. I want to know your theories about the *cause* of what you saw."

After a pause, Sergeant Andray said. "It looked to me as if he'd *jumped* through the window, your lordship. But I have no idea why he would do such a thing."

"You saw nothing that might have made him jump?"

Sergeant Andray frowned. "The only thing was that ball of light. Jaime and I mentioned it in my report."

"Yes. 'A ball of yellowish-white light that seemed to dance all over the room for a few seconds, then dropped to the floor and vanished,' you said. Is that right?"

"I should have said, 'dropped *toward* the floor,' your lordship. I couldn't have seen it actually hit the floor. Not from that angle."

"Very good, Sergeant! I wondered if you would correct that minor discrepancy, and you have done so to my satisfaction." Lord Darcy thought for a moment. "Now. You then went over to the body, examined it, and determined to your satisfaction that his lordship was dead. Did you touch him?"

"Only his wrist, to try to find a pulse. There was none, and the angle of his head . . ." He stopped.

"I quite understand. Meanwhile, you had sent Guardsman Jaime for the fire wagon. When it came, you used the extension ladder to go up and unlock the door, to let the other guardsmen in. Was the gaslight still on?"

"No. It had been blown out. I shut off the gas, and then went over and opened the door. There was enough light from the yardlamps for me to see by."

"And you found nothing odd or out of the way?"

"Nothing and nobody, your lordship," the sergeant said firmly. "Nor did any of the other guardsmen."

"That's straightforward enough. You searched the room then?"

"Not really searched it. We looked around to see if there was anyone there, using hand torches. But there's no place to hide in that room. We had called the Armsmen; when they came, they looked more carefully. Nothing."

"Very well. Now, when I arrived, that gaslight over the window was lit. Who lit it?"

"Chief Master-at-Arms Jaque Toile, your lordship."

"I see. Thank you, Sergeant." He looked at the others, one at a time. Their silence seemed interminable. "Lady Beverly, have you anything to add to this discussion?"

Lady Beverly looked at Father Villiers with her calm eyes.

The priest was looking at her. "My advice is to speak, my child. We must get to the bottom of this."

I see, Lord Darcy thought. *There is something here that has been discussed in the confessional. The Reverend Father* cannot *speak—but he can advise* her *to.*

Lady Beverly looked back to Lord Darcy. "You want a theory, my lord? Very well." There was a terrible sadness in her voice. "His late lordship, my father, was punished by God for his unbelief. Father Villiers has told me that this could not be so, but"—she closed her eyes —"I greatly fear that it is."

"How so, my lady?" Darcy asked gently.

"He was a Materialist. He was psychically blind. He denied that others had the God-given gift of the Sight and the Talent. He said it was all pretense, all hogwash. He was closed off to all emotion."

She was no longer looking *at* Lord Darcy; she was looking through and beyond him, as though her eyes were focused somewhere on a far horizon.

"He was not an evil man," she continued without shifting her gaze, "but he was sinful." Suddenly her eyes flickered, and she was looking directly into Lord Darcy's gray eyes. "Do you know that he forbade a wedding between my brother and the Demoselle Madelaine because he could not see the love between them? He wanted Gisors to marry Evelynne de Saint-Brieuc."

Darcy's eyes moved rapidly to Lord Gisors and Madelaine MacKenzie. "No, I did not know that. How many did?"

It was Captain Sir Roderique who spoke. "We all did, My Lord. He made a point of it. The Count forbade it, and I forbade it. But legally I had no right to forbid my daughter."

"But why did he—"

Lord Darcy's question was cut off abruptly by Lady Beverly.

"Politics, my lord. And because he could not see true love. So God punished him for his obstinacy. May I be excused, my lord? I would hear the Three Hours."

Quickly, Father Villiers said: "Would you excuse us both, my lord?"

"Certainly, Reverend Sir, Lady Beverly," Lord Darcy said, rising. His eyes watched them in silence as they left the room.

Half past noon.

Lord Darcy and Master Sean stood in the courtyard below the Red Tower gazing at a small sea of broken glass surrounded by a ring of armsmen and guardsmen.

"Well, my dear Sean, what did you think of our little breakfast conversation?"

"Fascinating, me lord," said the sorcerer. "I think I'm beginning to see where you're going. Lady Beverly's mind is not exactly straight, is it?"

"Let's put it that she seems to have some weird ideas about God," Lord Darcy said. "Are you ready for this experiment, Master Sean?"

"I am, me lord."

"Don't you need an anchor man for this sort of thing?"

Master Sean nodded. "Of course, me lord. Chief Jaque is bringing Journeyman Emile, forensic sorcerer for the County. I met him last night; he's a good man: he'll be a Master one day.

"Actually, me lord, the spells are quite simple. According to the Law of Contiguity, any piece of a structure remains a part of the structure. We can return it to the last state in which it was still a part of the contiguous whole—completely, if necessary, but you only want to return it to the point *after* the fracture but *before* the dispersal. Doing it isn't difficult; it's holding it in place afterwards. That's why I need an anchor man."

"I'll take my measurements and make my observations as quickly as possible." Lord Darcy promised. "Ah! There they are!"

Master Sean followed his lordship's gaze toward the main gate of the courtyard. Then, very solemnly, he said: "Ah, yes. One man is wearing the black-and-silver uniform of a Chief Master-at-Arms; the other is wearing the working garb of a Journeyman Sorcerer. By which I deduce that they are *not* a squad of Imperial Marines."

"Astute of you, my dear Sean: keep working at it. You will become an expert detective on the same day that I become a Master Sorcerer. Chief Jaque and I will go up to the tower room while you and Journeyman Emile work here. Carry on."

Lord Darcy toiled up eight flights of stairs, past several offices, vaguely wishing he were in the castle at Evreux, where the Countess D'Evreux's late brother had installed a steam-powered elevator. *No fool he*, Lord Darcy thought.

At the top landing, an armsman and a guardsman came immediately to attention as His Lordship appeared. He nodded at them. "Good afternoon." With thumb and forefinger he probed his left-hand waistcoat pocket. Then he probed the other. "Is that room locked?" he asked.

The armsman tested it. "Yes, your lordship."

"I seem to have mislaid the key. Is there another?"

"There is a duplicate, your lordship," said the guardsman, "but it's locked up in Captain Sir Roderique's office. I'll fetch it for you, if you like; it's only two floors down."

"No. No need." Lord Darcy produced the key from his right-hand waistcoat pocket. "I've found it. Thank you, anyway, Guardsman. Chief Jaque will be up in a few minutes."

He unlocked the door, opened it, went in, and closed the door behind him.

Some three minutes later, when Chief Jaque opened the door, he said: "Looking for something, my lord?"

Lord Darcy was on his knees, searching a cupboard, moving things aside, taking things out. "Yes, my dear Chief; I am looking for the wherewithal to hang a murderer. At first, I thought it more likely it would be in one of the high cupboards, but they contain nothing but glassware. So I decided it must be—ah!" He pulled his head back out of the cupboard and straightened up, still on his knees. From his fingers dangled a six-foot length of ordinary-looking cotton rope.

"Bit scanty to hang a man," Chief Jaque said dubiously.

"For this murderer, it will be quite adequate," said Lord Darcy, standing up. He looked closely at the rope. "If only it—"

He was interrupted by a halloo from below. He went to the shattered remains of the window and looked down. "Yes, Master Sean?" he called.

"We're ready to begin, my lord," the round little Irish sorcerer shouted up. "Please stand back."

In the courtyard, Armsmen and Guardsmen stood in a large circle, facing outward from the center, surrounding the fragments from the broken window. Journeyman Emile, a short, lean man with a Parisian accent, had carefully chalked a pale blue line around the area, drawing it three inches behind the bootheels of the surrounding guard.

"It is that I am ready, Master," he said in his atrocious patois.

"Excellent," said Master Sean. "Get the field set up and hold it. I will give you all the strength I can."

"But yes, master." He opened his symbol-decorated carpetbag—similar to in general, but differing from in detail, Master Sean's own—and took out two mirror-polished silvery wands which were so deeply incised with symbol engraving that they glittered in the early afternoon sunlight. "For the Cattell Effect, it is that it is necessary for the silver, no?"

"It is," agreed Master Sean. "You will be handling the static spells while I take care of the kinetic. Are you ready?"

"I am prepared," Journeyman Emile said. "Proceed."

He took his stance just inside the blue-chalked circle, facing the Red Tower and held up his wands in a ninety-degree *V*.

Master Sean took an insufflator from his own carpet-bag and filled it with a previously-charged powder. Then moving carefully around the circle, he puffed out clouds of the powder, which settled gently to the courtyard floor, touching each fragment of glass with at least one grain of the powder.

When he had completed the circle, Master Sean stood in front of Journeyman Emile. He put the insufflator back in his carpetbag and took out a short, eighteen-inch wand of pale yellow crystal, with which he inscribed a symbol in the air.

The Cattell Effect began to manifest itself.

Slowly at first, then more rapidly, the fragments from the shattered window began to move.

Like a reverse cascade in slow motion, they lifted and gathered themselves together, a myriad of sparkling shards moving upward, fountaining glitteringly toward the empty window casement eighty feet above. There was a tinkling like fairy bells as occasional fragments struck each other on the way up as they had struck on the way down.

Only the superb discipline of the armsmen and guardsmen kept them from turning to see.

Up, up, went the bits and pieces, like sharp-edged raindrops falling toward the sky.

At the empty opening, they coalesced and came together to form a window—that was not quite a window. It bulged.

Inside the late Count's upper room, Lord Darcy watched the flying fragments return whence they had come. When the stasis was achieved, Lord Darcy glanced at the Chief Master-at-Arms.

"Come, my dear Jaque; we must not tax our sorcerers more than necessary." He walked over to the window, followed by the Chief Armsman.

The lozenged window was neither a shattered wreckage nor a complete whole. It bulged outward curiously, each piece almost touching its neighbor, but not fitted closely to it. The leading between the lozenges was stretched and twisted outward, as if the whole window had been punched from within by a gigantic fist and had stopped stretching at the last moment.

"Not quite sure I understand this," said Chief Jaque.

"This is the way the window was a fraction of a second after his lordship, the late Count, struck it. At that time, it was pushed outward and broken, but the fragments had yet to scatter. I direct your attention to the central portion of the window."

The Chief Master-at-Arms took in the scene with keen eyes. "See what you mean. Like a mold, a casting. There's the chin—the chest—the belly—the knees."

"Exactly. Now try to get yourself into a position such that you would make an impression like that," Lord Darcy said.

The Chief grinned. "Don't need to. Obvious. Calves bent back at the knees. Head bent back so the chin hit first. Chest and belly hit first." He narrowed his eyes. "Didn't jump out: didn't fall out. Pushed from behind—violently."

"Precisely so. Excellent, Chief Jaque. Now let us make our measurements as rapidly and as accurately as possible," Lord Darcy said, "being careful not to touch that inherently unstable structure. If we do, we're likely to get badly-cut hands when the whole thing collapses."

Below, in the courtyard, an unmoving tableau presented itself. Armsmen and Guardsmen stood at parade rest, while the two sorcerers stood like unmoving statues, their eyes and minds on the window above, their wands held precisely and confidently.

Minute after minute went by, and the strain was beginning to tell. Then Lord Darcy's voice came: "Anytime you're ready, Master Sean!"

Without moving, Master Sean said sharply, "Sergeant! Get your men well back! Move 'em!"

The Sergeant-at-Arms called out orders, and both Armsmen and Guardsmen rapidly moved back toward the main gate. Then they turned to watch.

The magicians released control. The powerful forces which had held up the glass shards no longer obtained, and gravity took over. There was an avalanche, a waterfall of sparkling shards. They slid and tumbled down the stone wall with a great and joyous noise and subsided into a heap at the foot of the Red Tower.

The display had not been as spectacular as the reconstruction of the window had been, but it was quite satisfactory to the Armsmen and Guardsmen.

A few minutes later, Master Sean toiled his way up the stairs and entered the late Count's laboratory.

"Ah! Master Sean," said Lord Darcy, "Where is Journeyman Emile?"

The Irish sorcerer's smile was a little wan. "He's headed home, my lord. That's exhaustin' work, and he hasn't trained for it as I have."

"I trust you conveyed to him my compliments. That was a marvelous piece of work the two of you did."

"Thank you, my lord. I gave Journeyman Emile my personal compliments and assured him of yours. Did you get what you wanted, my lord?"

"I did, indeed. There is but one more thing. A simple test, but I'm sure it will be most enlightening. First, I will call your attention to those two five-gallon carboys which Chief Jaque and I have just discovered in one of the lower cupboards."

The carboys, which had been lifted up to the worktable, stood side by side, labels showing. One of them, with scarcely half an inch of pale yellowish liquid in it, was labeled *Concentrated Aqueous Spirit of Niter*. The other, half full of a clear oily-looking liquid, was *Concentrated Oil of Vitriol*.

"I suppose you knew you'd find 'em, me lord?" Master Sean said.

"I didn't *know;* I merely suspected. But their presence certainly strengthens my case. Do they suggest anything to you?"

Master Sean shrugged. "I know what they are, my lord, but I'm not a specialist in the Khemic Arts."

"Nor am I." Lord Darcy took out his pipe and thumbed tobacco into it. "But an Officer of the King's Justice should be widely read enough to be a jack-of-all-trades, at least in theory. Do you know what happens when a mixture of those acids is added to common cotton?"

"No—wait." Master Sean frowned, then shook his head. "I've read it somewhere, but—the details won't come."

"You get nitrated cotton." Lord Darcy said.

Chief Jaque coughed delicately. "Well, what does *that* do, your lordship?"

"I think I can show you." His lordship said with a rather mysterious smile. From his wallet, he took the four-inch piece of blackened rope he had found near the door the evening before. Then he picked up the six-foot piece of clean rope he had found half an hour before. Using his sharp pocketknife, he cut a small piece from the end of each and put them on the lab table about eighteen inches from each other. "Chief Jaque, take these long pieces and put them on the desk, well away from here. I shouldn't want to lose *all* my evidence. Thank you. Now watch."

He lit each bit with his pipe lighter. They both flared in a sudden hissing burst of yellow-white flame and were gone, leaving no trace. Lord Darcy calmly lit his pipe.

Master Sean's eyes lit up. "Aaa-hah!"

Chief Jaque said: "The demon!"

"Precisely, my dear Chief. Now we must go down and talk to the rest of the *dramatis personae.*"

As they went back down the stairs, Master Sean said:

"But why was the short piece covered with dirt, My Lord?"

"Not dirt, my dear Sean; lampblack."

"Lampblack? But why?"

"To render it invisible, of course."

"You are not preaching the Three Hours, Reverend Father?" Lord Darcy asked with a raised eyebrow.

"No, my lord," Father Villiers replied. "I am just a little too upset. Besides, I thought my presence here might be required. Father Dubois very kindly agreed to come over from the monastery and take my place."

Clouds had come, shortly after noon, to obliterate the bright morning sun, and a damp chill had enveloped the castle. The chill was being offset by the fire in the great fireplace in St. Martin's Hall, but to the ten people seated on sofas and chairs around the fireplace, there seemed to be a different sort of chill in the huge room.

The three MacKenzies, father, son, and daughter, sat together on one sofa, saying nothing, their eyes moving around, but always coming back to Lord Darcy. Lady Beverly sat alone near the fire, her eyes watching the flames unseeingly. Master Sean and Dr. Pateley were talking in very low tones on the opposite side of the fireplace. Chief Jaque stood stolidly in front of the mullioned window, watching the entire room without seeming to do so.

On the mantelpiece, the big clock swung its pendulum with muffled clicks.

Lord Gisors rose from his seat and came toward the sideboard where Lord Darcy and Father Villiers were talking.

"Excuse me, Lord Darcy, Father." He paused and cleared his throat a little, then looked at the priest. "We're all a little nervous, Reverend Sir. I know it's Good Friday, but would it be wrong to—er—to ask if anyone wants a glass of Xerez?"

"Of course not, my son. We are all suffering with Our

Lord this day, and may suffer more, but I do not think He would frown upon our use of a stiff dose of medicinal palliative. Certainly Our Lord did not. According to St. John, He said, 'I thirst,' and they held up to Him a sponge soaked in wine. After He had received it, He said, 'It is accomplished.' " Father Villiers stopped.

" 'And gave up His spirit,' " Lord Gisors quoted glumly.

"Exactly," said the priest firmly. "But by Easter Day His spirit had returned, and the only casualty among the faithful that weekend was Judas. I'll have a brandy, myself."

Only Lady Beverly and Chief Jaque refused refreshment—each for a different reason. When the drinks were about half gone, Lord Darcy walked casually to the fireplace and faced them all.

"We have a vexing problem before us. We must show how the late Count de la Vexin met his death. With the cooperation of all of you, I think we can do it. First, we have to dispense with the notion that there was any Black Magic involved in the death of his lordship. Master Sean?"

The Irishman rolled Xerez around on his tongue and swallowed before answering. "Me lords, ladies, and gentlemen, having thoroughly given the situation every scientific test, I would be willing to state in His Majesty's Court of Justice that by whatever means his lordship the Count was killed, there was no trace of any magic, black *or* white, involved. Not in any capacity by anyone."

Lady Beverly's eyes blazed suddenly. "By no *human* agency, I suppose you mean?" Her voice was low, intense.

"Aye, me lady," Master Sean agreed.

"But what of the punishment of God? Or the evil works of Satan?"

A silence hung in the air. After a moment, Master Sean said: "I think I'll let the Reverend Father answer that one."

Father Villiers steepled his fingers. "My child, God punishes transgressors in many ways—usually through the purgatorial torture of conscience, or, if the conscience is weak, by the reaction of the sinner's fellow men to his evildoing. The Devil, in hope that the sinner may die before he has a chance to repent, may use various methods of driving them to self-destruction.

"But you cannot ascribe an act like this to *both* God and Satan. There is, furthermore, no evidence whatever that your late father was so great a sinner that God would have resorted to such drastic punishment, nor that the Devil feared of his lordship's relenting in the near future of such minor sins as he may have committed.

"In any case, *neither God nor the Devil disposes of a man by grabbing him by the scruff of the neck and the seat of the pants and throwing him through a window!*

"Execution by defenestration, my child, is a peculiarly human act."

Lady Beverly bowed her head and said nothing.

Again a moment of silence, broken by Lord Darcy.

"My Lord Gisors, assuming that your father was killed by purely physical means, can you suggest how it might have been done?"

Lord Gisors, who had been at the sidetable pouring himself another drink, turned slowly around. "Yes, Lord Darcy. I can," he said thoughtfully.

Lord Darcy raised his left eyebrow again. "Indeed? Pray elucidate, my lord."

Lord Gisors lifted his right index finger. "My father was pushed out that window. Correct?" His voice was shaking a little.

"Correct," Lord Darcy acknowledged.

"Then, by God, somebody had to push him out! I don't know who, I don't know how! But there had to be someone in there to do it!" He took another swallow of his drink and then went on in a somewhat calmer voice. "Look at it this way. Someone was in there waiting for him. My father came in, walked toward the window, got up on his desk, and that someone, whoever he was, ran up behind him and pushed him out. I don't know who or why, but that's what *had* to have happened! You're the Duke's Investigator. You find out what happened and who did it. But don't try to put it on any of us, My Lord, because none of us was anywhere near that room when it happened!"

He finished his drink in one swallow and poured another.

Lord Darcy spoke quietly. "Assuming your hypothesis is true, my lord, how did the killer get into the room, and how did he get out?" Without waiting for an answer from Lord Gisors, Lord Darcy looked at Captain Sir Roderique. "Have you any suggestions, Sir Roderique?"

The old guardsman scowled. "I don't know. The laboratory was locked at all times, and always guarded when his lordship was in there. But it wasn't especially guarded when Lord Jillbert was gone. He didn't go in often—not more than once or twice a week. The room wasn't particularly guarded the rest of the time. Anyone with a key could have got in. Someone could have stolen the key from My Lord de la Vexin and had a duplicate made."

"Highly unlikely." Lord Darcy said. "His Lordship wanted no one in that room but himself. On the other hand, my dear Captain, *you* have a duplicate."

Roderique's face seemed to turn purple. He came suddenly to his feet, looking down at Lord Darcy. "Are you accusing *me?*"

Darcy lifted a hand, palm outward. "Not yet, my dear Captain; perhaps not ever. Let us continue with our discussion without permitting our emotions to boil over." The Captain of the Guard sat down slowly without taking his eyes from Lord Darcy's face.

"I assure you, my lord," the captain said, "that no other duplicate has ever been made from the key in my possession and that the key has never been out of my possession."

"I believe you, Captain; I never said that any duplicate was made from *your* key. But let us make a hypothesis.

"Let us assume," Lord Darcy continued, "that the killer *did* have a duplicate key. Very well. What happened then?" He looked at Sergeant Andray. "Give us your opinion, Sergeant."

Andray frowned as though concentration on the problem was just a little beyond his capabilities. His handsome features seemed to be unsure of themselves. "Well—uh—well, my lord, this is—I mean—well, if it were me—" He licked his lips again and looked at his wine-glass. "Well, now, my lord, supposing there were someone hidden inside the room, waiting for My Lord Count. Hm-m-m. His lordship comes in and climbs up on the desk. Then the killer would have run forward and pushed him out. Yes. That's the only way it could have happened, isn't it?"

"Then how did he get out of the room afterward, Sergeant? You have told us that there was no one in the room when you went in through the window, and that the guardsmen outside found no one in the room after you let them in. The room was under guard all that time, was it not?"

"Yes, my lord, it was."

"Then how did the killer get out?"

The sergeant blinked. "Well, my lord, the only other way out is through the trapdoor to the roof. He might have gone out that way."

Lord Darcy shook his head slowly. "Impossible. I looked at that rooftop carefully this morning. There is no sign that anyone has been up there for some time. Besides, how would he get down? The tower was surrounded by guardsmen who would have seen anyone trying to go down ninety feet on a rope, and there is hardly any other way. At any rate, he would have been seen. And he could hardly have come down the stairs;

the interior was full of the Guard." His Lordship's eyes shifted suddenly. "Do you have any suggestions, Demoselle Madelaine?"

She looked up at him with her round blue eyes. "No, my lord. I know nothing about such things. It still seems like magic to me."

More silence.

Well, that's enough of this, Lord Darcy thought. *Now we go on to the final phase.*

"Does anyone else have a suggestion?" Apparently, no one did. "Very well, then; perhaps you would like to know my theory of how the killer—a very solid and human killer—got in and out of that room without being seen. Better than merely telling you. I shall demonstrate. Shall we repair to the late Count's *sanctum sanctorum?* Come."

There was a peculiar mixture of reluctance and avidity in the general feeling of those present, but they rose without objection and followed Lord Darcy across the courtyard to the Red Tower and up the long stairway to the late Count's room.

"Now," said Lord Darcy after they were all in the room, "I want all of you to obey my instructions exactly. Otherwise, someone is likely to get hurt. I am sorry there are no chairs in this room—evidently My Lord de la Vexin liked to work on his feet—so you will have to stand. Be so good as to stand over against the east wall. That's it. Thank you."

He took the five-inch brass key from his waistcoat pocket, then went over to the door and closed it. "The door was locked, so." *Click.* "And barred, so." *Thump.*

He repocketed the key and turned to face the others. "There, now. That's approximately the way things were after Lord de la Vexin locked himself in his laboratory for the last time. Except, of course, for the condition of that ruined window." He gestured toward the casement, empty now save for broken shards of glass and leading around the edges.

He looked all around the room side to side and up

and down. "No, it still isn't right, is it? Well, that can soon be adjusted properly. Firstly, we'll need to get that unused oil lamp down. Yonder ladder is a full two feet short to reach a ten-foot beam. There are no chairs or stools. A thorough search has shown that the long-handled hook which is the usual accouterment for such a lamp is nowhere in the room. Dear me! What shall we do?"

Most of the others were looking at Lord Darcy as though he had suddenly become simple-minded, but Master Sean smiled inwardly. He knew that his lordship's blithering was to a purpose.

"Well! What have we here?" Lord Darcy was looking at the brass key in his hand as if he had never seen it before. "Hm-m-m, the end which engages the lock wards should make an excellent hook. Let us see."

Standing directly beneath the brass globe, he jumped up and accurately hooked the brass ring with the key. Then he lowered the big lamp down.

"What is this? It comes down quite easily! It balances the counterweight to a nicety. How odd! Can it be that it is not empty after all?" He took off the glass chimney, put it on the worktable of the east wall, went back and took out the wickholder. "Bless my soul! It is quite brimfull of fuel."

He screwed the wickholder back in and lowered the whole lamp to the fullest extent of the pulley chain. It was hardly more than an inch off the floor. Then he grabbed the chain firmly with both hands and lifted. The lamp came up off the floor, but the chain above Lord Darcy's hands went limp and did not move upward. "Ah! The ratchet lock works perfectly. The counterweight cannot raise the lamp unless one pulls the chain down a little bit and then releases it slowly. Excellent." He lowered the lamp back down.

"Now comes the difficult part. That lamp is quite heavy." Lord Darcy smiled. "But, fortunately, we can use the ladder for this."

He brought the ladder over to the locked and barred

door, bracing it against the wall over the lintel. Then his audience watched in stunned silence as he picked up the heavy lamp, carried it over to the ladder, climbed up, and hooked the chain over one of the apparatus hooks that the Count had fastened at many places in the ceiling.

"There, now," he said, descending the ladder. He looked up at the resulting configuration. The lamp chain now stretched almost horizontally from its supporting beam to the heavy hook in the ceiling over the door. "You will notice," said his lordship, "that the supporting beam for the lamp is not in the exact center of the room. It is two feet nearer the window than it is to the door. The center of the beam is eleven feet from the door, nine feet from the window."

"What *are* you talking about?" Lady Beverly burst out suddenly. "What has all this to do with—"

"If you please, my lady!" Lord Darcy cut her off sharply. Then, more calmly, "Restrain yourself, I pray. All will become clear when I have finished."

Good Lord, he thought to himself, *it should be plain to the veriest dunce...*

Aloud, he said, "We are not through yet: The rope, Master Sean."

Without a word, Master Sean O Lochlainn opened his big symbol-decorated carpetbag and took from it a coil of cotton rope; he gave it to Lord Darcy.

"This is plain, ordinary cotton rope." His Lordship said. "But it is not quite long enough. The other bit of rope, if you please, my dear Sean."

The sorcerer handed him another foot-long piece of rope that looked exactly like the coil he already held.

Using a fisherman's knot, Lord Darcy tied the two together.

He climbed up on the late Count's desk and tied the end of the rope to another hook above the gaslight—the end with the tied-on extra piece. Then he turned and threw the coil of rope across the room to the foot of the ladder. He went back across the room and climbed the ladder again, taking with him the other end of the rope.

Working carefully he tied the rope to the chain link just above the lamp, then taking the chain off the hook he looped the rope over the hook so that it supported the lamp.

He climbed back down the ladder and pointed. "As you see, the lamp is now supported solely by the rope, which is fastened at the hook above the gaslamp over the window, stretches across the room, and is looped over the hook above the door to support the weight."

By this time they all understood. There was tension in the room.

"I said," continued Lord Darcy, "that the rope I have used is ordinary cotton. So it is, except for that last additional foot which is tied above the gaslamp. That last foot is not ordinary cotton, but of specially treated cotton which is called nitred or nitrated cotton. It burns extremely rapidly. In the original death trap the entire rope was made of that substance, but there was not enough left for me to use in this demonstration.

"As you will notice, the end which supports the lamp is several inches too long after the knot was tied. The person who set this trap very tidily cut off the excess and then failed to pick up the discarded end. Well, we all make mistakes, don't we?"

Lord Darcy stood dramatically in the center of the room. "I want you all to imagine what it was like in this room last night. Dark—or nearly so. There is only the dim illumination from the courtyard lamps below." He picked up an unlit torch from the workbench a few feet away, then went to the door.

"My Lord Count has just come in. He has closed, locked, and barred the door. He has a torch in his hand." Lord Darcy lit the torch with his pipe lighter.

"Now, he walks across the room, to light the gaslamp

above the window, as is his wont." Lord Darcy acted out his words.

"He climbs up on his desk. He turns on the gas valve. He lifts his torch to light the gas."

The gas jet shot a yellow flame several inches high. It touched the nitrated cotton rope above it. The rope flared into hissing flame.

Lord Darcy leaped aside and bounced to the floor, well away from the desk.

On the opposite side of the room, the heavy lamp was suddenly released from its hold. Like some airborne juggernaut, it swung ponderously along the arc of its chain. At the bottom of that arc, it grazed the floor with the brass ring. Then it swung up and—as anyone could see —would have smashed the window, had it still been there. Then it swung back.

Everyone in the room watched the lamp pendulum back and forth dragging the cotton rope behind it. The nitrated section had long since vanished in flame.

Lord Darcy stood on the east side of the room with the pendulum scything the air between himself and the others.

"Thus you see how the late Count de la Vexin came to his death. The arc this thing cuts would have struck him just below the shoulder-blades. Naturally, it would not have swung so long as now, having been considerably slowed by its impact with the Count's body." He walked over, grabbed the chain and fought the pendulum to a standstill.

They all stared fascinated at the deadly weight which now swung in a modest two-inch wobble.

The young Lord Gisors lifted his head with a jerk and stared straight into Lord Darcy's eyes. "Surely my father would have seen that white rope, Darcy."

"Not if it were covered with lampblack—which it was."

Lord Gisors narrowed his eyes. "Oh, fine. So that's the end of it, eh? With the lamp hanging there, almost touching the floor. Then—*will you explain how it got back up to where it belongs?"*

"Certainly," said Lord Darcy.

He walked over to the lamp, removed the length of cotton rope, pulled gently on the chain to unlock the ratchet, and eased the lamp up. After it left his outstretched hand it moved on up quietly to its accustomed place.

"Like that," said Lord Darcy blandly. "Except, of course, that the glass chimney was replaced first. And the rope did not need to be removed since it had all been burnt up."

Before anyone else could speak, Father Villiers said: "Just a moment my lord. If someone had done that, he would have had to have been in this room—seconds after the death. But there is no way in or out of this room except the door—which was guarded—and the door to the roof, which you have said was not used. There is no other way in or out of this room."

Lord Darcy smiled. "Oh, but there is, Reverend Father."

The priest looked blank.

"The way My Lord de la Vexin took," Lord Darcy said gently.

Surely they understand now, Lord Darcy thought. He broke the silence by saying: "The lamp was down. There was no one in this room. Then someone climbed in through the window via the fire ladder, raised the lamp again and—

"Chief Jaque!" Lord Darcy shouted.

But he was a fraction of a second too late.

Sergeant Andray had drawn a concealed sidearm. Chief Jaque was just a little too late getting his own gun out.

There was the sudden ear-shattering shock of a heavy-caliber pistol firing in a closed room and Chief Jaque went down with a bullet in him.

Lord Darcy's hand darted toward the pistol at his

own hip but before it could clear the holster Captain Sir Roderique leaped toward his son.

"You fool! You—" His voice was agonized.

He grabbed the sergeant's wrist, twisted it up.

There came a second shattering blast.

Sir Roderique fell backwards; the bullet had gone in under his chin and taken the top of his head off.

Sergeant Andray screamed.

Then he spun around, leaped to the top of the desk, and flung himself out the window, still screaming.

The scream lasted just a bit over two seconds before Sergeant Andray was permanently silenced by the courtyard below.

The celebrations of Holy Saturday were over, Easter Season had officially begun. The bells were still ringing in the tower of the Cathedral of St. Ouen in the city of Rouen, the capital of the Duchy of Normandy.

His Royal Highness, Richard, Duke of Normandy leaned back in his chair and smiled across the cozy fireplace at his Chief Investigator. Both of them were holding warming glasses of fine Champagne brandy.

His Highness had just finished reading Lord Darcy's report.

"I see, my lord," he said. "After the trap had been set and triggered—after the late de la Vexin had been propelled through the window to his death—Sergeant Andray went up the fire ladder alone, raised the lamp back to its usual position and then opened the barred door to allow in the other guardsmen. The fox concealing himself among the hounds."

"Precisely, Your Highness. And you see the motive."

His Highness the Duke, younger brother of His Imperial Majesty, King John IV, was blond, blue-eyed, and handsome, like all the Plantagenets, but at this moment there was a faint frown upon his forehead.

"The motive was obvious from the beginning, my lord," he said. "I can see that Sergeant Andray wanted to get rid of my Lord de la Vexin in order to clear the way for a marriage which would be beneficial to his sister—and, of course, to the rest of the family. But your written report is incomplete." He tapped the sheaf of papers in his hand.

"I fear, Your Highness," Lord Darcy said carefully, "that it must remain forever incomplete."

Prince Richard leaned back and sighed. "Very well, Darcy. Give it to me orally. Off the record, as usual."

"As you command, Your Highness," Lord Darcy said, refilling his glass.

"Young Andray must be blamed for the murder. The evidence I have can go no further, now that both he and his father are dead. Chief Jaque, who will easily recover from the bullet wound in his shoulder, has no more evidence than I have.

"Captain Sir Roderique will be buried with military honors, since eyewitnesses can and will say that he tried to stop his son from shooting me. Further hypotheses now would merely raise a discussion that could never be resolved.

"But it was not Sergeant Andray who set the trap. Only Captain Sir Roderique had access to the key that unlocked the laboratory. Only he could have gone up there and set the death trap that killed the late Count."

"Then why," the Prince asked, "did he try to stop his son?"

"Because, Your Highness," Lord Darcy replied, "he did not think I had enough evidence to convict. He was trying to stop young Andray from making a fool of himself by giving the whole thing away. Andray had panicked—which I had hoped he would, but not, I must admit, to that extent.

"He killed his father, who had plotted the whole thing, and seeing what he had done, went into a suicidal hysteria which resulted in his death. I am sorry for that, Your Highness."

"Not your fault, Darcy. What about the Demoselle Madelaine?"

Lord Darcy sipped at his brandy. "She was the prime mover, of course. She instigated the whole thing—subtly. No way to prove it. But Lord Gisors sees through her now. He will wed the lady his father quite properly chose for him."

"I see," said the Prince. "You told him the truth?"

"I spoke to him, Your Highness," Lord Darcy said. "But he already knew the truth."

"Then the matter is settled." His Highness straightened up in his chair. "Now, about those notebooks you brought back with you. What do they mean?"

"They are the late Count's scientific-materialistic notes on his researches for the past twenty years, Your Highness. They present two decades of hard research.'"

"But—really, Darcy. Research on Materialism? Of what use could they possibly be?"

"Your Highness, the Laws of Magic tell us how the mind of man can influence the material universe. But the universe is more than the mind of man can possibly encompass. The mind of God may keep the planets and the stars in their courses, but, if so, then He has laws by which He abides."

Lord Darcy finished his brandy. "There are more things in this universe than the mind of man, Your Highness, and there are laws which govern them. Someday, those notebooks may be invaluable."

The Ipswich Phial

The pair-drawn brougham moved briskly along the Old Shore Road, moving westward a few miles from the little village of St.-Matthew's-Church, in the direction of Cherbourg.

The driver, a stocky man with a sleepy smile on his broad face, was well bundled up in a gray driving cloak, and the hood of his cowl was pulled up over his head and covered with a wide-brimmed slouch hat. Even in early June, on a sunshiny day, the Normandy coast can be chilly in the early morning, especially with a stiff wind blowing.

"Stop here, Danglars," said a voice behind him. "This looks like a good place for a walk along the beach."

"Yus, mistress," He reined in the horses, bringing the brougham to an easy stop. "You sure it's safe down there, Mistress Jizelle?" he asked, looking to his right, where the Channel stretched across to the north, toward England.

"The tide is out, is it not?" she asked briskly.

Danglars looked at his wristwatch. "Yus. Just at the ebb now."

"Very well, Wait for me here. I may return here, or I may walk on. If I go far, I will signal you from down the road."

"Yus, mistress."

She nodded once, sharply, then strode off toward the beach.

She was a tall, not unhandsome woman, who appeared to be in late middle age. Her gray-silver hair was cut rather shorter than the usual, but was beautifully arranged. Her costume was that of an upper-middle-class Anglo-French woman on a walking tour, but it was more in the British style than the Norman: well-burnished knee-high boots; a Scottish woolen skirt, the hem of which just brushed the boot-tops; a matching jacket; and a soft sweater of white wool that covered her from waist to chin. She wore no hat. She carried herself with the brisk, no-nonsense air of a woman who knows what she is and who she is, and will brook no argument from anyone about it.

Mistress Jizelle de Ville found a pathway down to the beach. There was a low cliff, varying from fifteen to twenty feet high, which separated the upper downs from the beach itself, but there were slopes and washes here and there which could be maneuvered. The cliff itself was the ultimate high-tide mark, but only during great storms did the sea ever come up that high; the normal high tide never came within fifteen yards of the base of the cliff, and the intervening space was covered with soft, dry sand which was difficult to walk in. Mistress Jizelle crossed the dry sand to the damper, more solidly packed area, and began walking westward.

It was a beautiful morning, in spite of the slight chill; just the sort of morning one would choose for a brisk, healthful walk along a pleasant beach. Mistress Jizelle was a woman who liked exercise and long walks, and she was a great admirer of scenic beauty. To her right, the rushing wind made scudding whitecaps of the ebbing tide and brought the "smell of the sea"—an odor never found on the open expanse of the sea itself, for it is composed of the aroma of the sea things which dwell in the tidal basins and the shallow coastal waters and the faint smell of the decomposition of dead and dying things beached by the rhythmic ebb and flow of tide and wave.

Overhead, the floating gulls gave their plaintive,

almost catlike cries as they soared in search of the rich sustenance that the sea and shore gave them.

Not until she had walked nearly a hundred yards along the beach did Mistress Jizelle see anything out of the ordinary. When she did, she stopped and looked at it carefully. Ahead and to her left, some eight or nine yards from the base of the cliff, a man lay sprawled in the dry sand, twenty feet or so above the high-tide line.

After a moment, she walked toward the man, carefully and cautiously. He was certainly not dressed for bathing; he was wearing the evening dress of a gentleman. She walked up to the edge of the damp sand and stopped again, looking at the man carefully.

Then she saw something that made the hairs on the back of her neck rise.

Danglars was sitting placidly in the driver's seat of the brougham, smoking his clay pipe, when he saw the approaching trio. He eyed them carefully as they came toward the carriage. Two young men and an older one, all dressed in the work clothes typical of a Norman farmer. The eldest waved a hand and said something Danglars couldn't hear over the sound of the waves and the wind. Then they came close enough to be audible, and the eldest said: "Allo! Got dee any trouble here?"

Danglars shook his head. "Nup."

The farmer ignored that. "Me an' m'boys saw dee stop up here, an' thought mayap we could help. Name's Champtier. Samel Champtier. Dese two a my tads, Evrit an' Lorin. If dou hass need a aid, we do what we can."

Danglars nodded slowly, then took his pipe from his mouth. "Good o' ya, Goodman Samel. Grace to ya. But I got no problem. Mistress wanted to walk along the beach. Likes that sort of thing. We head on pretty soon."

Samel cleared his throat. "Hass dou broke dy fast, dou an' d' miss-lady? Wife fixin' breakfast now. Mayap we bring du somewhat?"

Danglars took another puff and sighed. Norman farmers were good, kindly folk, but sometimes they overdid it. "Broke fast, Goodman Samel. Grace to ya. Mistress comes back, we got to be gettin' on. Again, grace to ya."

"Caffe, then," Samel said decisively. He turned to the elder son. "Evrit! Go tell dy mama for a pot a caffe an' two mugs! Run it, now!"

Evrit took off like a turpentined ostrich.

Danglars cast his eyes toward heaven.

Mistress Jizelle swallowed and again looked closely at the dead man. There was a pistol in his right hand and an ugly hole in his right temple. There was blood all over the sand around his head. And there was no question about his being dead.

She looked up and down the beach while she rather dazedly brushed at her skirt with the palms of her hands. Then, bracing her shoulders, Mistress Jizelle turned herself about and walked back the way she had come, paralleling her own footprints. There were no others on the beach.

Three men were talking to Danglars, and Danglars did not seem to be agitated about it. Determinedly, she strode onward.

Not until she was within fifteen feet of the brougham did Danglars deign to notice her. Then he tugged his forelock and smiled his sleepy smile. "Greeting, mistress. Have a nice walk?" He had a mug of caffe in one hand. He gestured with the other. "Goodman Samel and his boys, mistress, from the near farm. Brought a pot o' caffe."

The three farmers were tugging at their forelocks, too.

"I appreciate that," she said. "Very much. But I fear we have an emergency to attend to. Come with me, all of you."

Danglars widened his eyes. "Emergency, mistress?"

"That's what I said, wasn't it? Now, all of you follow

me, and I shall show you what I mean."

"But, mistress—" Danglars began.

"Follow me," she said imperatively.

Danglars got down from the brougham. He had no choice but to follow with the others.

Mistress Jizelle led them across the sparse grass to the edge of the cliff that overlooked the place where the dead man lay.

"Now look down there. There is a dead man down there. He has, I think, been shot to death. I am not much acquainted with such things, but that is what it looks like to me."

The four knelt and looked at the body below. There was silence for a moment, then Samel said, rather formally: "Dou be right, mistress. Dead he be."

"Who is he, goodman?" she asked.

Samel stood up slowly and brushed his trousers with calloused hands. "Don't rightly know, mistress." He looked at his two sons, who were still staring down with fascination. "Who be he, tads?"

They stood up, brushing their trousers as their father had. Evrit, the elder, spoke. "Don't know, Papa. Ee not from hereabout." He nudged his younger brother with an elbow. "Lorin?"

Lorin shook his head, looking at his father.

"Well, that does not matter for the moment," Mistress Jizelle said firmly. "There is Imperial Law to follow in such cases as this, and we must do so. Danglars, get in the brougham and return to—"

"But, Mistress Jizelle," Danglars cut in, "I can't—"

"You must do exactly as I tell you, Danglars," she said forcefully. "It is most important. Go back to St.-Matthew's-Church and notify the Rector. Then go on to Caen and notify the Armsmen. Goodman Samel and his boys will wait here with me and make sure nobody disturbs anything. Do you understand?"

"Yus, mistress. Perfec'ly." And off he went.

She turned to Samel. "Goodman, can you spare some

time? I am sure you have work to do, but I shouldn't like to be left here alone."

Samel smiled. "Mornin' chores all done, mistress. Eldest tad, Orval, can take care of all for a couple hours. Don't fret." He looked at the younger boy. "Lorin, go dou an tell dy mama an' dy brother what happen, but nobody else. An' say dey tell nobody. Hear?"

Lorin nodded and ran.

"And bring dou back somewat ta eat!" Evrit yelled after him.

Samel looked worried. "Mistress?"

"Yes, Goodman Samel?"

"Hass dou noticed somewat funny about d' man dere?"

"Funny?" She raised an eyebrow.

"Yea, mistress." He pointed down. "All round him, sand. Smooth. No footprints but dine own, an' dey come nowhere near him. Fresh dead, but—how he get dere?"

Five days later, Sir James le Lien, Special Agent of His Majesty's Secret Service, was seated in a comfortable chair in the studylike office of Lord Darcy, Chief Investigator for His Royal Highness, Richard, Duke of Normandy.

"And I still don't know where the Ipswich Phial is, Darcy," he was saying with some exasperation. "And neither do they."

Outside the open window, sounds of street traffic— the susurration of rubber-tired wheels on pavement, the clopping of horses' hooves, the footsteps and voices of a thousand people, and the myriad of other small noises that make up the song of a city—were wafted up from six floors below.

Lord Darcy leaned back in the chair behind his broad desk and held up a hand.

"Hold it, Sir James. You're leaping far ahead of yourself. I presume that by 'they' you mean the *Serka*—the

Polish Secret Service. But what is this Phial, anyway?"

"I can't tell you for two reasons. First, you have no need to know. Second, neither do I, so I couldn't tell you if I wanted. Physically, it's a golden cylinder the size of your thumb, stoppered at one end with a golden stopper, which is sealed over with soft gold. Other than that, I know nothing but the code name: The Ipswich Phial."

Sean O Lochlainn, Master Sorcerer, who had been sitting quietly in another chair with his hands folded over his stomach, his eyes half closed, and his ears wide open, said: "I'd give a pretty penny to know who assigned that code name; sure and I'd have him sacked for incompetence."

"Oh?" said Sir James. "Why?"

Master Sean opened his eyes fully. "If the Poles don't know that the Ipswich Laboratories in Suffolk, under Master Sir Greer Davidson, is devoted to secret research in magic, then they are so incredibly stupid that we need not worry about them at all. With a name like 'Ipswich Phial' on it, the *Serka* would *have* to investigate, if they heard about it."

"Maybe it's just a red herring designed to attract their attention while something else is going on," said Lord Darcy.

"Maybe," Master Sean admitted, "but if so, me lord, it's rather dear. What Sir James has just described is an auric-stabilized psychic shield. What would you put in such a container? Some Khemic concoction, like an explosive or a poison? Or a secret message? That'd be incompetence compounded, like writing your grocery list on vellum in gold. Conspicuous consumption."

"I see," said Lord Darcy. He looked at Sir James. "What makes you think the *Serka* hasn't got it already?"

"If they had it," Sir James said, "they'd have cut and run. And they haven't; they're still swarming all over the place. There must be a dozen agents there."

"I presume that your own men are all over the place, too?"

"We're trying to keep them covered," Sir James said.

"Then they know you don't have the Phial, either."

"Probably."

Lord Darcy sighed and began filling his silver-chased porcelain pipe. "You say the dead man is Noel Standish." He tapped a sheaf of papers with his pipestem. "These say he was identified as a man named Bourke. You say it was murder. These say that the court of His Majesty's Coroner was ready to call it suicide until you put pressure on to keep the decision open. I have the vague feeling, James, that I am being used. I should like to point out that I am Chief Criminal Investigator for the Duke of Normandy, not—repeat: *not*—an agent of His Majesty's Secret Service."

"A crime has been committed," Sir James pointed out. "It is your duty to investigate it."

Lord Darcy calmly puffed his pipe alight. "James, James." His lean, handsome face was utterly impassive as he blew out a long plume of smoke. "You know perfectly well I am not obliged to investigate every homicide in the Duchy. Neither Standish nor Bourke was a member of the aristocracy. I don't *have* to investigate this mess unless and until I get a direct order from either His Highness the Duke or His Majesty the King. Come on, James—convince me."

Master Sean did not smile, although it was somewhat of a strain to keep his face straight. The stout little Irish sorcerer knew perfectly well that his lordship was bluffing. Lord Darcy could no more resist a case like this than a bee can resist clover blossoms. But Sir James did not know that. He did know that by bringing the case before his superiors, he could eventually get an order from the King, but by then the whole thing would likely be over.

"What do you want, Darcy?" the King's agent asked.

"Information," his lordship said flatly. "You want me to go down to St.-Matthew's-Church and create a diversion while you and your men do your work. Fine. But I will not play the part of a dupe. I damn well want to know what's going on. I want the whole story."

Sir James thought it over for ten or fifteen seconds, then said: "All right, my lord. I'll give it to you straight."

For centuries, the Kings of Poland had been expanding, in an ebb-and-flow fashion, the borders of their territories, primarily toward the east and south. In the south, they had been stopped by the Osmanlis. In the east, the last bite had been taken in the early 1930's, when the Ukraine was swallowed. King Casimir IX came to the throne in 1937 at the age of twenty, and two years later had plunged his country into a highly unsuccessful war with the Empire and her Scandinavian allies, and any further thought of expansion to the east was stopped by the threat of the unification of the Russian States.

Poland was now, quite literally, surrounded by enemies who hated her and neighbors who feared her. Casimir should have taken a few years to consolidate and conciliate, but it was apparent that the memory of his father and his own self-image as a conqueror were too strong for him. Knowing that any attempt to march his armies into the German buffer states that lay between his own western border and the eastern border of the Empire would be suicidal as things stood, Casimir decided to use his strongest non-military weapon: the *Serka*.

The nickname comes from a phrase meaning roughly: "The King's Right Arm." For financial purposes, it is listed in the books as the Ministry of Security Control, making it sound as if it were a division of the King's Government. It is not; none of His Slavonic Majesty's ministers or advisors know anything about, or have any control over, its operation. It is composed of fanatically loyal men and women who have taken a solemn vow of obedience to the King himself, *not* to the Government. The *Serka* is responsible to no one but the King's Person.

It is composed of two main branches: The Secret Police (domestic), and the Secret Service (foreign). This separation, however, is far from rigid. An agent of one branch may at any time be assigned to the other.

The *Serka* is probably the most powerful, most ruthless instrument of government on the face of the Earth today. Its agents, many of them Talented sorcerers, infest every country in Europe, most especially the Anglo-French Empire.

Now, it is a historical fact that Plantagenet Kings do not take kindly to invasion of their domain by foreign sovereigns; for eight centuries they have successfully resisted such intrusive impudence.

There is a saying in Europe: "He who borrows from a Plantagenet may repay without interest; he who steals from a Plantagenet will repay at ruinous rates."

His present Majesty, John IV—by the Grace of God, King of England, Ireland, Scotland, and France; Emperor of the Romans and Germans; Premier Chief of the Moqtessumid Clan; Son of the Sun; Count of Anjou and Maine; Prince Donator of the Sovereign Order of St. John of Jerusalem; Sovereign of the Most Ancient Order of the Round Table, of the Order of the Leopard, of the Order of the Lily, of the Order of the Three Crowns, and of the Order of St. Andrew; Lord and Protector of the Western Continents of New England and New France; Defender of the Faith—was no exception to that rule.

Unlike his medieval predecessors, however, King John had no desire to increase Imperial holdings in Europe. The last Plantagenet to add to the Imperial domain in Europe was Harold I, who signed the original Treaty of Kobnhavn in 1420. The Empire was essentially frozen within its boundaries for more than a century until, during the reign of John III, the discovery of the continents of the Western Hemisphere opened a whole new world for Anglo-French explorers.

John IV no longer thought of European expansion, but he deeply resented the invasion of his realm by Polish *Serka* agents. Therefore, the theft of a small golden phial from the Ipswich Laboratories had provoked instant reaction from the King and from His Majesty's Secret Service.

"The man who actually stole it," Sir James explained, "is irrelevant. He was merely a shrewd biscuit who accidentally had a chance to get his hands on the Phial. Just how is immaterial, but rest assured that that hole has been plugged. The man saw an opportunity and grabbed it. He wasn't a Polish agent, but he knew how to get hold of one, and a deal was made."

"How much time did it take him to deal, after the Phial was stolen?" Lord Darcy asked.

"Three days, my lord. Sir Greer found it was missing within two hours of its being stolen, and notified us straight away. It was patently obvious who had taken it, but it took us three days to trace him down. As I said, he was a shrewd biscuit.

"By the time we'd found him, he'd made his deal and had the money. We were less than half an hour too late. A *Serka* agent already had the Phial and was gone.

"Fortunately, the thief was just that—a thief, not a real *Serka* agent. When he'd been caught, he freely told us everything he knew. That, plus other information received, convinced us our quarry was on a train for Portsmouth. We got hold of Noel Standish at the Portsmouth office by teleson, but . . ."

The plans of men do not necessarily coincide with those of the Universe. A three-minute delay in a traffic jam had ended with Noel Standish at the slip, watching the Cherbourg boat sliding out toward the Channel, with forty feet between himself and the vessel.

Two hours later, he was standing at the bow of H.I.M.S. *Dart,* staring southward into the darkness, listening to the rushing of the Channel waters against the hull of the fast cutter. Standish was not in a good mood.

In the first place, the teleson message had caught him just as he was about to go out to dine with friends at the Bellefontaine, and he had had no chance to change; he felt silly as hell standing on the deck of a Navy cutter in full evening dress. Further, it had taken better than an hour to convince the Commanding Admiral at the Portsmouth Naval Docks that the use of a cutter was imperative—and then only at the cost of a teleson connection to London.

There was but one gem in these otherwise bleak surroundings: Standish had a firm psychic lock on his quarry.

He had already had a verbal description from London. *Young man, early to middle twenties. Five feet nine. Slender, but well-muscled. Thick, dark brown hair. Smooth shaven. Brown eyes. Well formed brows. Face handsome, almost pretty. Well-dressed. Conservative dark green coat, puce waistcoat, gold-brown trousers. Carrying a dark olive attache case.*

And he had clearly seen the quarry standing on the deck of the cross-Channel boat as it had pulled out of Portsmouth, heading for Cherbourg.

Standish had a touch of the Talent. His own name for a rather specialized ability was "the Game of Hide and Seek," wherein Standish did both the hiding and the seeking. Once he got a lock on someone he could follow him anywhere. Further Standish became psychically invisible to his quarry; even a Master Sorcerer would never notice him as long as Standish took care not to be located visually. Detection range, however, was only a matter of miles, and the man in the puce waistcoat, Standish knew, was at the limit of that range.

Someone tapped Standish on the shoulder. "Excuse me, sir—"

Standish jerked round nervously. *"What? What?"*

The young officer lifted his eyebrows, taken aback by the sudden reaction. This Standish fellow seemed to have every nerve on edge. "Begging your pardon, sir, but the Captain would have a word with you. Follow me, please."

Senior Lieutenant Malloix, commanding H.I.M.S. *Dart,* wearing his royal blue uniform, was waiting in his cabin with a glass of brandy in each hand. He gave one to Standish while the junior officer quietly disappeared. "Come in, Standish. Sit and relax. You've been staring off the starboard bow ever since we cast off, and that's no good. Won't get us there any the faster, you know."

Standish took the glass and forced a smile. "I know, Captain. Thanks." He sipped. "Still, do you think we'll make it?"

The captain frowned, sat down, and waved Standish to a chair while he said: "Hard to say, frankly. We're using all the power we have, but the sea and the wind don't always do what we'd like 'em to. There's not a damn thing we can do about it, so breathe deep and see what comes, eh?"

"Right you are, Captain." He took another swallow of brandy. "How good a bearing do we have on her?"

S/Lt Malloix patted the air with a hand. "Not to worry. Lieutenant Seamus Mac Lean, our navigator, has a Journeyman's rating in the Sorcerer's Guild, and this sort of thing is his speciality. The packet boat is two degrees off to starboard and, at our present speed, forty-one minutes ahead of us. That's the good news."

"And the bad news?"

Malloix shrugged. "Wind variation. We haven't gained on her in fifteen minutes. Cheer up. Pour yourself another brandy."

Standish cheered up and drank more brandy, but it vailed him nothing. The *Dart* pulled into the dock at

Cherbourg one minute late, in spite of all she could do.

Nevertheless, Goodman Puce-Weskit was less than a hundred yards away as Standish ran down the gangplank of the *Dart,* and the distance rapidly closed as he walked briskly toward his quarry, following his psychic compass that pointed unerringly toward Puce-Weskit.

He was hoping that Puce-Weskit was still carrying the Phial; if he wasn't, if he had passed it on to some unknown person aboard the packet, the whole thing was blown. The thing would be in Krakowa before the month was out.

He tried not to think about that.

The only thing to do was follow his quarry until there came a chance to waylay and search him.

He had already given a letter to the captain of the *Dart,* to be delivered as soon as possible to a certain address on the Rue Queen Brigid, explaining to the agent in charge of the Cherbourg office what was going on. The trouble was, Standish was not carrying a tracer attuned to the Cherbourg office; there was no way to get in touch with them, and he didn't dare leave Puce-Weskit. He couldn't even set up a rendezvous, since he had no idea where Puce-Weskit would lead him.

And, naturally, when one needed an Armsman, there wasn't one in sight.

Twenty minutes later, Puce-Weskit turned on to the Rue Queen Brigid.

Don't tell me he's headed for the Service office, Standish thought. *My dear Puce-Weskit, surely you jest.*

No fear. A dozen squares from the Secret Service office, Goodman Puce-Weskit turned and went into a caffe-house called the Aden. There, he stopped.

Standish had been following on the opposite side of the street, so there was less chance of his being spotted. Dodging the early morning traffic; narrowly avoiding the lead horse of a beer lorry, he crossed the Rue Queen Brigid to the Aden.

Puce-Weskit was some forty feet away, toward the rear of the caffe-house. Could he be passing the Phial on to some confederate?

Standish was considering what to do next when the decision was made for him. He straightened up with a snap as his quarry suddenly began to move southward at a relatively high rate of speed.

He ran into the Aden. And saw his mistake.

The rear wall was only thirty feet away. Puce-Weskit had gone through the rear door, and had been standing *behind* the Aden!

He went right on through the large room, out the back door. There was a small alleyway there, but the man standing a few feet away was most certainly not his quarry.

"Quick!" Standish said breathlessly. "The man in the puce waistcoat! Where did he go?"

The man looked a little flustered. "Why—uh—I don't know, sir. As soon as his horse was brought—"

"Horse? Where did he get a horse?

"Why, he left it in the proprietor's charge three or four days ago. Four days ago. Paid in advance for the keeping of it. He asked it to be fetched, then he went. I don't know where."

"Where can I rent a horse?" Standish snapped.

"The proprietor—"

"Take me to him immediately!"

"And that," said Sir James le Lien, "is the last trace we were able to uncover until he reported in at Caen two days later. We wouldn't even know that much if one of our men hadn't been having breakfast at the Aden. He recognized Standish, of course, but didn't say anything to him, for obvious reasons."

Lord Darcy nodded. "And he turns up dead the following morning near St.-Matthew's-Church. Any conjecture on what he may have been doing during those two days?"

"It seems fairly clear. The proprietor of the Aden told us that our quarry—call him Bourke—had his saddlebags packed with food packets in protective-spell wrappers, enough for a three, maybe four-day trip. You know the Old Shore Road that runs southeast from Cherbourg to the Vire, crosses the river, then goes westward, over the Orne, and loops around to Harfleur?"

"Of course," Lord Darcy said.

"Well, then, you know it's mostly farming country, with only a few scattered villages, and no teleson connections. We think Bourke took that road, and that Standish followed him. We think Bourke was headed for Caen."

Master Sean lifted an eyebrow. "Then why not take the train? 'Twould be a great deal easier and faster, Sir James."

Sir James smiled. "It would be. But not safer. The trouble with public transportation is that you're essentially trapped on it. When you're fleeing, you want as much freedom of choice as possible. Once you're aboard a public conveyance, you're pretty much constrained to stay on it until it stops, and that isn't under your control."

"Aye, that's clear," said Master Sean. He looked thoughtful. "This psychic lock-on you mentioned—you're sure Standish used it on Bourke?"

"Not absolutely certain, of course," Sir James admitted. "But he certainly had that Talent; he was tested by a board of Masters from your own Guild. Whether he used it or not at that particular time, I can only conjecture, but I think it's a pretty solid assumption."

Lord Darcy carefully watched a column of pipesmoke rise toward the ceiling and said nothing.

"I'll agree with you," Master Sean said. "There's no doubt in me mind he did just that, and I'll not say he was wrong to do so. *De mortuis non disputandum est.* I just wonder if he knew how to handle it."

"How do you mean?" Sir James asked.

"Well, let's suppose a man could make himself perfectly transparent—'invisible,' in other words. The poor lad would have to be very careful, eh? In soft ground or in snow, he'll leave footprints; in a crowd, he may brush up against someone. Can you imagine what it would be like if you grabbed such a man? There you've got an armful of air that feels fleshy, smells sweaty, sounds excited, and would taste salty if you cared to try the experiment. You'll admit that such an object would be suspect?"

"Well, yes," Sir James admitted, "but—"

"Sir James," Master Sean continued, "you have no idea how conspicuous a psychically invisible person can be in the wrong circumstances. There he stands, visible to the eye, sensible to the touch, audible to the ear, and all the rest—*but there's nobody home!*

"The point I'm making, Sir James, is this: How competent was Noel Standish at handling his ability?"

Sir James opened his mouth, shut it, and frowned. After a second, he said: "When you put it that way, Master Sean, I must admit I don't know. But he handled it successfully for twelve years."

"And failed once," said Master Sean. "Fatally."

"Now hold, my dear Sean," Lord Darcy said suddenly. "We have no evidence that he failed in that way. That he allowed himself to be killed is a matter of cold fact; that he did so in that way is pure conjecture. Let's not leap to totally unwarranted conclusions."

"Aye, me lord. Sorry."

Lord Darcy focused his gray eyes on Sir James. "Then I have not been called in merely to create a diversion, eh?"

Sir James blinked. "I beg your pardon, my lord?"

"I mean," said his lordship patiently, "that you actually want me to solve the problem of 'who killed Noel Standish?' "

"Of course! Didn't I make that clear?".

"Not very." Lord Darcy picked up the papers again.

"Now let's get a few things straight. How did the body come to be identified as Bourke, and where is the real Bourke? Or whoever he was."

"The man Standish was following checked into the Green Seagull Inn under that name," Sir James said. "He'd used the same name in England. He was a great deal like Standish in height, weight, and coloring. He disappeared that night, and we've found no trace of him since."

Lord Darcy nodded thoughtfully. "It figures. Young gentleman arrives at village inn. Body of young gentleman found next morning. Since there is only one young gentleman in plain sight, they are the same young gentleman. Identifying a total stranger is a chancy thing at best."

"Exactly. That's why I held up my own identification."

"I understand. Now, exactly how did you happen to be in St.-Matthew's-Church that night?" Lord Darcy asked.

"Well, as soon as Standish was fairly certain that his quarry had settled down at the Green Seagull, he rode for Caen and sent a message to my office, here in Rouen. I took the first train, but by the time I got there, they were both missing."

"Yes." Lord Darcy sighed. "Well, I suppose we'd best be getting down there. I'll have to ask His Royal Highness to order me to, so you may as well come along with me and explain the whole thing all over again to Duke Richard."

Sir James looked pained. "I suppose so. We want to get there as soon as possible, or the whole situation will become impossible. Their silly Midsummer Fair starts the day after tomorrow, and there are strangers showing up already."

Lord Darcy closed his eyes. "That's all we need. Complications."

Master Sean went to the door of the office. "I'll have

Ciardi pack our bags, me lord. Looks like a long stay."

The little village of St.-Matthew's-Church was transforming itself. The Fair proper was to be held in a huge field outside of town, and the tents were already collecting on the meadow. There was, of course, no room in the village itself for people to stay; certainly the little Green Seagull couldn't hold a hundredth of them. But a respectable tent-city had been erected in another big field, and there was plenty of parking space for horse-wagons and the like.

In the village, the storefronts were draped with bright bunting, and the shopkeepers were busy marking up all the prices. Both pubs had been stocking up on extra potables for weeks. For nine days, the village would be full of strangers going about their hectic business, disrupting the peace of the local inhabitants, bringing with them a strange sort of excitement. Then they would go, leaving behind acres of ugly rubbish and bushels of beautiful cash.

In the meanwhile, a glorious time would be had by all.

Lord Darcy cantered his horse along the River Road up from Caen and entered St.-Matthew's-Church at noon on that bright sunshiny day, dressed in the sort of riding clothes a well-to-do merchant might wear. He wasn't exactly incognito, but he didn't want to attract attention, either. Casually, he made his way through the already gathering throngs toward the huge old church dedicated to St. Matthew, which had given the village its name. He guided his mount over to the local muffin square, where the array of hitching posts stood, tethered his horse, and walked over to the church.

The Reverend Father Arthur Lyon, Rector of the Church of St.-Matthew, and, *ipso facto,* Rector of St.-Matthew's-Church, was a broad-shouldered man in his fifties who stood a good two inches taller than six feet. His bald head was fringed with silvery hair, and his authoritative, pleasant face was usually smiling. He was sitting behind his desk in his office.

There came a rap at his office door. A middle-aged woman came in quickly and said: "Sorry to bodder dee, Fahder, but dere's a Lord Darcy to see dee."

"Show him in, Goodwife Anna."

Lord Darcy entered Father Art's office to find the priest waiting with outstretched hand. "It's been some time, my lord," he said with a broad smile. "Good to see you again."

"I may say the same. How have you been, old friend?"

"Not bad. Pray, sit down. May I offer you a drink?"

"Not just now, Father." He took the proffered seat. "I understand you have a bit of a problem here."

Father Art leaned back in his chair and folded his hands behind his head. "Ahh, yes. The so-called suicide. Bourke." He chuckled. "I thought higher authority would be in on that, sooner or later."

"Why do you say 'so-called suicide,' Father?"

"Because I know people, my lord. If a man's going to shoot himself, he doesn't go out to a lonely beach for it. If he goes to a beach, it's to drown himself. A walk into the sea. I don't say a man has never shot himself by the seaside, but it's so rare that when it happens I get suspicious."

"I agree," Lord Darcy said. He had known Arthur Lyon for some years, and knew that the man was an absolutely dedicated servant of his God and his King. His career had been unusual. During the '39 war, he had risen to the rank of Sergeant-Major in the Eighteenth Infantry. Afterwards, he had become an Officer of the King's Peace, and had retired as a Chief Master-at-Arms before taking up his vocation as a priest. He had shown himself to be not only a top-grade priest, but also a man with the Talent as a brilliant Healer, and had been admitted, with honors, to the Order of St. Luke.

"Old friend," Lord Darcy said, "I need your help.

What I am about to tell you is most confidential; I will have to ask you to disclose none of it without official permission."

Father Art took his hands from behind his head and leaned forward with a gleam in his eyes. "As if it were under the Seal of the Confessional, my lord. Go ahead."

It took better than half an hour for Lord Darcy to give the good father the whole story as he knew it. Father Art had leaned back in his chair again with his hands locked behind his head, smiling seraphically at the ceiling. "Ah, yes, my lord. Utterly fascinating. I remember Friday, sixth June, very well. Yes, very well indeed." He continued to smile at the ceiling.

Lord Darcy closed his right eye and cocked his left eyebrow. "I trust you intend to tell me what incident stamped that day so indelibly on your mind."

"Certainly, my lord. I was just reveling in having made a deduction. When I tell my story, I dare say you'll make the same deduction." He brought his gaze down from the ceiling and his hands from behind his head. "You might say it began late Thursday night. Because of a sick call which had kept me up most of the previous night, I went to bed quite early Thursday evening. And, naturally, I woke up a little before midnight and couldn't get back to sleep. I decided I might as well make use of the time, so I did some paper work for a while and then went into the church to say the morning office before the altar. Then I decided to take a walk in the churchyard. I often do that; it's a pleasant place to meditate.

"There was no moon that night," the priest continued, "but the sky was cloudless and clear. It was about two hours before dawn. It was quite dark, naturally, but I know my way about those tombstones pretty well by now. I'd been out there perhaps a quarter of an hour when the stars went out."

Lord Darcy seemed to freeze for a full second. "When the *what?*"

"When the stars went out." Father Art repeated. "One moment, there they were, in their accustomed constellations—I was looking at Cygnus in particular—and the next moment the sky was black all over. Everywhere. All at once."

"I see," said Lord Darcy.

"Well, *I* couldn't," the priest said, flashing a smile. "It was black as the Pit. For a second or two, I confess, I was almost panicky. It's a weird feeling when the stars go out."

"I dare say," Lord Darcy murmured.

"But," the Father continued, "as a Sensitive, I knew that there was no threat close by, and, after a minute, I got my bearings again. I could have come back to the church, but I decided to wait for a while, just to find out what would happen next. I don't know how long I stood there. It seemed like an hour, but it was probably less than fifteen minutes. Then the stars came back on the same way they'd gone out—all at once, all over the sky."

"No dimming out?" Lord Darcy asked. "No slow brightening back on?"

"None, my lord. *Blink:* off. *Blink:* on."

"Not a sea fog, then."

"Impossible. No sea fog could move that fast."

Lord Darcy focused his eyes on a foot-high statue of St. Matthew that stood in a niche in the wall and stared at the Apostle without actually seeing him.

After a minute, Lord Darcy said: "I left Master Sean in Caen to make a final check of the body. He should be here within the hour. I'll talk to him, but . . ." His voice trailed off.

Father Art nodded. "Our speculation certainly needs to be confirmed, my lord, but I think we're on the right track. Now, how else can I help?"

"Oh, yes. That." Lord Darcy grinned. "Your revelation of the extinguished stars almost made me forget why I came to talk to you in the first place. What I'd like you to do, Father, is talk to the people that were at the Green Seagull on the afternoon and late evening of the fifth. I'm a stranger, and I probably wouldn't get much out of them—certainly not as much as you can. I want to know the whole pattern of comings and goings. I don't have to tell an old Armsman like yourself what to look for. Will you do it?"

Father Art's smile came back. "With pleasure, my lord."

"There's one other thing. Can you put up Master Sean and myself for a few days? There is, alas, no room at the inn."

Father Art's peal of laughter seemed to rock the bell tower.

Master Sean O Lochlainn had always been partial to mules. "The mule," he was fond of saying, "is as much smarter than a horse as a raven is smarter than a falcon. Neither a raven nor a mule will go charging into combat just because some human tells him to." Thus it was that the sorcerer came riding toward St.-Matthew's-Church, clad in plain brown, seated in a rather worn saddle, on the back of a very fine mule. He looked quite pleased with himself.

The River Road had plenty of traffic on it; half the population of the duchy seemed to be converging on the little coastal village of St.-Matthew's-Church. So Master Sean was mildly surprised to see someone headed toward him, but that feeling vanished when he saw that the approaching horseman was Lord Darcy.

"Not headed back to Caen, are you, me lord?" he asked when Lord Darcy came within speaking distance.

"Not at all, my dear Sean; I rode out to meet you. Let's take the cutoff road to the west; it's a shortcut that bypasses the village and takes us to the Old Shore Road, near where the body was found." He wheeled his horse around and rode beside Master Sean's mule. Together, they cantered briskly toward the Old Shore Road.

"Now," Lord Darcy said, what did you find out at Caen?"

"Conflicting evidence, me lord; conflicting evidence. At least as far as the suicide theory is concerned. There was evidence at the cliff edge that he had fallen or been pushed over and tumbled down along the face of the cliff. But he was found twenty-five feet from the base of the cliff. He had two broken ribs and a badly sprained right wrist—to say nothing of several bad bruises. All of these had been inflicted some hours before death."

Lord Darcy gave a rather bitter chuckle. "Which leaves us with two possibilities. *Primus:* Goodman Standish stands on the edge of the cliff, shoots himself through the head, tumbles to the sand below, crawls twenty-five feet, and takes some hours to die of a wound that was obviously instantly fatal. Or, *secundus:* He falls off the cliff, crawls the twenty-five feet, does nothing for a few hours, then decides to shoot himself. I find the second hypothesis only slightly more likely than the first. That his right wrist was sprained badly is a fact that tops it all off. Not suicide; no, not suicide." Lord Darcy grinned. "That leaves accident or murder. Which hypothesis do you prefer, my dear Sean?"

Master Sean frowned deeply, as if he were in the awful throes of concentration. Then his face brightened as if revelation had come. "I have it, me lord! He was accidentally murdered!"

Lord Darcy laughed. "Excellent! Now, having cleared that up, there is further evidence that I have not given you yet."

He told Master Sean about Father Art's singular experience with the vanishing stars.

When he had finished, the two rode in silence for a minute or two. Then Master Sean said softly: "So *that's* what it is."

*   *   *

There was an Armsman standing off the road at the site of the death, and another seated, who stood up as Lord Darcy and Master Sean approached. The two riders dismounted and walked their mounts up to where the Armsmen were standing.

"I am sorry, gentlemen," said the first Armsman with an air of authority, "but this area is off bounds, by order of His Royal Highness the Duke of Normandy."

"Very good; I am happy to hear it," said his lordship, taking out his identification. "I am Lord Darcy; this is Master Sorcerer Sean O Lochlainn."

"Yes, my lord," said the Armsman. "Sorry I didn't recognize you."

"No problem. This is where the body was found?"

"Yes, my lord. Just below this cliff, here. Would you like to take a look, my lord?"

"Indeed I would. Thank you."

Lord Darcy, under the respectful eyes of the two Armsmen, minutely examined the area around the cliff edge. Master Sean stayed with him, trying to see everything his lordship saw.

"Everything's a week old," Lord Darcy muttered bitterly. "Look at that grass, there. A week ago, I could have told you how many men were scuffing it up; today, I only know that it was more than two. I don't suppose there's any way of reconstructing it, my dear Sean?"

"No, me lord. I am a magician, not a miracle worker."

"Thought not. Look at the edge of this cliff. He fell, certainly. But was he pushed? Or thrown? No way of telling. Wind and weather have done their work too well. To quote my cousin de London: *'Pfui!'*"

"Yes, me lord."

"Well, let's go down to the beach and take a look from below."

That operation entailed walking fifty yards or so down the cliff edge to a steep draw which they could clamber down, then back again to where Standish had died.

There was a pleasant breeze from landward that brought the smell of growing crops. A dozen yards away, three gulls squabbled raucously over the remains of some dead sea-thing.

Lord Darcy was still in a bitter mood. "Nothing, damn it. *Nothing*. Footprints all washed away long ago. Or blown away by the wind. Damn, damn, *damn*! All we have to go by is the testimony of eyewitnesses, which is notoriously unreliable."

"You don't believe 'em, me lord?" Master Sean asked.

Lord Darcy was silent for several seconds. Then, in a calmer voice, he said: "Yes. Oddly enough, I do. I think the testimony of those farmers was absolutely accurate. They saw what they saw, and they reported what they saw. But they did not—they *could* not have seen everything!"

One of the Armsmen on the cliff above said: "That's the spot, right there, my lord. Near that flat rock." He pointed.

But Lord Darcy did not even look at the indicated spot. He had looked up when the Armsman spoke, and was staring at something on the cliff face about two feet below the Armsman's boot toes.

Master Sean followed his lordship's gaze and spotted the area immediately. "Looks like someone's been carving his initials, me lord."

"Indeed. How do you make them out?"

"Looks like S. . .S. . .O. Who do we know with the initials SSO?"

"Nobody connected with this case so far. The letters may have been up there for some time. But . . ."

"Aye, me lord," said Master Sean. "I see what you mean. I'll do a time check on them. Do you want 'em preserved?"

"Unless they're more than a week old, yes. By the by, did Standish have a knife on him when he was found?"

"Not so far as I know, me lord. Wasn't mentioned in the reports."

"Hmmm." Lord Darcy began prowling around the whole area, reminding Master Sean of nothing so much as a leopard in search of his evening meal. He finally ended up at the base of the cliff, just below where the glyphs had been carved into the clay wall. He went down on his knees and began digging.

"It has to be here somewhere," he murmured.

"Might I ask what you're looking for, me lord?"

"A piece of steel, my dear Sean; a piece of steel."

Master Sean put his carpetbag on the sand and opened it, taking out a thin, dark, metallic-blue wand just as Lord Darcy said: "A*aha!*"

Master Sean, wand still in hand, said: "What is it, me lord?"

"As you see," Lord Darcy said, standing up and displaying the object in the palm of his hand. "Behold and observe, old friend: A man's pocketknife."

Master Sean smiled broadly. "Aye. I presume you'll be wanting a relationship test, me lord? Carving, cutter, and corpse?"

"Of course. No, don't put away your wand. That's your generalized metal detector, is it not?"

"Aye, me lord. It's been similarized to all things metallic."

"Good. Put this knife away for analysis, then let's go over to where the body was found. We'll see if there isn't something else to be dug up."

The Master Sorcerer pointed the wand in his right hand at the sand and moved back and forth across the area, his eyes almost closed, his left hand held above his head, fingers spread. Every time he stopped, Lord Darcy would dig into the soft sand and come up with a bit of metal—a rusty nail, a corroded brass belt-buckle, a copper twelfth-bit, a bronze farthing, and even a silver half-sovereign—all of which showed evidence of having been there for some time.

While the two of them worked, the Armsmen on the cliff above watched in silence. It is not wise to disturb a magician at work.

Only one of the objects was of interest to Lord Darcy: a small lump of lead. He dropped it into a waistcoat pocket and went on digging.

At last, Master Sean, having covered an area of some eight by twelve feet, said: "That's it, me lord."

Lord Darcy stood up, brushed the sand from his hands and trousers, and looked at the collection of junk he had put on the big flat rock. "Too bad we couldn't have found a sixth-bit. We'd be an even solidus ahead. No gold in the lot, either."

Master Sean chuckled. "You can't expect to find a complete set of samples from the Imperial Mint, me lord."

"I suppose not. But here—" he took the small lump of lead from his waistcoat pocket, "—is what I expected to find. Unless I am very much mistaken, this bullet came from the .36 Heron that the late Standish carried, and is the same bullet which passed through his head. Here; check on it, will you, my good Sean?"

Master Sean put the bullet in one of the carefully insulated pockets of his capacious carpetbag, and the two men trudged back across the sand, up the slope to the top of the cliff again.

Master Sean spread himself prone and looked over the edge of the cliff. After a minute inspection of the carving in the sandy clay of the cliff face, he got up, took some equipment from his carpetbag, and lay down again to go to work. A simple cohesion spell sufficed to set the clay so that it would not crumble. Then, he deftly began to cut out the brick of hardened clay defined by the spell.

In the meantime, Lord Darcy had called the senior of

the two Armsmen to one side and had asked him a question.

"No, my lord, we ain't had any trouble," the Armsman said. "We been runnin' three eight-hour shifts out here ever since the body was found, and hardly nobody's come by. The local folk all know better. Wouldn't come near it, anyway, till the whole matter's been cleared up and the site's been blessed by a priest. 'Course, there was that thing this morning."

"This morning?" Lord Darcy lifted an eyebrow.

"Yes, my lord." He glanced at his wristwatch. "Just after we come on duty. Just on six hours ago—eight-twelve."

"And what happened?" his lordship asked with seemingly infinite patience.

"Well, these two folk come along the beach from the east. Romany, they was. Whole tribe of 'em come into St.-Matthew's-Church fairground early this morning. These two—man and a woman, they was—come along arm in arm. Dan—that's Armsman Danel, over there—warned 'em off, but they just smiled and waved and kept coming. So Dan went down to the beach fast and blocked 'em off. They pretended they didn't speak no Anglo-French; you know how these Romany are. But Dan made it clear they wasn't to come no farther, so off they went. No trouble."

"They went back without any argument, eh?"

"Yes, my lord, they did."

"Well, no harm done there, then. Carry on, Armsman."

"Yes, my lord."

Master Sean came back from the cliff edge with a chunk of thaumaturgically-hardened clay further loading his symbol-decorated carpetbag. "Anything else, me lord?"

"I think not. Let's get some lunch."

In a tent near the fairgrounds, an agent of *Serka*, Mission Commander for this particular operation, was opening what looked on the outside like a battered, scuffed, worn, old leather suitcase. The inside was new and in the best condition, and the contents were startingly similar to those of Master Sean's symbol-decorated carpetbag.

Out came two small wands, scarcely six inches long, of ruby-red crystal wound with oddly-spaced helices of silver wire that took exactly five turns around the ruby core. Each wand was a mirror image of the other; one helix wound to the right, the other to the left. Out came two small glass flacons, one containing a white, coarsely-ground substance, the other an amber-yellow mass of small granules. These were followed by a curiously-wrought golden candlestick some four inches high, an inch-thick candle, and a small brazier.

Like any competent sorcerer, the Commander had hands that were strong and yet capable of delicate work. The beeswax candle was being fitted into the candlestick by those hands when there came a scratching at the closed tent flap.

The Commander froze. "Yes?"

"One-three-seven comes," said a whispered voice.

The Commander relaxed. "Very well; send him in."

Seconds later, the tent flap opened, and another *Serka* agent ducked into the tent. He glanced at the thaumaturgical equipment on the table as he sat down on a stool. "It's come to that, eh?" he said.

"I'm not certain yet," said the Commander. "It may. I don't want it to. I want to avoid any entanglement with Master Sean O Lochlainn. A man with his ability and power is a man to avoid when he's on the other side."

"Your pardon, Mission Commander, but just how certain are you that the man you saw on the mule this morning was actually Master Sean?"

"Quite certain. I heard him lecture many times at the University at Buda-Pest when I was an undergraduate there in 'sixty-eight, 'sixty-nine, and 'seventy. He was taking his ThD in theoretics and analog math. His King paid for it from the Privy Purse, but he supplemented his income by giving undergrad lectures."

"Would he recognize you?"

"Highly unlikely. Who pays any attention to undergraduate students at a large university?"

The Commander waved an impatient hand. "Let's hear your report."

"Yes, Mission Commander," Agent 137 said briskly. "I followed the man on muleback, as you ordered. He met another man, ahorse, coming from thc village. He was tall, lean but muscular, with handsome, rather English-looking features. He was dressed as a merchant, but I suspected . . ."

The Commander nodded. "Lord Darcy. Obviously. Continue."

"You said they'd go to the site of the death, and when they took the left-hand bypass I was sure of it. I left off following and galloped on to the village, where Number 202 was waiting with the boat. We had a good westerly breeze, so we made it to the cove bcfore them. We anchored and lay some two hundred yards off-shore. Number 202 did some fishing while I watched through field glasses.

"They talked to the Armsmen atop the cliff for a while, thcn went down to the beach. One of the Armsmen pointed to where the body had been. Darcy went on talking to him for a while. Then Darcy walked around, looking at things. He went over to the base of the cliff and began digging. He found something; I couldn't see what.

"Master Sean put it in his bag, then, for ten minutes or so, he quartered the area where the body'd been, using one of those long, blue-black metal wands—you know—"

"A metal detector," said the Commander. "Yes. Go on."

"Yes. Lord Darcy dug every time O Lochlainn

pointed something out. Dug up an awful lot of stuff. But he found *some*thing interesting. Don't know what it was; couldn't see it. But he stuck it in his pocket and gave it to the sorcerer later."

"I know what it was," said the Commander in a hard voice. "Was that the only thing that seemed to interest him?"

"Yes, as far as I could tell," said 137.

"Then what happened?"

137 shrugged. "They went back topside. Darcy talked to one of the Armsman; the other watched the sorcerer dig a hole in the cliff face."

The Mission Commander frowned. "Dig a hole? A *hole*?"

"That's right. Lay flat on his belly, reached down a couple of feet over the edge, and dug something out. Couldn't see what it was. Left a hole about the size of a man's two fists—maybe a bit bigger."

"Damn! Why couldn't you have watched more carefully?"

Agent 137's face stiffened. "It was very difficult to see well, Mission Commander. Any closer than two hundred yards, and we would have drawn attention. Did you ever try to focus six-by field glasses from a light boat bobbing up and down on the sea?"

"Calm down. I'm not angry with you. You did well. I just wish we had better information." The Commander looked thoughtful. "That tells us something. We can forget about the beach. Order the men to stay away; they are not to go there again for any reason.

"The Phial is not there now, if it ever was. If Master Sean did not find it, it wasn't there. If he *did* find it, it is gone now, and he and Lord Darcy know where it is. And that is a problem I must consider. Now get out of here and let me think."

Agent 137 got out.

The public room at the Green Seagull, as far as population went, looked like a London railway car at the rush hour.

Amidst all the hubbub, wine and beer crossed the bar in one direction, while copper and silver crossed it in the other, making everyone happy on both sides.

In the club bar, it was somewhat quieter, but the noise from the public bar was distinctly audible. The inn-keeper himself was taking care of the customers in the club bar; he took a great deal of pride in his work. Besides, the tips were larger and the work easier.

"Would dere be anyting else for dce?" he asked as he set two pints of beer on one of the tables. "Someting to munch on, mayhap?"

"Not just now, Goodman Dreyque," said Father Art. "This will do us for a while."

"Very good, Fahder. Tank dee." He went quietly away.

Lord Darcy took a deep draught of his beer and sighed. "Cool beer is a great refresher on a midsummer evening. The Green Seagull keeps an excellent cellar. Food's good, too; Master Sean and I ate here this afternoon."

"Where is Master Sean now?" the priest asked.

"In the rooms you assigned us in the Rectory, amidst his apparatus, doing lab work on some evidence we dug up." His voice became soft. "Did you find out what happened here that night?"

"Pretty much," Father Art replied in the same low tones. "There are a few things which are still a little hazy, but I think we can fill in most of those areas."

Standish's quarry had arrived at the Green Seagull late in the afternoon of the fifth, giving the name "Richard Bourke." He was carrying only an attache case, but since he had a horse and saddle and saddlebags, they were considered surety against indebtedness.

There were only six rooms for hire in the inn, all on the upper floor of the two-storied building. Two of these were already occupied. At two-ten, the man Danglars had come in and registered for himself and his mistress, Jizelle de Ville.

"Bourke," said Father Art, "came in at five-fifteen. Nobody else at all checked in during that evening. And nobody saw a young man wearing evening clothes." He paused and smiled brightly. "How-*ev*-er . . ."

"Ahhh. I knew I could depend on you, my dear Arthur. What was it?"

Still smiling seraphically, the good father raised a finger and said: "The Case of the Sexton's Cloak."

"You fascinate me. Pray elucidate."

"My sexton," said Father Art, "has an old cloak, originally made from a couple of used horse blankets, so it wasn't exactly beautiful when new. But it *is* warm. He uses it when he has to work outside in winter. In summer, he hangs it in the stable behind the church. Claims it keeps the moths out—the smell, I mean.

"On the morning of sixth June, one of the men who works here in the inn brought it over to the church, asked my sexton if it were his. It was. Want to take a wild, silly guess where it was found?" Father Art asked.

"Does the room used by Bourke face the front or the rear?"

"The rear."

"Then it was found on the cobblestones at the rear of the building."

Smiling even more broadly, Father Art gently clapped his hands together once. "Precisely, my lord."

Lord Darcy smiled back. "Let's reconstruct. Bourke went to his room before five-thirty. Right?"

"Right. One of the maids went with him, let him in, and gave him the key."

"Was he ever seen again?"

"Only once. He ordered a light meal, and it was brought up about six. That's the last time he was seen."

"Were either of the other guests in the house at the time?"

"No. The man Danglars had left about four-thirty,

and hadn't returned. No one saw Mistress Jizelle leave, but the girl who turns down the beds says that both rooms were empty at six. Bourke was still there at the time."

"Hmmmm."

Lord Darcy looked into the depths of his beer. After half a minute, he said: "Reverend Father, was a stranger in an old horse-blanket cloak actually seen in this inn, or are we speculating in insubstantial mist?"

Father Art's mouth twisted in a small grimace. "Not totally insubstantial, my lord, but not strong, either. The barmaid who was on duty that night says she remembers a couple of strangers who came in, but she doesn't remember anything about them. She's not terribly bright."

Lord Darcy chuckled. "All right, then. Let's assume that Standish actually came in here in a stolen—and uncomfortably warm—cloak. How did that come about, and what happened afterwards?"

Father Art fired up his old briar and took another sip from his seidel of beer. "Well, let's see. Standish comes into the village an hour after Bourke—perhaps a little more. But he doesn't come in directly; he circles round behind the church. Why? Not to steal the cloak. How would he know it was there?" He took two puffs from his pipe, then his eyes brightened. "Of course. To tether his horse. He didn't want it seen in the public square, and knew it would be safe in the church stable." Two more puffs.

"Hmmm. He sees the cloak on the stable wall and realizes that it will serve as a disguise, covering his evening dress. He borrows it and comes here to the inn. He makes sure that Bourke is firmly in place, then goes back to his horse and hightails it for Caen to send word to Sir James. Then he comes back here to the Green Seagull. He waits until nobody's looking, then sneaks up the stairs to Bourke's room."

The priest stopped, scowled, and took a good, healthy

drink from his seidel. "Some time later, he went out the window to the courtyard below, losing the cloak in the process." He shook his head. "But what happened between the time he went upstairs and the time he dropped the cloak, and what happened between then and his death, I haven't the foggiest conjecture."

"I have several," Lord Darcy said, "but they are all very, very foggy. We need more data. I have several questions." He ticked them off on his fingers. "One: Where is Bourke? Two: Who shot Standish? Three: *Why* was he shot? Four: What happened here at the inn? Five: What happened on the beach? And, finally: *Where is the Ipswich Phial?*"

Father Art lifted his seidel, drained its contents on one extended draught, set it firmly on the table, and said: "I don't know. God does."

Lord Darcy nodded. "Indeed; and one of His greatest attributes is that if you ask Him the right question in the right way, He will always give you an answer."

"You intend to pray for answers to those questions, my lord?"

"That, yes. But I have found that the best way to ask God about questions like these is to go out and dig up the data yourself."

Father Art smiled. "*Dominus vobiscum.*"

"*Et cum spiritu tuo,*" Lord Darcy responded.

"*Excavemus!*" said the priest.

In his room in the Rectory, Master Sean had carefully set up his apparatus on the table. Noel Standish's .36 Heron was clamped securely into a padded vise which stood at one end of the table. Three feet in front of the muzzle, the bullet which Lord Darcy had dug from the sand had been carefully placed on a small pedestal, so that it was at exactly the same height as the muzzle. He was using certain instruments to make sure that the axis of the bullet was accurately aligned with the axis of the Heron's barrel when a rhythmic code knock came at the door. The sorcerer went over to the door, unbolted it, opened it, and said: "Come in, me lord."

"I hope I didn't interrupt anything," Lord Darcy said.

"Not at all, me lord." Master Sean carefully closed and bolted the door again. "I was just getting ready for the ballistics test. The similarity relationship tests have already assured me that the slug was the one that killed Standish. There's only to see if it came from his own gun. Have you found any further clues?"

"None," Lord Darcy admitted. "I managed to get a good look at the guest rooms in the Green Seagull. Nothing. Flat nothing. I have several ideas, but no evidence." Then he gestured at the handgun. "Pray proceed with your work, I will be most happy to wait."

"It'll only be a minute or so," Master Sean said apologetically. He went back to the table and continued his preparations while Lord Darcy watched in silence. His lordship was well aware of the principle involved; he had seen the test innumerable times. He recalled a lecture that Master Sean had once given on the subject.

"You see," the sorcerer had said, "the Principle of Relevance is important here. Most of the wear on a gun is purely mechanical. It don't matter *who* pulls the trigger, you see; the erosion caused by the gases produced in the chamber, and the wear caused by the bullet's passing through the barrel will be the same. It's not relevant *to the gun* who pulled the trigger or what it was fired at. But, *to the bullet* it *is* relevant which gun it was fired from and what it hit. All this can be determined by the proper spells."

In spite of having seen it many times, Lord Darcy always liked to watch the test because it was rather spectacular when the test was positive. Master Sean sprinkled a small amount of previously charged powder on both the bullet and the gun. Then he raised his wand and said an incantation under his breath.

At the last syllable of the incantation, there was a

sound as if someone had sharply struck a cracked bell as the bullet vanished. The .36 Heron shivered in its vise.

Master Sean let out his breath. "Just like a homing pigeon, me lord. Gun and bullet match."

"I've often wondered why the bullet does that," Lord Darcy said.

Master Sean chuckled. "Call it an induced return-to-the-womb fixation, me lord. Was there something you wanted?"

"A couple of things." Lord Darcy walked over to his suitcase, opened it, and took out a holstered handgun. It was a precision-made .40 caliber MacGregor—a heavy man-stopper.

While he checked out the MacGregor itself, he said: "This is one. The other is a question. How long before his body was found did Standish die?"

Master Sean rubbed the side of his nose with a thick finger. "Well, the investigative sorcerer at Caen, a good journeyman, placed the time as not more than fifteen minutes before the body was discovered. My own tests showed not more than twenty-five minutes, but not even the best preservative spell can keep something like that from blurring after a week has passed."

Lord Darcy slid the MacGregor into its snugly-fitted holster and adjusted his jacket to cover it. "In other words, there's the usual hazy area. The bruises and fractures were definitely inflicted before death?"

"Definitely, my lord. About three hours before, give or take that same fifteen minutes."

"I see. Interesting. Very interesting." He looked in the wall mirror and adjusted his neckpiece. "Have you further work to do?"

"Only the analysis on the knife," Master Sean said.

Lord Darcy turned from the mirror. "Will you fix me up with a tracer? I'm going out to stroll about the village and possibly to the fairgrounds and the tent city. I anticipate no danger, but I don't want to get lost, either."

"Very well, me lord," the sorcerer said with resignation. He opened his symbol-decorated carpetbag and took out a little wooden box. It held what looked remarkably like one-inch toothpicks, except that they were evenly cylindrical, not tapered, and they were made of ash instead of pine. He selected one and put the box back in his bag. He handed the little cylinder to Lord Darcy, who took it between the thumb and forefinger of his right hand.

Then the master sorcerer took a little scented oil on his right thumb from a special golden oil stock and rubbed it along the sliver of ash, from Lord Darcy's thumb to the other end. Then he grasped that end in his own right thumb and forefinger.

A quick motion of both wrists, and the ashen splinter snapped.

But, psychically and symbolically, the halves were still part of an unbroken whole. As long as each man carried his half, the two of them were specially linked.

"Thank you, my dear Sean," Lord Darcy said. "And now I shall be off to enjoy the nightlife of the teeming metropolis surrounding us."

With that, he was gone, and Master Sean returned to his work.

The sun was a fat, squashed-looking, red-orange ellipsoid seated neatly on the horizon when Lord Darcy stepped out of the gate of the churchyard. It would be gone in a few minutes. The long shadow of the church spire reached out across the village and into the fields. The colors of the flags and banners and bunting around the village were altered in value by the reddish light. The weather had been beautiful and clear all day, and would continue to be, according to the Weather Bureau predictors. It would be a fine night.

"Please, my lord—are you Lord Darcy?"

Lord Darcy had noticed the woman come out of the church, but the village square was full of people, and he had paid little attention. Now he turned his full attention on her and was pleasantly surprised. She was quite the loveliest creature he had seen in a long time.

"I am, Damoselle," he said with a smile. "But I fear you have the advantage of me."

Her own smile was timid, almost frightened. "I am named Sharolta."

Her name, her slight accent, and her clothing all proclaimed her Romany. Her long, softly dark hair and her dark eyes, her well-formed nose and her full, almost too-perfect lips, along with her magnificently lush body, accentuated by the Romany costume, proclaimed her beautiful.

"May I be of help to you, Damoselle Sharolta?"

She shook her head. "No, no. I ask nothing. But perhaps I can be of help to you." Her smile seemed to quaver. "Can we go somewhere to talk?"

"Where, for instance?" Lord Darcy asked carefully.

"Anywhere you say, my lord. Anywhere, so long as it is private." Then she finished. "I—I mean, not *too much* private. I mean, where we can talk. You know."

"Of course. It is not yet time for Vespers; I suggest that we go into the church," Lord Darcy said.

"Yes, yes. That would be fine." She smiled. "There were not many folk in there. It should be fine."

The interior of the Church of St.-Matthew was darkened, but far from being gloomy. The flickering clusters of candles around the statues and icons were like twinkling, multicolored star clusters.

Lord Darcy and the Damoselle Sharolta sat down in one of the rear pews. Most of the dozen or so people who were in the church were farther up toward the altar, praying; there was no one within earshot of the place Lord Darcy had chosen.

Lord Darcy waited in silence for the girl to speak. The Romany become silent under pressure; create a vacuum for them to fill, and the words come tumbling over each other in eloquent eagerness.

"You are the great Lord Darcy, the great Investigator," she began suddenly. "You are looking into the death of the poor Goodman Standish who was found on the beach a week ago. Is all this not so?"

Lord Darcy nodded silently.

"Well, then, there must be something wrong about that man's death, or you would not be here. So I must tell you what I know."

"A week ago, there came to our tribe a group of five men. They said they were from the tribe of Chanro—the Sword—which is in the area of Buda-Pest. Their leader, who calls himself Suv—the Neddle—asked our chief for aid and sanctuary, as it is their right, and it was granted. But they are very secretive among themselves. They behave very well, mind you; I don't mean they are rude or boorish, or anything like that. But there is—how do I say it?—there is a *wrongness* about them.

"This morning, for instance. I must tell you of that. The man who calls himself Suv wanted me to walk along the beach with him. I did not want to, for I do not find him an attractive man—you understand?"

Again his lordship nodded. "Of course."

"But he said he meant nothing like that. He said he wanted to walk along the sea, but he did not want to walk alone. He said he would show me all the shore life —the birds, the things in the pools, the plants. I was interested, and I thought there would be no harm, so I went.

"He was true to his word. He did not try to make love to me. It was nice for a while. He showed me the tide pools and pointed out the different kinds of things in them. One had a jellyfish." She looked up from her hands, and there was a frown on her face.

"Then we got near to that little cove where the body was found. I wanted to turn back, but he said, no, he wanted to look at it. I said I wouldn't and started back. Then he told me that if I didn't, he'd break my arm. So I went." She seemed to shiver a little under her bright dress. "When the Armsman showed up, he kept on going, pretending he didn't understand Anglo-French. Then we saw that there were two of them, the Armsmen, I mean, so we turned around and went back. Suv was very furious."

She stopped and said no more.

"My dear," he asked gently, "why does one of the Romany come to the authorities with a story like this? Do not the Romany take care of their own?"

"Yes, my lord. But these men are not Rom."

"Oh?"

"Their tent is next to mine. I have heard them talking when they think no one is listening. I do not understand it very well, but I know it when I hear it; they were speaking *Burgdeutsch*."

"I see," said Lord Darcy softly and thoughtfully. The German of Brandenburg was the court language of Poland, which suddenly made everything very interesting indeed.

"Do you suppose, Damoselle," he said, "that you could point out this Suv to me?"

She looked up at him with those great wonderful eyes and smiled. "I'm sure I could, my lord. Come; wrap your cloak about you and we shall walk through the village."

Outside the church, the darkness was relieved only by the regulation gaslamps of the various business places, and by the quarter moon hanging high in the sky, like a half-closed eye.

In the deeper darkness of the church porch, Lord Darcy, rather much to his surprise, took the girl in his arms and kissed her, with her warm cooperation. It was several wordless minutes before they went out to the street.

Master Sean woke to the six o'clock Angelus bell feeling vaguely uneasy. A quick mental focus on his half of the tracer told him that Lord Darcy was in no danger.

Actually, if he had been, Sean would have wakened immediately.

But he still had that odd feeling when he went down to Mass at seven; he had trouble keeping in his mind his prayers for the intercession of St. Basil the Great, and couldn't really bring his mind to focus until the Sanctus.

After Mass, he went up to Father Art's small parlor in the rectory, where he had been asked to break his fast, and was mildly surprised to find Sir James le Lien with the priest.

"Good morning, Master Sean," Sir James said calmly. "Have you found the Phial yet?"

The sorcerer shook his head. "Not so far as I know."

Sir James munched a buttered biscuit and sipped hot black caffe. Despite his calm expression Master Sean could tell that he was worried.

"I am afraid," Sir James said carefully, "we've been outfoxed."

"How so?" Father Art asked.

"Well, either the *Serka* have got it, or they think we have it safely away from them. They seem to have given the whole thing over." He drank more caffe. "Just after midnight, every known *Serka* agent in the area eluded our men and vanished. They dropped out of sight, and we haven't spotted a single one in over eight hours. We have reason to believe that some of them went south, toward Caen; some went west, toward Cherbourg; others are heading east, toward Harfleur."

Master Sean frowned. "And you think—"

"I think they found the Ipswich Phial and one of their men is carrying it to Krakowa. Or at least across the Polish border. I rode to Caen and made more teleson calls than I've ever made in so short a time in my life. There's a net out now, and we can only hope we can find the man with the Phial. Otherwise . . ." He closed his eyes. "Otherwise, we may be faced with an overland attack by the armies of His Slavonic Majesty, through one or more of the German states. God help us."

After what seemed like a terribly long time, Master Sean said: "Sir James, is there any likelihood that Noel Standish would have used a knife on the sealed Phial?"

"I don't know. Why do you ask?"

"We found a knife near where Standish's body was discovered. My tests show gold on the knife edge."

"May I see it?" Sir James asked.

"Certainly. I'll fetch it. Excuse me a minute."

He left the parlor and went down the rather narrow hallway of the rectory. From the nearby church came the soft chime of a small bell. The eight o'clock Mass was beginning.

Master Sean opened the door of his room . . .

. . . and stood stock still, staring, for a full fifteen seconds, while his eyes and other senses took in the room.

Then, without moving, he shouted: "Sir James! Father Art! Come here! Quickly!"

Both men came running. They stopped at the door. "What's the matter?" Sir James snapped.

"Somebody," said Master Sean in an angry rumble, "has been prowlin' about in one room! And a trick like that is likely to be after gettin' me Irish up!" Master Sean's brogue varied with his mood. When he was calmly lecturing or discussing, it became almost nonexistent. But when he became angry . . .

He strode into the room for a closer look at the table which he had been using for his thaumaturgical analyses. In the center was a heap of crumbled clay. "They've destroyed me evidence! Look at that!" Master Sean pointed to the heap of crumbled clay on the table.

"And what is it, if I may ask?"

Master Sean explained about the letters that had been cut in the cliff face, and how he had taken the chunk of clay out for further examination.

"And this knife was used to cut the letters." He gestured toward the knife on the table nearby. "I haven't been able to check it against Standish's body yet."

"That's the one with the gold traces on the blade?" Sir James asked.

"It is."

"Well, it's Standish's knife, all right. I've seen it many times. I could even tell you how he got that deep cut in the ivory hilt." He looked thoughtful. "S. . .S. . .O. . ." After a moment, he shook his head. "Means nothing to me. Can't think what it might have meant to Standish."

"Means nothing to me, either," Father Art admitted.

"Well, now," said the stout little Irish sorcerer, "Standish must have been at the top of the cliff when he wrote it. What would be right side up to him would be inverted to anyone standing below. How about OSS?"

Again Sir James thought. Again he shook his head. "Still nothing, Master Sean. Father?"

The priest shook his head. "Nothing, I'm afraid."

Sir James said: "This was obviously done by a *Serka* agent. But why? And how did he get in here without your knowing it?"

Master Sean scowled. "To a sorcerer, that's obvious. First, whoever did it is an accomplished sorcerer himself, or he'd never have made it past that avoidance spell, which is keyed only to meself and to his lordship. Second, he picked exactly the right time—when I was at Mass and had me mind concentrated elsewhere so I wouldn't notice what he was up to. Were I doing it meself, I'd have started just as the Sanctus bell was rung. After that—no problem." He looked glum. "I just wasn't expecting it, that's all."

"I wish I could have seen that carving in the clay," Sir James said.

"Well, you can see the cast if they didn't—" Master Sean pulled open a desk drawer. "No, they didn't." He pulled out a thick slab of plaster. "I made this with quick-setting plaster. It's reversed, of course, but you can look at it in the mirror, over there."

Sir James took the slab, but didn't look at it immediately. His eyes were still on the heap of clay. "Do you suppose that Standish might have buried the Ipswich Phial in that clay to keep it from being found?"

Master Sean's eyes widened. "Great Heaven! It could be! With an auric-stabilized psychic shield around it, I'd not have perceived it at all!"

Sir James groaned. "That answers the question, *Why?* —doesn't it?"

"So it would seem," murmured Father Art.

Bleakly, Sir James held the plaster slab up to the mirror above the dresser. "SSO. No. Wait." He inverted it, and his lean face went pale. "Oh, no. God," he said softly. "Oh, please. No."

"What is it?" the priest asked. "Does OSS mean something?"

"Not OSS," Sir James said still more softly. "055. Number 055 of the *Serka*. Olga Polovski, the most beautiful and the most dangerous woman in Europe."

It was at that moment that the sun went out.

* * *

The Reverend Father Mac Kennalty had turned to the congregation and asked them to lift up their hearts to the Lord that they might properly assist at the Holy Sacrifice of the Altar, when a cloud seemed to pass over the sun, dimming the light that streamed in through the stained glass windows. Even the candles on the Altar seemed to dim a little.

He hardly noticed it; it was a common enough occurrence. Without a pause, he asked the people to give thanks to the Lord God, and continued with the Mass.

* * *

In the utter blackness of the room, three men stood for a moment in silence.

"Well, that tears it," said Sir James's voice in the darkness. There was a noticeable lack of surprise or panic in his voice.

"So you lied to his lordship," said Master Sean.

"He did indeed," said Father Art.

"What do you mean?" Sir James asked testily.

"You said," Master Sean pointed out with more than a touch of acid in his voice, "that you didn't know what the Ipswich Phial is supposed to do."

"What makes you think I *do*?"

"In the first place, this darkness came as no surprise to you. In the second, you must have known what it was, because Noel Standish knew."

"I had my orders," Sir James le Lien said in a hard voice. "That's not the point now. The damned thing is being used. I—"

"*Listen!*" Father Art's voice cut in sharply. "*Listen!*"

In the blackness, all of them heard the sweet triple tone of the Sanctus bell.

Holy . . . Holy . . . Holy . . . Lord God Sabaoth . . .

"What—?" Sir James's low voice was querulous.

"Don't you understand?" Father Art asked. "The field of suppression doesn't extend as far as the church. Father Mac Kennalty could go on with the Mass in the dark, from memory. But the congregation wouldn't be likely to. They certainly don't sound upset."

"You're right, Father," Master Sean said. "That gives us the range, doesn't it? Let's see if we can feel our way out of here, toward the church. His lordship may be in trouble."

"Follow me," said the priest. "I know this church like I know my own face. Take my hand and follow me."

Cautiously, the three men moved from the darkness toward the light. They were still heading for the stairway when the sun came on again.

Lord Darcy rode into the stableyard behind the Church of St.-Matthew, where four men were waiting for him. The sexton took his horse as he dismounted, and led it away to the stable. The other three just waited, expectantly.

"I could do with a cup of caffe, heavily laced with brandy, and a plate of ham and eggs, if they're available," said Lord Darcy with a rather dreamy smile. "If not, I'll just have the caffe and brandy."

"What's happened?" Sir James blurted abruptly.

Lord Darcy patted the air with a hand. "All in good time, my dear James; all in good time. Nothing's amiss, I assure you."

"I think a breakfast such as that could be arranged," Father Art said with a smile. "Come along."

The caffe and brandy came immediately, served by Father Art in a large mug. "The ham and eggs should be along pretty quickly," the priest said.

"Excellent! You're the perfect host, Father." Lord Darcy took a bracing jolt from the mug, then fished in his waistcoat pocket with thumb and forefinger. "Oh, by the by, Sir James, here's your play-pretty." He held up a small golden tube.

Sir James took it and looked at it while Master Sean scowled at it in a way that made him seem rather cross-eyed.

"The seal has been cut," Sir James said.

"Yes. By your man, Standish. I suggest you give the thing to Master Sean for resealing until you get it back to Ipswich."

Sir James gave the Phial to Master Sean. "How did you get it back from them?" the King's Agent asked.

"I didn't." Lord Darcy settled himself back in the big chair. "If you'll be patient, I'll explain. Last evening, I was approached by a young woman . . ."

His lordship repeated the entire conversation verbatim, and told them of her gestures and expressions while they were talking inside the church.

"And you went with her?" Sir James asked incredulously.

"Certainly. For two very good reasons. *Primus:* I had to find out what was behind her story. *Secundus:* I had fallen in love."

Sir James gawked. Master Sean's face became expressionless. Father Art cast his eyes toward Heaven.

Sir James found his voice first. "In *love*?" It was almost a squawk.

Lord Darcy nodded calmly. "In love. Deeply. Madly. Passionately."

Sir James shot to his feet. "Are you mad, Darcy? Don't you realize that that woman is a *Serka* agent?"

"So indeed I had surmised. Sit down, James; such outbursts are unseemly." Sir James sat down slowly. "Now pay attention," Lord Darcy continued. "Of course I knew she was a spy. If you had been listening closely when I quoted her words, you would have heard that she said I was investigating the death of *Standish*. And yet everyone here knows that the body was identified as *Bourke*. Obviously, she had recognized Standish and knew his name."

"Standish had recognized her, too," Sir James said. "Secret Agent Number 055, of *Serka*. Real name: Olga Polovski."

"Olga," Lord Darcy said, savoring the word. "That's a pretty name, isn't it?"

"Charming. Utterly enchanting. And in spite of the fact that she's a Polish agent, you love the wench?"

"I didn't say that, Sir James," said Lord Darcy. "I did not say I loved her; I said I was 'in love' with her. There is a fine distinction there, and I have had enough experience to be able to distinguish between the two states of mind. Your use of the word 'enchanting' is quite apropos, by the way. The emotion was artificially induced. The woman is a sorceress."

Master Sean suddenly snapped his fingers. "*That's* where I heard the name before! Olga Polovski! Six years ago, she was an undergraduate at the University in Buda-Pest. A good student, with high-grade Talent. No wonder you 'fell in love' with her."

Sir James narrowed his eyes. "I see. The purpose was to get information out of you. Did she succeed?"

"In a way." Lord Darcy chuckled. "I sang like a nightingale. Indeed, Darcy's *Mendacious Cantata,* sung *forte e claro,* may become one of the most acclaimed works of art of the twentieth century. Pardon me; I am euphoric."

"You have popped your parietals, my lord," Sir James said, with a slight edge to his voice. "What was the result of this baritone solo?"

"Actually, it was a duet. We alternated on the versicles and responses. The theme of my song was simply that I was a criminal investigator and nothing more. That I hadn't more than a vague notion of what His Imperial Majesty's Secret Service was up to. That, for some reason, the apprehension of this murderer was most important to the Secret Service, so their agents were hanging around to help me. That they were more hindrance than help." He paused to take another swallow of laced caffe, then continued: "And—oh, yes—that they must be going to England for more men, because, four days ago, a heavily armed group of four men took a Navy cutter from Harfleur for London."

Sir James frowned for a second, then his face lit up. "Ah, yes. You implied that we had already found the Phial and that it was safely in England."

"Precisely. And since she had not heard of that oh-so-secret departure, she was certain that it could not be a bluff. As a result, she scrubbed the entire mission. Around midnight, she excused herself for a moment and spoke to someone—I presume it was the second in command, the much-maligned Suv. Her men took off to three of the four winds."

"And she didn't?"

"Of course not. Why arouse my suspicions? Better to keep me under observation while her men made good their escape. I left her shortly after dawn, and—"

"You were there from sunset till dawn? What took you so long?"

Lord Darcy looked pained. "My dear James, surely you don't think I could simply hand her all that misinformation in half an hour without her becoming suspicious. I had to allow her to draw it from me, bit by bit. I had to allow her to give me more information than she intended to give in order to get the story out of me. And, of course, *she* had to be very careful in order not to arouse *my* suspicions. It was, I assure you, a very delicate and time-consuming series of negotiations."

Sir James did his best not to leer. "I can well imagine."

Father Art looked out the window, solemnly puffing his pipe as though he were in deep meditation and could hear nothing.

Rather hurriedly, Master Sean said: "Then it was you who broke the clay brick I dug out of the cliff, me lord."

"It was; I'm sorry I didn't tell you, but you were at Mass, and I was in somewhat of a hurry. You see, there were only two places where the Phial could possibly be, and I looked in the less likely place first—in that lump of clay. Standish *could* have hidden it there, but I thought it unlikely. Still, I had to look. It wasn't there.

"So I got my horse and rode out to where the body was found. You see, Standish *had* to have had it with him. He opened it to get away from his pursuers. I presume Master Sean knows how the thing works, but all I know is that it renders everyone blind for a radius of about a mile and a half."

Master Sean cleared his throat. "It's akin to what's called hysterical blindness. Nothing wrong with the eyes, ye see, but the mind blocks off the visual centers of the brain. The Phial contains a charged rod attached to the stopper. When you open it and expose the rod everything goes black. That's the reason for the auric-stabilized psychic shield which forms the Phial itself."

"Things don't go black for the person holding it,"

said Lord Darcy. "Everything becomes a colorless gray, but you can still see."

"That's the built-in safety spell in the stopper," said the little Irish sorcerer.

"Well, where *was* the blasted thing?" Sir James asked.

"Buried in the sand, almost under that big rock where his body was found. I just had to dig till I found it." Lord Darcy looked somber. "I fear my analytical powers are deserting me; otherwise, Master Sean and I would have found it yesterday. But I relied on his metal detector to find it. And yet, Master Sean clearly told me that a psychic shield renders anything psychically invisible. He was talking about Standish, of course, but I should have seen that the same logic applied to the Ipswich Phial as well."

"If ye'd told me what ye were looking for, me lord . . ." Master Sean said gently.

Lord Darcy chuckled mirthlessly. "After all our years together, my dear Sean, we still tend to overestimate each other. I assumed you had deduced what we were looking for, though you are no detective; you assumed I knew about psychic shielding, though I am no thaumaturge."

"I still can't quite see the entire chain of events," Father Art said. "Could you clarify it for us? What was Standish doing out on that beach, anyway?"

"Well, let's go back to the night before he was killed. He had been following the mysterious Bourke. When Bourke was firmly ensconced in the Green Seagull, Standish rode for Caen, notified you via teleson, then rode back. He borrowed the sexton's cloak and went over to the inn. When he saw his chance, he dodged upstairs fast and went to Bourke's room presumably to get the Phial.

"Now, you must keep in mind that all this is conjecture. I can't prove it, and I know of no way to prove it. I do not have, and cannot get, all the evidence I would need for *proof*. But all the data I *do* have leads inescapably to one line of action.

"Master Sean claims I have a touch of the Talent—the ability to leap from an unwarranted assumption to a foregone conclusion. That may be so. At any rate, I *know* what happened.

"Very well, then. Standish went into Bourke's room to arrest him. He *knew* Bourke was in that room because he was psychically locked on to Bourke.

"But when he broke into the room he was confronted by a woman—a woman he knew. The woman was just as surprised to see Standish.

"I don't know which of them recovered first, but I strongly suspect it was the woman. Number 055 is very quick on the uptake, believe me.

"But Standish was stronger. He sustained a few good bruises in the next several seconds, but he knocked her unconscious. I saw the bruise on her neck last night.

"He searched the room and found the Phial. Unfortunately, the noise had attracted two, possibly three, of her fellow *Serka* agents. He had to go out the window, losing his cloak in the process. The men followed him.

"He ran for the beach, and—"

"Wait a minute," Sir James interrupted. "You mean Bourke was actually Olga Polovski in disguise?"

"Certainly. She's a consummate actress. The idea was for Bourke to vanish completely. She knew the Secret Service would be after her, and she wanted to leave no trace. But she didn't realize that Standish was so close behind her because he was psychically invisible. That's why she was shocked when he came into her room.

"At any rate, he ran for the beach. There was no place else to go at that time of night, except for the church, and they'd have him trapped there.

"I must admit I'm very fuzzy about what happened during that chase, but remember he had ridden for two days without much rest, and he was battered a little by the blows Olga had landed. At any rate, he eventually found himself at the edge of that cliff, with *Serka* closing in around him. Remember, it was a moonless night, and there were only stars for him to see by. But at least one of the Polish agents had a lantern.

"Standish was trapped on the edge of a cliff, and he had no way to see how far down it went, nor what was at the bottom. He lay flat and kept quiet, but the others were getting close. He decided to get rid of the Phial. Better to lose it than have it fall into King Casimir's hands. He took out his knife and carved the '055' in the side of the cliff, to mark the spot and to make sure that someone else would see it if he were killed. I'm sure he intended to dig a hole and bury it there. I don't believe he was thinking too clearly by then.

"The *Serka* men were getting too close for comfort. He might be seen at any moment. So he cut the seal of the Phial and opened it. Blackout.

"Since he could see his pursuers—however dimly—and they couldn't see him, he decided to try to get past them, back to the village. If he had a time advantage, he could find a place to hide.

"He stood up.

"But as he turned, he made a misstep and fell twenty feet to the sand below." Lord Darcy paused.

Father Art, looking thoughtful, said: "He had a gun. Why didn't he use it?"

"Because they had guns, too, and he was outnumbered. He didn't want to betray his position by the muzzle flash unless he had to," Lord Darcy said. "To continue: The fall is what broke those ribs and sprained that wrist. It also very likely knocked him out for a few minutes. Not long. When he came to, he must have realized he had an advantage greater than he had thought at first. The *Serka* couldn't see the muzzle flash from his handgun. Badly hurt as he was, he waited for them."

"Admirable," said Father Art. "It's fantastic that he didn't lose the two parts of the Phial when he fell. Must have hung on for dear life."

"Standish would," said Sir James grimly. "Go on, my lord."

"Well, at that point, the *Serka* lads must have realized the same thing. They had no way of knowing how badly Standish was hurt, nor exactly where he was. He could be sneaking up on them, for all they knew. They got out of there. Slowly, of course, since they had to feel their way, but once they reached the Old Shore Road, they made better time.

"But by that time, Standish was close to passing out again. He still had to hide the Phial, so he buried it in the sand where I found it."

"Me lord," said Master Sean, "I still don't understand who killed Standish and why."

"Oh, that. Why that was patently obvious from the first. Wasn't it, Father Art?"

The good father stared at Lord Darcy. "Begging your pardon, my lord, but not to *me* it wasn't."

Lord Darcy turned his head. "Sir James?"

"No."

"Oh, dear. Well, I suppose I shall have to back up a bit, then. Consider: The Damoselle Olga, to cover her tracks, has to get rid of 'Bourke.' But if 'Bourke' disappears into nowhere, and someone else appears from nowhere, even a moron might suspect that the two were the same. So a cover must be arranged. Someone else, not connected in any way with 'Bourke,' must appear at the Green Seagull *before* 'Bourke' shows up.

"So, what happenes? A coachman named Danglars shows up; a servant who registers for himself and his mistress, Jizelle de Ville. (Danglars and Suv were almost certainly the same man, by the way.) But who sees Mistress Jizelle? Nobody. *She is only a name in a register book until the next morning!*

"The original plan was to have Mistress Jizelle show up in the evening, then have Bourke show up again, and so on. The idea was to firmly establish that the two people were separate and not at all connected. The arrival and intrusion of Standish changed all that, but things worked out fairly well, nonetheless.

"It *had* to be 'Mistress Jizelle' who killed him. Look at the evidence. Standish died—correct me if I'm wrong, Master Sean—within plus or minus fifteen minutes of the time Standish was found."

Master Sean nodded.

"Naturally," his lordship continued, "we always assume a minus time. How could the person be killed *after* the body was found?

"But there was no one else around who could have killed him! A farmer and his two sons were close enough to the road during that time to see anyone who came along unless that someone had walked along the beach. But there were no footprints in that damp sand except those of 'Mistress Jizelle'!

"Picture this, if you will: Number 055, still a little groggy, and suffering from a sore neck, is told by her returning henchmen that they have lost Standish. But she is clever enough to see what must have happened. As soon as possible, she puts on her 'Mistress Jizelle' *persona* and has her lieutenant drive her out to that section of the beach. She walks down to take a look. She sees Standish.

"Standish, meanwhile, has regained his senses. He opens his eyes and sees Olga Polovski. His gun is still in his hand. He tries to level it at her. She jumps him, in fear of her life. A struggle. The gun goes off. *Finis.*"

"Wouldn't the farmers have heard the shot?" Master Sean asked.

"At that distance, with a brisk wind blowing, the sea pounding, and a cliff to baffle the sound, it would be hard to hear a pistol shot. That one was further muffled by the fact that the muzzle was against Standish's head. No, it wouldn't have been heard."

"Why did her footprints only come up to some five yards from the body?" Sir James asked. "There were no prints in the dry sand."

"Partly because she smoothed her prints out, partly because of the wind, which blew enough to cover them. She was shaken and worried, but she did take time to search the body for the Phial. Naturally, she didn't want any evidence of that search around. She went back to consult Danglars-Suv about what to do next. When she saw the farmers, there was nothing she could do but bluff in through. Which, I must say, she did magnificently."

"Indeed." Sir James le Lien looked both cold and grim. "Where is she now?"

"By now, she has taken horse and departed."

"Riding sidesaddle, no doubt." His voice was as cold as his expression. "So you let her get away. Why didn't you arrest her?"

"On what evidence? Don't be a fool, Sir James. What would you charge her with? Could you swear in His Majesty's Court of High Justice that 'Mistress Jizelle' was actually Olga Polovski? If I had tried to arrest her, I would have been a corpse by now in that Romany camp, even if I'd had the evidence. Since I did not and do not have that evidence, there would be no point.

"I would not call it a satisfactory case, no. But you have the Phial, which was what you wanted. I'm afraid the death of Noel Standish will have to be written off as enemy action during the course of a war. It was not first degree murder; it was, as Master Sean put it yesterday, a case of accidental murder."

"But—"

Lord Darcy leaned back in the chair and closed his eyes. "Drop it, Sir James. You'll get her eventually."

Then, very quietly, he began to snore.

"I'll be damned!" said Sir James. "I worked all night on my feet and found nothing. He spends all night in bed with the most beautiful woman in Europe and gets all the answers."

"It all depends on your method of approach," Master Sean said. He opened his symbol-decorated carpetbag and took out a large, heavy book.

"Oh, certainly," said Sir James bitterly. "Some work vertically, some horizontally."

Father Arthur Lyon continued to stare out the window, hearing nothing he didn't mean to hear.

"What are you looking up there, in that grimoire?" he asked Master Sean after a moment.

"*Spells, infatuation; removal of,*" said Master Sean calmly.

The Sixteen Keys

"Naval treaties with Roumeleia are all very well," said Lord Sefton, with a superior smile on his jovial, round face, "but tell me, Your Highness, doesn't it strike you as intrinsically funny that a Greek at Constantinople should sit on a golden throne, wearing the imperial purple of the Caesars, and claim to be the representative before God of the Senate and People of Rome?"

"Indeed it does, my lord," said Prince Richard, Duke of Normandy, as he poured himself a bit more brandy. "I think it even funnier that a Frenchified Viking barbarian should sit on the ancient Throne of Britain and claim exactly the same thing. But that's politics for you, isn't it?"

The florid face of Lord Sefton appeared to approach the apoplectic. He seemed about to rebuke the Prince with something like "By Heaven, sir! How *dare* you? Who do you think you are?" Then, as though he had suddenly realized who Richard of Normandy thought he was, he paled and drowned his confusion in a hurriedly swallowed brimfull glass of Oporto.

Across the table, the Lord High Admiral had roared with laughter. Then, still chuckling, he said: "Only difference is that the people of the City of Rome agree with John of England, not with Kyril of Byzantium. And have for seven centuries or thereabouts. Wasn't it King Henry III who was the first Holy Roman Emperor, Your Highness?"

The Lord High Admiral, Richard knew, was giving Lord Sefton a chance to recover himself. "That's correct," he said. "Elected in 1280. But he didn't become *King* Henry until '83, when John II died. Let's see . . . the next four Kings were elected Emperor, then, after the end of the First Baltic War in 1420, when Harold I was on the Throne, the Imperial Crown was declared to be hereditary in the Anglo-French Kings and the Plantagenet line. So Richard the Great was actually the first to *inherit* the office and title."

"Well," said Lord Sefton, apparently himself again, "I don't suppose it matters much what Kyril wants to call himself. I mean, after all, does it? Long as he does his part in the Mediterranean.

"Speaking of which, I suppose we shall have to find a way to come to some understanding with the Osmanlis, too, on this."

"Oh, yes. We'll certainly have to get an agreement with the Sultan." Not for the first time that evening, Richard wondered whatever had possessed his brother the King to appoint Sefton as Secretary for Foreign Affairs. The man was not very bright; he was certainly slow on the uptake; and he had a provincial air of superiority over anyone and anything that he could classify as "foreign." Well, whatever the King's reasons, they were good ones; if there was more to this than appeared on the surface, the Royal Duke had no desire to even speculate on what it was. If John wanted him to know, he would be told. If not . . . well, that was the business of His Most Dread and Sovereign Majesty the King.

On the other hand, Peter de Valera ap Smith, Lord High Admiral of the Imperial Navy, Commander of the Combined Fleets, Knight Commander of the Order of the Golden Leopard, and Chief of Staff for Naval Operations, was a known quantity. He was a man of middle age, with dark, curly hair that showed traces of gray. His forehead was high and craggy, his eyes heavy-lidded and deep-set beneath thick, bushy eyebrows, his nose large, wide, and slightly twisted, as though it had been broken and allowed to heal without the services of a Healer. The moustache over his wide, straight mouth was thick and bushy, spreading out to either side like a cat's whiskers. The beard was full but cut short, and was as wiry and curly as his moustache. His voice, even when muted, sounded as though its slightly rasping baritone should be bellowing orders from a quarterdeck.

On first meeting the Lord High Admiral, one got the impression of forbidding ruthlessness and remorseless purpose; it required a little time to find that these qualities were modified by both wisdom and humor. He was a man with tremendous inner power and the ability to control and use it both wisely and well.

The three men were sitting around a large table in a well-appointed drawing room, waiting for a fourth man to return. It had been one of those warm late spring days when no air moves and nothing else wants to. Not oppressively hot—just warm enough to enervate and to cause attacks of acute vernal inertia. In spite of that, the four men had worked hard all day, and now, in the late evening, they were relaxing over drinks and cigars.

At least, three of them were.

"Where the Devil is Vauxhall?" Lord Sefton asked. "He's been an infernally long time about getting that leather envelope."

Prince Richard glanced at his wristwatch. "He does seem to be taking his time. Would you be a good fellow, my lord, and go see what's delaying him? It's not like Lord Vauxhall to keep people waiting."

"Certainly, Your Highness." Lord Sefton rose and left the room.

"I thought for a moment," said the Lord High Admiral with a grin, "that you were going to say it was not like Lord Vauxhall to dally, and I was going to ask in what sense you meant the word."

Duke Richard laughed. "No comment."

A few minutes later, Lord Sefton returned, looking worried. "Can't seem to find him, Your Highness," he said. "Looked everywhere. Chap seems to have disappeared."

"Everywhere?"

"Library, office, and so on. Went upstairs and checked his bedroom and bathroom. Didn't search the whole house, of course. Might be in the kitchen, getting a snack or something. Perhaps we ought to turn out the servants?"

"Not just yet, I think," said the Lord High Admiral. He was looking out the west window. "Would you come here a moment, Your Highness?"

Duke Richard walked over to the window, followed by Lord Sefton.

Lord Peter pointed out the window. "Isn't that Lord Vauxhall's summer cottage, just beyond the little grove of trees?"

"Yes. That's what he calls it," said His Highness. "It looks as though every light in the place were on. How odd." He frowned. "Lord Sefton, you stay here and wait, in case Lord Vauxhall should return. The Admiral and I will take a stroll down there and see what's going on."

The "summer cottage" was a quarter of a mile away from the main house on the Vauxhall estate. The two men took a flagstoned pathway that went down a gentle grassy slope and through the grove of trees. Halfway up the sky, a gibbous moon leered balefully at the world beneath, casting a weird silvery radiance over the landscape, making ghostly glimmerings between the shadows of the trees.

"All the lights are on, all right," said Lord Peter as they approached the small house. "All the drapes drawn back. Looks as if there were a party going on, except it's far too quiet."

"No fear;" said the Duke, "if it were one of Vauxhall's parties, we'd have heard it long before now." He went up the four steps to the front door and knocked loudly. "Vauxhall! Lord Vauxhall! It is I! De Normandy!"

"Belay that, Your Highness," said the Admiral. "It won't do any good. Look here."

The Lord High Admiral was standing to one side, looking through the big window to the left of the door.

"You seem to find a great deal by looking through windows, Lord Peter," Prince Richard grumbled. But when he looked, he had nothing to say. His face seemed to freeze, and the Lord High Admiral fancied for a moment that it looked like the handsome face on the famous marble statue of Robert, Prince of Britain, who had died so tragically young in 1708.

The body of Lord Vauxhall was lying on its back in front of the fireplace, its dead, glazed eyes staring sightlessly at the ceiling overhead. In the outstretched right hand was a heavy .44 calibre MMP, the Imperial service pistol.

After what seemed a terribly long time, Prince Richard spoke. His voice, while perfectly calm, had a curiously distant quality about it. "I see the body, but are you sure it's he? Where is the Lord Vauxhall whose dashing good looks fascinated the grand ladies of half the courts of Europe?"

"It is he," the Lord High Admiral said grimly. "I knew his father when I was a boy."

For the face of the corpse was that of an old, old man. Lord Vauxhall had aged half a century in less than an hour.

Lord Darcy, Officer of the King's Justice and Chief Investigator for His Royal Highness de Normandy, was in his sitting room, firmly planted in an easy chair, wearing one of his favorite dressing gowns—the crimson silk —smoking his favorite pipe—the big, straight-stemmed meerschaum—and reading his favorite newspaper—the London *Courier*.

Outside the half-opened window, what little breeze there was brought the faint sounds of a city which had prepared itself for sleep—small, unidentifiable sounds from the streets of Rouen. In the distance, a late night omnibus rolled over the pavement, drawn by its six-horse team.

Lord Darcy reached for the nightcap Ciardi had prepared and took a long sip of the cool drink. He had only a vague idea of what Ciardi put in the thing—rum, he knew, and lime juice and Spanish orange-blossom honey, but there were other things as well. He never asked. Let Ciardi have his little secrets; the man was far too good a servant to upset by excessive indulgence in the satisfaction of one's own curiosity. Hmmm. Did he detect, perhaps, just the slightest touch of anise? Or was it . . .

His thoughts were distracted by the increased loudness of horses' hooves in the street one story below. He had been aware of their approach for some seconds now, he realized, but now they sounded as if they were going to go right by the house. Had there been only one or two, at a slow canter, he would have paid no attention, but there were at least seven horses, and they were moving quite rapidly.

Good heavens, what a din, he thought. *You'd think it was a troop of cavalry going by.* He was torn between his natural curiosity to see who these late night riders were and the feeling of lassitude and comfort that made it seem like a terrible effort to get up and go to the window.

It seemed quite clear that comfort had won over curiosity—just when the horses pulled up to a halt in front of the house. Lord Darcy was on his feet and out of his chair to the window in as close to nothing flat as was humanly possible.

By the time the imperturbable Ciardi arrived, his lordship was already dressed.

"My lord . . ." Ciardi began.

"Yes, Ciardi; I know. It really *was* a troop of cavalry."

"Yes, my lord. Lieutenant Coronel Edouin Danvers, commanding the Duke of Normandy's Own 18th Heavy Dragoons, presents his compliments. He requested me to give you this." He handed over an envelope. "He says he will wait, my lord."

Lord Darcy tore open the envelope and read the short letter.

"Ciardi, rouse Master Sean. Then rouse Gabriel and tell him to get the light carriage ready. Master Sean and I will be accompanying Coronel Danvers to Lord Vauxhall's estate—that's five miles out of the city, on the River Road toward Paris. I don't know how long we shall be there, so I'm taking my traveling case. If we need anything more, I shall send word. Did you offer the Coronel a drink?"

"Yes, my lord. He took ouiskie and water, and I left him with the decanter on the sideboard. Will there be anything else, my lord?"

"Not at the moment. I shall go down and talk to the Coronel."

Lieutenant Coronel Danvers was a spare man of medium height with a clipped, dark, military moustache and a tanned face; he looked alert and wide awake, neatly turned out in crisp field dress. He turned round from the sideboard as the tall, handsome Chief Investigator entered the downstairs receiving room.

"Evening, Lord Darcy. Get you out of bed, did I? Sorry. Orders, you know. Have a little ouiskie; fix you right up."

"No, thanks, Coronel. I see Ciardi has thoughtfully prepared the caffe service. As soon as the water's hot, I'll make a pot."

"Never drink caffe after noon, myself, my lord. Fine stuff in the morning, though. Fine stuff."

"Yes. See here, Danvers, what the devil is this all about?"

"Be damned if I know, my lord." Coronel Danvers looked genuinely surprised. "Expected *you'd* tell *me*. Thought perhaps His Highness put it all down in that letter I brought, eh? No? Well, all I was told was to fetch you and Master Sean and Dr. Pateley and Chief Master-at-Arms Donal Brennan and a Journeyman Sorcerer named Torquin Scoll and a troop of fifty horsemen." He turned back to the sideboard, added ouiskie and water to his glass, and went on: "I came for you and Master Sean, and sent Captain Broun and Senior Captain Delgardie after the others. They'll be joining us on the road."

"Wait a second," Lord Darcy said, "I'm missing data here. You weren't out at Vauxhall's with His Highness?"

"Oh, no! Rather not." He shook his massive head. "I was at home when Sir Ramsey came charging into my yard as though the Hunnish cavalry were after him to deliver those letters from His Highness. Didn't stay; said he was heading back out."

The copper kettle over the gas flame was bubbling happily now. Lord Darcy poured boiling water into the silver funnel that held freshly-ground caffe and watched as the dark liquid filtered through. "Somebody's hurt or dead," he said, more to himself than to Coronel Danvers, "and perhaps a crime's been committed. That would account for calling in Master Sean, Dr. Pateley and myself. And Chief Donal. But why fifty horsemen? And why does he need *two* magicians?"

"That's a good question, me lord," said a voice from the door. "Why does His Grace need two magicians? Who's the other one?"

The short, sturdy figure in sorcerer's robes was Master Sean O Lochlainn, Chief Forensic Sorcerer for the Duchy of Normandy.

The Coronel spoke before Lord Darcy could. "Ah! Evening, Master Sean! Got you out of bed, did I?"

"'Fraid you did, Coronel Danvers." Master Sean stopped a yawn.

"Terribly sorry. Here, though; I'm fixing myself a bit of ouiskie and splash; let me fix you one. Best thing for you, this time of night."

"No, thanks, Coronel; I'll have some of the caffe his lordship is making. What other magician, my lord?"

"Journeyman Torquin Scoll, according to the Coronel."

"Oh. The locksman. Good man, in his field. He's a nut on locks. Absolutely dotes on 'em, me lord. Couldn't cast a simple preservative spell over a prune, he couldn't—but give him a simple padlock, and he'll have it singing the Imperial Anthem in four-part harmony in five minutes."

"Interesting," said Lord Darcy, handing Master Sean a cup of caffe. "Opens up all kinds of speculations. Far too many, in fact. For now, we'll just have to—"

He was interrupted by the entrance of the tall, lean, silver-haired Ciardi. "Your carriage is ready, my lord. I took the liberty of packing a basket of refreshments, my lord, just in case. Your traveling case is in the luggage compartment. As is yours, Master Sean, along with your instrument bag."

"Thank you, Ciardi," said Master Sean. With the obvious exception of Lord Darcy himself, Ciardi was the only man in the world that Master Sean would trust to handle the symbol-decorated carpetbag that carried the instruments and tools of his profession.

"Excellent, Ciardi," Lord Darcy said. "Shall we finish our caffe and be off, then, gentlemen?"

The Coronel downed his drink. "I'll get my men ready, my lord."

* * *

As the cavalcade moved through the gates of the Vauxhall estate some time later, Lord Darcy remarked: "Frankly, what I miss are the flags and banners, the band music and the cheering crowds."

Master Sean, seated across from him in the carriage, lifted both brows. "Beg your pardon, me lord?"

"Well, I mean, after all, my dear Sean, if we're going to have a parade, we should do it properly. The Duke's Own should be in full dress, with sabres, not field dress, with sidearms. The dozen Armsmen should be wearing full decorations. And, above all, we should be going at a leisurely, dignified pace, at high noon, not galloping along in the middle of the night, as though we were fleeing the country. No, no; I fear that, as a parade, it has left a great deal to be desired."

Master Sean grinned. "As your cousin de London would say, my lord, 'Most unsatisfactory.' "

"Precisely. Ho! We're stopping." Lord Darcy put his head out the window, looking toward the head of the column. "It's His Highness. He's talking to Coronel Danvers, gesturing all around, as if he were including the whole countryside. What the devil *is* going on? Come along, Master Sean."

Lord Darcy opened the carriage door and climbed out, followed by the stout little Irish sorcerer. He didn't bother to give any instructions to Gabriel; that tough old horse handler would know what to do.

The Chief Sergeant Major with Coronel Danvers took a small pipe from his jacket pocket and sounded *Officers Assemble,* followed by *Senior NCOs Assemble.* The Coronel and the CSM trotted their mounts out to a broad section of the lawn, and were joined by seven other dragoons.

"This night will be one the troops will remember, regardless of what happens next," Lord Darcy said with a low chuckle as he and Master Sean walked toward where His Royal Highness was now talking to Chief

Master-at-Arms Donal Brennan.

"How's that, me lord?"

"They're top heavy," his lordship said. "We've got two squadrons with us. Out there, you have two lieutenants as squadron commanders and a captain as troop commander, which is all very fine. You've got two squadron sergeants and the troop first sergeant. Still fine. But, in addition, you have the regimental commander, the regimental exec, and the regimental CSM, who will be running all around trying to get something done while trying not to give any orders except to the captain in charge of the troop. The CSM can't even do that, so he'll be trying not to tell the first what to do. Oh, it will be fun, all right." He chuckled again. "It will be all right here, where the gas lamps by the driveway give plenty of light, but wait till they're milling about in those woods with nothing but a three-quarter moon overhead."

Master Sean frowned. "Why would they be milling about in the woods, my lord?"

"Searching for something or somebody. Surely you noticed that every man Jack of 'em has a search lamp slung at his saddle. Lieutenant Coronel Edouin Danvers didn't tell me everything he knew. Which is all right; we'll get it straight from His Highness now."

Prince Richard had caught sight of Lord Darcy and Master Sean. "Ah, there you are, my lord. Sorry to drag you and Master Sean out at this time of night, but there's no help for it. Where is Goodman Torquin?"

"Right here, Your Highness," said a mellow, baritone voice from somewhere behind and below Lord Darcy's head. His lordship turned round.

The man in the working dress of a journeyman Sorcerer was not over five-two, and was built like a wrestler. He was not a dwarf, merely short—although his head seemed a trifle large for the rest of him. He had a pleasantly ugly face that made Lord Darcy suspect he practiced pugilism on the side, large warm brown eyes, and, like Master Sean, he carried a symbol-decorated carpetbag in his left hand.

Introductions were made all round, including Donal Brennan, the grim-looking black-uniformed Chief Master-at-Arms of the City of Rouen.

"Let's walk down toward the summer cottage, while I explain what all this ruckus is about," said the Duke.

Briefly, but completely, he told the story. The only thing he did not mention was the contents of the "important papers" that Lord Vauxhall had been carrying when last seen. Nor did he describe the body; they would see that soon enough.

"You must understand," he concluded, "that it is vitally important that we find those papers."

"You think they are in the diplomatic case, then, Your Highness?" Lord Darcy asked.

"Fairly certain. Vauxhall took the papers with him to put them in it. He had left it on his desk in his office, and we couldn't find it anywhere."

Lord Darcy nodded. "Yes. The obvious conclusion is that the papers are in that leather envelope. I tend to agree with Your Highness."

"That's why I called out a troop of the regiment," said the Duke. "I want these grounds searched thoroughly, and cavalrymen are trained for that sort of thing. Besides, I didn't want to pull that many Armsmen out of the city. A dozen is enough to search all the buildings, and that's what *they're* trained for."

Chief Donal nodded, apparently impressed by the Duke's sagacity.

The five men heard running footsteps behind them, and they all turned to look. Running down the grassy slope in the silvery moonlight was a figure carrying a black leather bag.

"It's Dr. Pateley," said Master Sean.

"Sorry to be late, gentlemen," puffed the gray-haired chirurgeon. "Sorry, Your Highness. Unavoidable delay.

Sorry." He stopped to get his breath and to adjust the pince-nez glasses which had become awry. "Where's the body?"

"That's where we're headed now, Doctor," Prince Richard said. "Come along." The men followed.

"Sister Elizabeth had to call me in," Dr. Pateley was saying in a low voice to Master Sean. "She's a midwife and Healer of the Order of St. Luke. A little unexpected post-parturition trouble. Nothing serious. Stitching job. Baby doing fine."

"Glad to hear it," murmured Master Sean.

Ahead of them, the lights gleamed from the windows of Lord Vauxhall's summer cottage. Near the door stood a bearded man in a Naval uniform of royal blue that was lavishly decorated with gold. Lord Darcy recognized him immediately, even in the moonlight.

After the introductions had been made, Lord Darcy gripped the Lord High Admiral by the arm and said, in a low voice, "Peter, you old pirate, how are you?"

"Not bad at all, Darcy. I can't say I'm much enamored over this particular situation, but otherwise everything's fine. And you?"

"The same, I'm glad to say. Shall we go inside and view the remains?"

"You can view 'em through the window until the locksman gets that door open," Lord Peter said.

Lord Darcy looked round quickly at Prince Richard. "You mean nobody's been inside that house yet?"

"No, my lord," the Duke said. "I thought it best not to break in until you came to take charge."

"I see." He looked searchingly at the Duke's calm face. Prince Richard knew what he was doing; Plantagenets always did. But if the papers were found in that house after Richard had called in the cavalry to search for it, he'd look an awful fool. That was the chance he'd have to take. Another hour's delay, if the papers were *not* in the house, might have been disastrous.

Lord Darcy looked back at the house. The windows

were of the modern "picture window" type, with only narrow transoms at top and bottom to allow for air circulation—too narrow to allow a man to enter. Without the key, it would be a major smashing job to get in. Lord Darcy could see why the Prince had made the decision he had.

"Very well, then, Your Highness; let's get started. I assume Journeyman Sorcerer Torquin designed and built those locks and designed and cast the spells on them; otherwise you'd have let Master Sean do the unlocking work."

The Duke nodded. "That's right, my lord."

Master Sean said: " 'Tis a good thing Your Highness brought him. I, meself, would hate to try to unravel one o' Goodman Torquin's lock spells in less than an hour—"

"Meanin' no disrespect, Master," Torquin Scoll put in, "but would ye care to make a small wager ye can't do it in an hour and a half?"

"—without the key," Master Sean went on. "Of course, *with* the key—"

"I'll give ye the key and two hours and still bet ye a gold sovereign."

"I will not," said Master Sean firmly. "You already have more o' my gold sovereigns than I'd care to tot up. Taking lessons from you is expensive."

"You gentlemen can talk shop elsewhen," Lord Darcy said. "Right now, I want that door unlocked."

"Yes, my lord." Goodman Torquin opened his bag and knelt down to peer at the lock, looking somehow gnomelike in the moon's radiance. He took a small lamp from his bag, lit it, and went to work.

Lord Darcy went over and peered through the window. "*How* long did you say he's been dead, Your Highness?" he said, staring.

"Less than three hours," the Duke replied. "He looked bad enough when we found him. But now . . ." He turned his head away.

"If that's what I think it is," Master Sean said softly, "I'd better get in there fast with a preservative spell."

There was the approaching thud of hooves on turf. Coronel Danvers came up at a fast canter and sprang lightly from the saddle. In the distance, through the trees, Lord Darcy could see search lamps flickering like large, slow-moving fireflies.

"Your Highness." The Coronel saluted. The Prince was, after all, the Honorary Coronel of the 18th, and Lieutenant Coronel Danvers was in uniform. "I have the perimeter surrounded and the remainder of the men on search, as you ordered. Senior Captain Delgardie will report here to me, directly anything's found."

"Very good, Coronel."

"Er—Your Highness." Danvers seemed suddenly unsure of himself. "Lord Sefton—er—presents his compliments, and wishes to know when Your Highness intends to begin interrogation of the prisoners."

"Prisoners?" said the Lord High Admiral. "What's this? What prisoners?"

"His lordship means the servants," said Prince Richard with forced calmness. "They are not prisoners. I merely asked them to remain until this thing was cleared up. I left them in Lord Sefton's care. If those papers can't be found . . ." He paused and frowned slightly. "Chief Donal—"

He was cut off by Journeyman Torquin's voice. "There ye go, my lords and gentlemen."

The front door of the little cottage swung open.

"Everyone stay out until Master Sean is through," Lord Darcy said crisply.

Master Sean went in to cast the special spell which would stop the dissolution of the corpse. Everyone left him alone, as they had Goodman Torquin; nobody but a fool disturbs a magician when his is working at his Art. It was over quickly.

The other six men came into the room.

There is something about death which fascinates all

human beings, and something about horror which seems even more deeply fascinating. The thing which lay on the floor in front of the big cold fireplace, illuminated brightly by the mantled gas lamps in the wall brackets, embodied both.

The big fireplace had facings of fine marble, white, mottled with pink and gold, the great mirror over the mantelpiece reflected the walls of the room, covered by smooth brocade paper that picked up the pink-and-gold motif. The woven brocade upholstery of the furniture repeated the pattern of the walls. It was a light, airy, beautiful room that did not deserve the insult which lay on the pale eggshell carpet.

The air was thick with the smell.

The Lord High Admiral was opening transoms above and below the windows. Nobody closed the door.

"Here, Your Highness! Sit down!" At the sound of Coronel Danvers' voice, Lord Darcy turned away from the thing on the floor.

Prince Richard's face had gone gray-white, and he swallowed a couple of times as the Coronel eased him into one of the big, soft chairs. "I'm all right," the Duke managed. "It—it's rather warm in here."

"Ah. Yes. It is that," Danvers agreed. "Where did Vauxhall keep his spirits? Must be . . . Ah!" He had opened a waist-high cabinet against the west wall. "Here we are! A good stiff one will brace you right up, Your Highness. Ouiskie? Or brandy?"

"Brandy, thank you."

"There you are, Your Highness. Believe I'll have a little ouiskie, myself. Shocking sight. Absolutely shocking."

Lord Darcy, seeing that the Duke was all right and in good hands, knelt beside the corpse with Master Sean and Dr. Pateley. "Whatever killed him," his lordship murmured, "it wasn't a bullet from this." He disengaged the heavy .44 MMP from the right hand of the corpse.

The Lord High Admiral was standing, looking down

over Dr. Pateley's shoulder. "No. A Morley military pistol makes rather large, easily visible holes."

Lord Darcy knew Lord Peter wasn't being sardonic—just blunt. He handed the weapon to the Lord High Admiral. "Look like it's been fired to you?"

The Naval officer's strong, capable hands unloaded the handgun, field stripped it, put it back together again. "Not recently."

"Thought not. Well, well; what's this?" Lord Darcy had been searching the clothing of the late Lord Vauxhall and had come up with a small leather case which, when opened, proved to contain a series of keys, all very much alike, numbered from *1* to *16*, all neatly arrayed in order and attached to the case so that each could swing free separately. "Very pretty. Wonder what it's for? He has another set of keys of various sizes on a ring; this must be something special."

"Oh, yes; that it is, my lord," said Journeyman Sorcerer Torquin Scoll. "Made that set special for his lordship, I did. His lordship was a man of rare taste, he was." A broad grin suddenly came over the little man's face. "That is to say, my lord, he enjoyed locks as much as I do, if ye see what I mean." The grin vanished. "I shall miss him. We enjoyed talkin' locks together. And workin' with 'em. Very knowledgeable he was, and clever with his hands. I shall certainly miss him."

"I'm sure." Lord Darcy looked back down at the keys during a moment of silence, then looked up again and said: "What do they fit, if I may ask?"

"Why, they're the keys to this house, your lordship."

"*This* house? *All* of them?"

The grin came back to the pleasantly ugly face. "That's right, your lordship. There's sixteen doors in this house, and every blessed one of 'em locks with a different key—from either side. Here, I'll show ye." He opened up his symbol-decorated carpetbag and brought out a thick loose-leaf notebook. After a moment of search, he selected a sheet of paper, made a small cross-mark on it, detached it carefully, and handed it to Lord Darcy. "There ye are, your lordship. That's a plan sketch I made of this house. We're right here in the receiving room, d'ye see, where I made the cross. Those slidin' doors lead into the gallery, the dinin' room, and the library. That small door over there goes to the front bedroom. All the doors 're numbered to match the keys."

"What's this 'green room' that's all glassed in?" Lord Darcy asked.

"It's a sort of a greenhouse, your lordship. Lord Vauxhall called this a summer cottage, but he used it durin' the winter, too, when he was home. That's the reason for the fireplaces. One here, one in the library, one in the dinin' room, an' those little corner fireplaces in the bedrooms."

"How many sets of keys are there?"

"Just that one, my lord. Oh, the gard'ner has duplicates for keys three and four, so's he can tend the plants, but that's all."

Lord Darcy could sense a certain depressing tension in the room. Prince Richard was staring blankly at a half-full glass of brandy; Coronel Danvers was pouring himself a drink; Lord Peter was staring out the window; Chief Donal was watching Master Sean and Dr. Pateley go over the body.

Then he realized that the momentary shock that had hit the Duke had gone, and realized, too, what His Highness was waiting for. He had given charge of the case over to Lord Darcy and was now trying to be patient. Lord Darcy walked over to where he was sitting.

"Would Your Highness care to inspect the rest of the house?" he asked quietly.

Prince Richard looked up and smiled. "I thought you'd never ask." He finished off the brandy.

"There's nothing more I can learn from the body until Master Sean and Dr. Pateley give me their findings. I can detect no sign of struggle. Apparently he walked in here with a gun in his hand and—died."

"Why the gun, I wonder?" Prince Richard said musingly. "Had he been frightened by something, do you suppose?"

"I wish I knew. He wasn't wearing a holster, so he must have picked it up from somewhere after he left you."

"Yes. He wasn't wearing a coat, so he couldn't have concealed a weapon that big. Oh. Excuse me a moment. Chief Donal?"

"Yes, Your Highness?" said the grim-looking Chief Master-at-Arms, turning away from the body to face his Duke.

"When you have finished here, go up to the main house and take charge. Keep the servants calm and don't tell them anything. They don't even know their master is dead. If one of them does, it might tell us something. And I don't want any interrogation of any kind until Lord Darcy says so."

"I'm through now, Your Highness. Got all I need. From now on, it's up to Lord Darcy." He flashed a smile which looked very uncomfortable on his face, and must have been, for it went away immediately. "Cases involving Black Magic are way over my head, anyway. Don't like 'em at all." With no further ceremony, he left.

"Well, let's see if we can find those papers," Lord Darcy said. "Might as well try the gallery first."

"Mind if I come along?" the Lord High Admiral asked.

"Of course not, my lord," the Duke said. "How about you, Coronel? Want to take the tour with us?"

Danvers frowned and glanced at his nearly empty glass. "I think not, begging Your Highness' leave; I'd best be at hand in case Delgardie or the Sergeant Major come with news."

The sliding doors were locked, and Lord Darcy had inserted the key marked "5". It turned easily—too easily. It went right on round and clicked back into place. A turn in the other direction had the same result. The bolt remained solidly in place.

"Beggin' your pardon, my lord," said Torquin Scoll, "but I guess I'll have to come along with ye. The wrong key won't even turn the cylinder; the right key will, but it won't engage the bolt unless the right man is holdin' the key. It'll be a little tricky, even for me, since these keys are tuned to his late lordship."

He took the key case, fitted No. 5 in again, closed his eyes, and turned the key carefully. Click.

"There we go, my lords, Your Highness."

The four men went into the gallery.

"Don't you have a set of these keys tuned to yourself, Goodman Torquin?" Lord Darcy inquired.

"Do, indeed, my lord; used 'em just a week ago to do the regular spell maintenance. I'd have brought 'em with me if I'd've known what was afoot. But all that Captain —whatisname?—Broun. If that Captain Broun'd've told me where we were going. But no, he just says the Duke wants me, so I saddled up and came along."

"My apologies, Goodman Torquin," said His Highness.

"Oh, no need, Highness; no need. Not your fault. Military mind, you know. Take orders; give orders; don't explain, especially to civilians. Not your fault at all, Highness." Then he gestured with a broad sweep of a hand. "How do you like the gallery, gentle sirs?"

"Fascinating," murmured Lord Darcy. "Utterly fascinating."

The west wall was almost all glass—seven windows, six feet wide, with only narrow pillars between them. The heavy theater-type drapes which would cover them had been drawn up to the ceiling. Outside, in the darkness, one could see the occasional gleam of search lamps, the only sign that the dragoons were at work.

But that was not the vista that Lord Darcy had found fascinating.

The east wall was covered with paintings. None of

them were obscene, and not all were erotic, but they all spoke of beauty, love, and romance.

"These must have run him into quite a bit of money over the years," the Lord High Admiral remarked. "Beautiful work, all of 'em. There! That's a Van Gaughn; always admired his work."

"Some of them," said the Duke, "were done especially by his late lordship's order. This one, for instance."

"That," said Lord Peter authoritatively, "is a Killgore-Spangler. I'd recognize her style anywhere."

"I also recognize the model," Lord Darcy said in a slightly dreamy voice.

"That, too," said the Lord High Admiral.

Prince Richard looked surprised. "Both of you are acquainted with Doña Isabella Maria Constanza Diaz y Carillo de la Barra?"

The Lord High Admiral burst out laughing. "Oh, yes, Your Highness. Oh, yes. Recognized her in spite of the red wig, eh, Darcy?"

"In that pose, I'd have recognized her with a sack over her head." Lord Darcy began to chuckle.

"What *is* so funny?" Prince Richard asked in a tone that held more than a touch of irritation.

"Your Highness," Lord Darcy said, "that woman is no more a Spanish noblewoman than the Coronel's horse is. That happens to be Olga Vasilovna Polovski, Number 055 of *Serka*, the Polish Secret Service. She's the most beautiful and the most dangerous woman in Europe."

"Good God!" The Prince looked shocked. "Did Vauxhall know?"

"I hope so," said Lord Darcy. "I sincerely hope so."

"Oh, he knew, all right," said Lord Peter. "He was making special reports to Naval Intelligence at the time. That's what made the whole affair so delicious."

"I can well imagine," said Lord Darcy.

They walked on.

Lord Darcy cast a practiced eye over the long gallery.

If someone had wanted to hide it, the eleven-by-fifteen, two-inch-thick diplomatic case could be concealed—with difficulty—in the theater drapes that hung in graceful curves above the windows. Or there might be some secret niche behind one of the paintings. But for now he would assume that it was in plain sight—or pretty much so.

Torquin the Locksman had gone on ahead to unlock doors. The three noblemen followed in his wake. The next door led into a small but comfortable bedroom. The wallpaper here had a pattern similar to that in the receiving room, but here it was pastel blue and gold. The upholstery on the two chairs and the spread on the double bed matched it. No fancy marble on the corner fireplace, however; it was of plain fieldstone, with an unfinished ruggedness that contrasted nicely with the patterned smoothness of the rest of the room.

"Wonder how old this house is?" the Lord High Admiral asked idly as they searched the room.

"Not very, in comparison to the manor house," Lord Darcy said. "That's late Robertian—1700 or thereabout."

"It's practically brand new," Prince Richard said. "Vauxhall built it himself in 1927 or '28. It's been redecorated a couple of times since, I understand, but no drastic changes. It's rather nice, I think. And the picture gallery is much more inspiring than the one up the hill. All those ghastly old ancestors staring at you."

"Your Highness ought to know," murmured Lord Darcy.

"Oh, God, yes! Have you seen that portrait of my thrice-great grandfather, Gwiliam IV? The big one that hangs in Westminster? It was painted in 1810, just two years before he died. Really grim-looking old boy at eighty. Well, that picture used to scare the devil out of me when I was a boy. I wouldn't go anywhere near it. The eyes aren't quite looking at you, you know, but you get the feeling that if the old man just shifted them a little, he'd see you straight on. At least *I* thought so. And I had the feeling that if he ever looked straight at me he would see what a wicked little boy I was, and would leap down from his frame and devour me upon the spot. Well, there's nothing in this clothespress."

"And nothing in the bathroom," said Lord Darcy.

"It's dark under this bed," the Lord High Admiral said. "Lend me your pipe lighter, Lord Darcy. Thanks. Mmmm. No. Nothing under there." He stood up and brushed off the knees of his trousers.

Lord Darcy was looking up at the skylight. "That doesn't look as though it opens."

The other two looked up. "No," said the Lord High Admiral. "Except for that narrow transom on the leeward side."

"Yes," the Duke said, pointing. "It's operated by that cord that hangs down the wall. It goes up through that pulley, there, you see."

"I suppose all of the inner rooms have skylights, Your Highness?" Lord Darcy said.

"Oh, yes, my lord. Even the library has one, as you'll see. It has no windows, since the walls are covered with bookshelves. The only other light in there would be from the glass double doors that lead into the garden." The Duke looked all around. "Well, the next stop is the service pantry."

They went out into the north wing of the L-shaped gallery, turned right, and went to the door of the service pantry. It swung open at a touch; Torquin had been there before them.

The room was, in effect, a very small kitchen. Vauxhall did not throw big dining parties here; when he wanted food served, the servants brought it down from the main house.

"Not very big," the Lord High Admiral said, "but lots of places to look." He opened the warming oven, saw nothing, closed it, and went on to the cabinets.

Lord Darcy climbed up on a little three-legged stool

and began going through shelves. "Your Highness," he said, "would I be out of order if I asked just what these 'important papers' are?"

"They're the only copies, in three languages, of our new naval treaty with Roumeleia."

"Oh, *ho*. I see."

"As ambassador to the Basileus at Constantinople, Lord Vauxhall was instrumental in persuading Kyril to agree to all the terms. The Greeks, of course, control the Bosphoros and the Dardanelles, which means they have the Black Sea bottled off from the Mediterranean.

"Casimir of Poland is still trying to get around our naval blockade of the North Sea and the Baltic. By the treaty we forced on him after the '39 war, no Polish armed vessel is to pass the Fourteenth Meridian, and no Imperial armed vessel is to pass the Tenth Meridian going the other way."

"Nobody here but us Scandinavians," growled the High Admiral.

"Right," said Prince Richard. "And the treaty also permits Scandinavian or Imperial naval vessels to stop and search *any* Polish vessel between the Eighth and Fourteenth Meridians for contraband—arms and ammunition—and to seize any that's found.

"But the situation's different in the Mediterranean. The Greeks didn't like what Poland pulled during the '39 War, and took advantage of our winning it to say that no armed vessel of *any* nation—except Roumeleia, of course—would be allowed in the Sea of Marmara. But they didn't quite have guts enough to put a stop-search-and-seizure clause in that fiat.

"Emperor Kyril is ready to do that now, provided we'll back him up in the Mediterranean. The Roumeleian Navy isn't strong enough by a long sight to patrol the Black, the Marmara, *and* the Mediterranean, and they're still worried about the Osmanlis, to say nothing of North Africa. This treaty arranges for all that."

"I see," Lord Darcy said. He was silent for a moment, then: "May I ask, Your Highness, why all this sudden need for a search of King Casimir's merchant ships?"

The Lord High Admiral's chuckle was unpleasant. "May I tell him, Your Highness?"

"Certainly. The King my brother has trusted Lord Darcy with state secrets far more crucial than this one."

That was not what the Lord High Admiral had meant, but he let it pass. He said: "His Slavonic Majesty, Casimir IX, has concocted a scheme to get himself a fleet in the Atlantic. It's a lovely scheme—and it could work. In fact—*it may already have worked*. We may have caught on just a little too late for comfort."

"Three ships is hardly a fleet," the Duke objected.

"Three ships *that we know of*, Your Highness. At any rate, what has happened is this: A few years ago, Poland started expanding her merchant fleet with a new type of vessel—a little faster, a little more sturdily built. They started making them first up in the Pomeranian Bay area. Six months later, they began tooling up for them in the Black Sea—at Odessa.

"More time goes by. At some time—which we haven't nailed down yet—the game of Shells-and-Pea begins."

"The papers don't seem to be in here," the Duke interrupted. "Shall we go into the green room?"

"Yes," said Lord Darcy. "Let's see if naval treaties grow on bushes."

There were no bushes. The room, like the gallery, had two outside walls that were practically all glass. Greenery and flowers grew in pots and tubs all over the place. Nothing spectacular, but it was colorful and pleasant.

The search continued.

"Thank goodness the roses are the thornless variety," said the Lord High Admiral as he pushed leaves and blooms aside. "Where was I?"

"You were playing the Shells-and-Pea Game with Polish merchant vessels," said Lord Darcy.

"Oh, yes. Now, you must understand that these ships

are all alike. We call 'em the *Mielic* class; the *Mielic* was the first one off the ways, and they're all named after small cities. And you can't tell one from the next, except for the name painted on 'em.

"Here's what happens. Let's say the *Zamość* sails from—oh, Danzig. She stops at the Helsingør-Hälsingborg Naval Check Point for inspection, which she passes with flying colors."

"I was afraid you'd say that," murmured Lord Darcy as he peered under a long wooden bench.

"From there," Lord Peter continued remorselessly, "she continues to Antwerp. This time, *we* check her. She's clean."

"And her colors are still flying," said Lord Darcy.

"Exactly. So she works her way south. Bordeaux, San Sebastián, La Coruña, Lisbon, and finally through the Strait of Gibraltar. She does business around the Mediterranean for a while. Finally, she heads east, through the Dardanelles and the Bosphorous, into the Black Sea, and straight for Odessa. A week later—Ouch! That rose *does* have thorns! A week later, she's coming back again. The *Zamość* goes back through the Bosphorous, the Dardanelles, the Mediterranean, the Straits of Gibraltar, and heads south again, for the coast of Africa. A few months later, here comes the *Zamość* again, back to Bordeaux with a hold full of zebra hides or something. Then, on north and turn east again and back to Danzig, passing every inspection with utter innocence."

"Only the name has been changed to protect the guilty," Lord Darcy remarked.

"You are so right. I won't ask how you knew."

"It was obvious. Tell me: Were the crew allowed liberty at port?"

The Lord High Admiral grinned through his beard. "Not likely, eh? No, they weren't. And would it surprise you to know that the hull of a *Mielic*-class vessel looks astonishingly like that of a light cruiser? I thought not."

Lord Darcy said: "I see what you mean by the Shells-

and-Pea game. It means that three different ships are involved. Number One—the *Zamość*—is a genuine merchantman. But when it gets to Odessa, there's a heavily-armored light cruiser hull that looks exactly like her, with the name *Zamość* lettered neatly on her bow and stern. Her cargo is heavy naval guns, ready to be mounted in some shipyard in Africa. Where?"

"Abidjan, we think."

"The Ashanti, eh? Well, well. Anyhow, the second *Zamość*, with the same officers, but a different crew, gets by the Greeks easily because they can't board and search. Off she goes to Abidjan, where the third *Zamość*, another genuine merchantman, is waiting. Same officers; third crew. And back to Danzig as pure as the snows of Pamir. Clever. And what happens to the original *Zamość*?"

"Why, pretty soon the *Berdichev* comes sliding down the ways. Brand new ship. Says so in her papers."

"And this has happened three times?"

"Three times that we know of," said the Lord High Admiral. "We still haven't been able to check out every one of those ships and follow their official courses, much less try to deduce their *un*official shenanigans. The point is that we have to put a stop to it immediately."

"There is evidence," Prince Richard said, "that two more will be sailing out of the Black Sea within the week. They're stepping up operations, my lord. That's why all the worry about that damned missing diplomatic case. It has already been signed by Kyril, but he won't act on it until he sees the Imperial Seal and my signature on it. There's an official letter with it from His Majesty, signed, sealed, and everything, authorizing my own signature as proxy, and all that. It was done that way because the King my brother cannot come to Normandy at this time, and it would take just enough extra time to get the thing over there and back that we would be skating too close to the edge. Two—or even one more of King Casimir's ships out of the blockade could mean more trouble than we can handle right now.

"The Napoli Express leaves Calais in—" He pushed back the lace at his cuff and looked at his wristwatch. "—five hours and twenty-one minutes. That train only runs twice a week. If we can put that treaty on it in Paris, it will be in Brindisi in less than thirty-six hours. From there to Athens by ship is another twenty-four hours. The Basileus will be there, waiting for it, and the Greek Navy will be enforcing it in another twenty-four.

"If we don't have it on that train, we're lost."

"I don't think it's as bad as all that, Your Highness," the Lord High Admiral said. "We can get it to—"

But the Duke cut him off sharply. "Don't be an optimistic fool, my lord! If we haven't found that thing by then, it will mean that somehow—I don't know how—it has come into the hands of the *Serka*.

"Kyril trusted and liked Vauxhall. With him dead, we'd find it hard going to re-negotiate the treaty. Kyril would think us fools to lose the first copy, and he'd be right. He'd likely balk at signing another. Besides, Casimir would know all about it and be taking steps to do something else."

It was not until that point that Lord Darcy realized how much on edge the Prince was. Outbursts of that kind were not like him.

"I think you need not worry yourself unduly on that score, Your Highness," he said quietly. "I believe I can guarantee that the treaty will be on the Napoli Express in the morning." He knew he was sticking his neck out, and he knew that the axe blade was sharp. But he had that feeling . . .

The Prince took a deep breath, held it for a second, then eased it out. "I am relieved to hear that, my lord. I have never known you to be wrong on something of that kind. Thank you."

Lord Darcy felt a ghostly prickle at the back of his neck. The axe had grown a bit more solid.

"Well, wherever it is," said the Lord High Admiral,

"it is not here with the vegetation. I guess the library's next."

They slid aside the double doors and went in.

And stopped.

The room was wall-to-wall and floor-to-ceiling with bookshelves. And they were full of books.

"Help us, Blessed Mary," Prince Richard said earnestly. "We'll have to look behind every one of them."

"Just a moment, Your Highness; let me check something," said Lord Darcy. He went over to the doors that led back into the front room and slid them open. Master Sean was over by the fireplace, talking in low tones with Journeyman Torquin. Coronel Danvers was sipping a drink and staring moodily out the front window. There was no sign of either Dr. Pateley or the body. Three heads turned as Lord Darcy opened the doors.

"I see the clay has been removed," Lord Darcy said.

"Aye, me lord," Master Sean said. "The hearse came. The doctor went along to make arrangements for the autopsy. I made all the tests possible for now."

"Excellent. Tell me, my good Sean, how long would it take you—possibly with the assistance of your colleague —to remove all the privacy spells around here so that an ordinary clairvoyant could find what we're looking for?"

Master Sean blinked, then looked at Goodman Torquin. "Are any of these yours?"

Torquin shook his head. "Not much good at that sort of thing, Master. Locks are my specialty. I don't know who he got to renew his privacy spells."

Master Sean looked around and seemed to feel the air. "They've been here a long while, me lord. Fifty years or so—give or take ten percent. Strong; well reinforced. Complex, too. Fine, competent workmanship. Master grade, I'd say—or a specialist. Ummm." He reached down, opened his symbol-decorated carpetbag, and took out a thin silver wand with a flat, five-pointed star on the end, looking rather like a long nail with a five-pointed head. He closed his eyes and twirled it slowly between the thumb and forefinger of his right hand. "Some of the basics are even older. This house is new, but the grounds have been private property for centuries. There was a castle up on the hill where the manor house is now, but it was torn down in the Fifteenth Century. But they had good, solid privacy spells, even then. And the more modern ones are built on an old, very solid foundation."

He opened his eyes and returned the wand to his bag. "Nine hours, my lord—if I'm lucky."

Lord Darcy sighed. "Forget it. Thank you very much, Master Sean." He slid the doors shut again.

"It was a nice idea while it lasted," said the Lord High Admiral. "Let's get on with it."

"I suggest," Lord Darcy said, "that we give it a quick look and then go on to the dining room and the other bedroom. We can come back here if we don't find it there, but we'd feel silly if we pulled out all these books and then found it in the bath of the front bedroom."

A quick search revealed nothing.

"Dining room, then," Lord Darcy said, opening the sliding doors. "Well! What have we here?"

There was a large, bare table of polished walnut, big enough to seat ten, set lengthwise in the room. At the southern end, near the door to the front room, was an open bottle of wine and an empty glass. Lord Darcy went over and looked at them carefully. *Schwartzschlosskellar* '69. A very good Rhenish. One drink gone, and the bottle's abominably warm. Bottom of the glass still has a sticky drop or two in it."

"His last drink," said Prince Richard.

"I think so, yes. Leave them alone; we'll have Master Sean look them over later, if it becomes necessary."

They found nothing in the dining room.

The front bedroom was very like the rear one, except that the wallpaper pattern was green and silver.

"Notice the way the bedrooms are separated," Lord Peter remarked. "Only a partition between them, but you have to go through at least two other rooms to go from one to the other. Vauxhall had a fine and very subtle sense of psychology."

"That's why he became a diplomat," said the Duke.

There was no diplomatic case in the bedroom, either.

"Back to the library," muttered the Lord High Admiral.

It took them nearly an hour, even with the help of Master Sean, Goodman Torquin, and the Coronel. They found all sorts of little odds and ends about, but nothing of importance. Certainly no Roumeleian naval treaty.

"Well, Your Highness," said the Coronel, "if it's not in this house, it must be outside, eh? Just you wait, though; one of my lads will turn it up. Old Vauxhall probably dropped it somewhere between here and the manor house. That's where I set my sharpest lads to work. I know it's disappointing, though. Tell you what! Let's all have a good stiff drink. Do us no end of good after all that dusty work. What say?"

With the exception of the two sorcerers, everybody agreed with him, for once.

They were all standing around silently, holding their glasses, or staring at walls, when a knock came at the front door, followed immediately by the entrance of Lord Sefton, the Foreign Secretary.

He was perspiring, which gave an oily look to his red, jowly face. "Ah! Your Highness, my lords, gentlemen. Thought I'd find you here." He glanced quickly at the men, not knowing any of them but the Duke and the Lord High Admiral. Prince Richard made introductions.

"Just dropped down to tell Your Highness that the Armsmen have finished searching the house. Haven't found the blasted thing, so Chief Donal is having them go over it all again. Looking for secret panels and the like. I thought maybe you'd found it here."

"No such luck," Prince Richard said. He looked at Lord Darcy. "How about that, my lord? Should we look for secret panels?"

Lord Darcy shook his head. "I've looked. Wallpapered walls like this don't lend themselves to such things. There's no way to hide the cracks. Everywhere they *could* be, I checked. I'm going to go out to the gallery again and look behind the pictures, though; if there are any secret hiding places, that's where they'll be."

"Well, then, Lord Darcy," Lord Sefton said importantly, "have you determined who committed the murder?"

"Good God!" Coronel Danvers almost dropped his glass. *"Murder?* What murder?" He jerked his head around to look at Lord Darcy. "You didn't say anything about a murder. Has there been a murder? What the devil is the fellow talking about?"

"I'm sure I don't know," said Lord Darcy. "Nobody's said anything about a murder. What *are* you talking about, Lord Sefton?"

"Yes," said Prince Richard, "please explain yourself, my lord."

Lord Sefton's flabby mouth opened, closed, and opened again. "Wuh—wuh—why, Lord *Vauxhall!* I saw him through the window when you called me down! He was right there! With a gun in his hand! Looked like an Egyptian mummy!" He stopped, swallowed, then, more calmly: "Oh. Was it suicide, then?"

Lord Darcy looked at the Duke. "You know, Your Highness, I think that might explain the gun. I believe he was thinking of it—before he died."

"I think you're right," the Duke said solemnly. "He might have thought it would be an easier way to go. Perhaps it would have been. It might have been less—painful."

Master Sean shook his head. " 'Tisn't painful, Your Highness. Except mentally. Seeing yourself go all to pieces that way. But the nervous system goes pretty fast. Numbness sets in quite rapidly toward the last."

Lord Sefton seemed ready to go to pieces himself. "Buh—buh—but what are you talking about? Chief Donal said Vauxhall'd been killed by Black Magic! Why are you all taking it so calmly? *Why?*"

"My lord, please calm yourself and sit down," Prince Richard said firmly.

"Yes, my lord, do sit down," said the Coronel. "Here, let me fetch you a glass of brandy. Straighten you right up."

Lord Sefton took the brandy with a shaking hand. "I don't understand," he said weakly.

"Perhaps Master Sean would be good enough to explain," said His Highness.

Master Sean thought for a couple of seconds, then said: "How old would you say Lord Vauxhall was, my lord?"

"Thuh—thirty. Thirty-five."

"He was over seventy," said Master Sean.

Sefton said nothing. He just looked stunned.

"These days, thanks to modern healing methods," Master Sean went on, "a man can expect the Biblical three-score-and-ten as a minimum, if accident or other violence doesn't carry him off before that. Because of the tremendous psychic burdens they bear, Kings don't get much past that, but an ordinary fellow can look forward with reasonable confidence to his hundredth birthday, and a quarter of a century more is far from uncommon. We call a man in his sixties 'middle-aged', and quite rightly, too.

"But Healers and sorcerers aren't miracle-workers. We can all expect to get older; there's no cure for that. A man slows down; his reflexes aren't what they were; he gets wrinkles and gray hair and all that sort of thing.

We all know it, and we expect it. And, until about a century ago—a little more—there was nothing could be done about it.

"Then, in 1848, in the early part of the reign of Gwiliam V, two medical thaumaturgists, working independently, discovered a method for retaining the appearance and the vigor of youth. One was a Westphalian named Reinhardt von Horst; the other an Ulsterman named Duivid Shea.

"Essentially, what they discovered was a method of keeping the entire body in balance, as it were. I'll not go into the thaumaturgical terminology, but what happens, under the effect of the treatment, is that the body keeps katabolism and anabolism so perfectly balanced that each part contributes to the support of every other part. Do you see?"

Lord Sefton nodded and held his empty glass out to Coronel Danvers, who promptly refilled it along with his own.

Lord Darcy had heard Master Sean lecture on this subject before, but he enjoyed listening to Master Sean when he got into his pedagogical mood. For one thing, he lost almost all of his brogue, and for another, he always showed a new facet of any subject, no matter how many times he'd spoken on it before.

"Now, that sounds awfully good in theory, doesn't it, my lord?"

"Unfortunately, it doesn't work out that way. Take the skin, for instance. It's one of the first things to go as age progresses. That's why we get wrinkles and gray hair. The skin loses its youthful elasticity and its ability to pigment hair. The heart, on the other hand, is one of the toughest organs we have. It has to be. It keeps going, day and night, year after year, with only a tiny bit of rest between beats. If a man sees his Healer regularly, the old ticker will keep going strong until the very end. It can be the last thing to go, long after the rest of the body has given up and, to all intents and purposes, died.

"But this treatment I've been talking about spreads the wearing-out process all over the whole body evenly. In order to keep such things as the purely cosmetic functions of the skin going, the heart, the liver, the pancreas, and so on, all have to give up some of their own life expectancy.

"Eventually, the body reaches the point where every organ in it, every individual cell, is on the verge of death. And when they begin dying, it happens all over, with terrifying rapidity. A matter of minutes, never more than an hour. Everything goes at once. The enzymes go wild. Connecting fibers dissolve. Resistance to microorganisms vanishes.

"Well—you saw the result. Lord Vauxhall had taken that treatment."

"*Ugh,*" Lord Sefton said. "That's horrible."

"In effect," Master Sean continued relentlessly, "what Lord Vauxhall did was trade fifty extra years of life for fifty extra years of youth. All of us who knew him suspected it, and it came as no surprise—only as a shock."

"Great God," Lord Sefton said. "A man like Vauxhall, tied in with Black Magic. Horrible."

"Well, now, as to that," said Master Sean, "it is and it isn't. Black Magic, I mean. It's not done with evil intent. No ethical thaumaturgist in the Empire would do it, but I understand it's not considered a bad exchange in some parts of Islam. Leading the sex life of an eighteen-year-old for half a century might appear to some as a good thing. Depends on your outlook, I suppose. But the end is pretty messy."

"Tell me, Master Sean," Prince Richard said, "how many treatments does it take?"

"Oh, you have to take the treatments regularly, Your Highness. It's like an addictive drug, in a way. After a certain length of time, the withdrawal symptoms are pretty bad. The whole body has been weakened, you see, and without the support of additional spells you'd go to pieces. And more slowly. If Lord Vauxhall had stopped, say, twenty-five years ago, he might have lasted a year. But it would have been a rather horrible year.

"In the long run, of course, there's nothing a sorcerer can do. I have heard that some sorcerers using the treatment have had patients collapse and die in the middle of a treatment session. I don't think I'd care for that, meself."

"Why have I never heard of this before?" Lord Sefton asked.

"It's rarely done," Master Sean said. "Few magicians *can* do it; even fewer *would* do it. And it's a devilish difficult job. Accordingly, the price is high. Very high. Only a rich man like Lord Vauxhall could afford it. And, o' course, it's not widely advertised. We'd rather it were not discussed very much, if you follow me, Lord Sefton."

"I do indeed." The Foreign Secretary drained his glass, and then sat blinking for a minute. At last he said: "Poor old boy. Bad way to go." He forced a smile. "Damned inconvenient, too. For us, I mean. What do you suppose he did with the treaty?" He looked up at Lord Darcy.

Lord Darcy had been thumbing tobacco into what he called his "knockabout briar" and drawing it alight. He slowly blew out a cloud of smoke and said: "Welll—let's reconstruct what he must have done.

"He left the table where my lords had been talking in order to get the leather diplomatic case to put the papers in. While he was gone, he received some sign that the end was near. What would that be, Master Sean?"

"Probably his hair started coming out, me lord," the stout little Irish sorcerer replied. "That's usually the first indication. Then the skin around the eyes. And a sudden feeling of lassitude and weakness."

"We can picture the scene, then," Lord Darcy went on. "I don't know how I, personally, would react if I suddenly saw myself going like that, but Vauxhall was a pretty tough-minded man and he had known what the end would be like for years. He was prepared for it, in a way. But at the moment of realization, everything else became suddenly unimportant. He didn't want others to see him; his vanity precluded that. What went through his mind?

"Lord Vauxhall's greatest conquests were made in the field of diplomacy, but many of his most pleasurable ones were made right here in this house. He had built it himself and was proud of it and happy with it. I think he wanted to see it one last time. He could die here in peace.

"I think the gun must have been in a desk drawer or the like; we can check that later, up at the manor. It's of no matter, really, except that it shows his state of mind.

"We can imagine him making his decision and coming down here. The important thing we must imagine is what he might have done with that leather-encased treaty. He had, I think, forgotten about it. There it was, under his left arm or in his left hand, and he didn't even notice it. Like a man who has shoved his spectacles up to his forehead and forgotten them."

"Why do you say his left hand, my lord?" Prince Richard asked with a frown.

"Because he was thinking about his right hand," Lord Darcy said gently. "There was a handgun in it."

The Duke nodded silently.

"Now, at some time between then and the moment of his death, he *did* notice it—and put it down somewhere. I hardly think he deliberated concealed it. He had suddenly noticed it and it was rather heavy, so he unburdened himself of it.

"He came here, poured himself a glass of wine, and—"

Lord Darcy stopped.

"The wine," he said after a half minute.

"What about it?" Lord Peter asked. "Perfectly good wine, wasn't it?"

"Oh, yes. But he wouldn't drink a Rhenish warm. He wouldn't keep it in a place where it would become warm. Oh, it's warm now, but it was cool when he opened it. Had to be."

He turned away from them suddenly and looked out the front window at the wanly moonlit scene. "I can't picture it," he said, almost as if to himself. "I just can't see him coming down that slope with a bottle of wine, a gun, and a diplomatic case. Even if he left the case in the manor house, would he have gone all the way down to the cellar for a bottle? No. It would have to be picked up on the way—" He swung round and looked at the Prince.

"Were the four of you drinking wine this evening?"

"No, my lord," said Prince Richard. "Oh, there was Oporto and Xerez on the sideboard with the spirits, but nothing that would have been brought up from the wine cellar."

"Then where the devil did he get that bottle of Rhenish?"

Prince Richard put his hand over his eyes with a sudden gesture. "I forgot all about it! There's a small cellar right here. Come! I'll show you."

They all trooped after him, through the dining room, back to the service pantry. He strode over to one wall and knelt on the parquet floor. Lord Darcy saw that there was a small, finger-sized hole in one of the wooden blocks that made up the floor and mentally cursed himself for not having seen it before.

The Duke stuck his finger in the hole and lifted. A block of the wood came up. Beneath it was a heavy steel ring which lay flat until His Highness grasped it and lifted as he stood up. The ring made a handle, and a twenty-eight by twenty-eight section of the floor swung upward on hinges. Below, a ladder led down into gloom.

Lord Darcy was already getting a candle from the supply he had noticed when the room had been searched previously. He lit it with his pipe lighter, and, pipe clenched between his teeth, descended into the little wine cellar.

Once on the floor of the underground room, he lifted his candle and looked around.

"Not much here," he said after a minute. "Most of the shelves are empty. A few good reds. And, yes, seven bottles of the *Schwartzschlosskellar* '69 and a couple of dozen of the '70. Want to come down and help me look, Peter? There's a candle here in a holder—probably the one Vauxhall used. It looks fresh."

The Lord High Admiral came down the ladder as if he were on a ship.

The men above waited with what can only be called stolid impatience. After what seemed a God-awful long time, they heard:

"Well, Darcy, so much for that."

"Yes. Nothing here. Dammit, where *is* it?"

The two men came back up the ladder looking utterly dispirited.

"A fine big buildup to a big letdown," Lord Darcy said. "Sorry, Your Highness." They all went back to the front room.

Once there, Coronel Danvers went over to the liquor cabinet, finished his drink, picked up his dragoon officers' cap, adjusted it smartly on his head, turned, and saluted His Highness the Duke.

"With Your Highness' permission, I'll go out and take a look around between here and the manor house. I'm getting a bit fidgety waiting for someone else to find that package."

"Certainly, Coronel. Let me know immediately when you find it."

"I shall, Your Highness." And he went briskly out the door.

"Amazing man, the Coronel," said the Duke.

"A good officer," said the Lord High Admiral. "What he needs is to see some action. Which he may, if we don't find that treaty."

"I believe I'll go with him," said Lord Sefton. "Maybe I can be of some help. I'm of no use hanging about here. With your permission, Your Highness?"

"Of course, my lord."

He went out, leaving Lord Darcy with the Prince, the Lord High Admiral, Master Sean, and Goodman Torquin.

"Well," Lord Darcy said with a sigh, "I suppose there's nothing for it but to look behind all the pictures in the gallery. I wish I knew what rooms Vauxhall actually went to."

"Why, he went to all of 'em, ye know," said Torquin.

Lord Darcy looked down at the small man. "He did?"

"Oh, yea. Took a complete tour of the house, he did. The locks had just been freshly serviced by myself d'ye see, so I could tell when I opened 'em. Nobody but him had been in the house since. Funny thing—he went through every door once. And only once. Unlocked the door, went through, locked it behind him. Extraordinary. Must have wanted the house left in tip-top form, eh?"

There seemed to come a great calm over Lord Darcy as he said: "Yes. Most interesting. May I see that sketch plan again?"

"Of course, my lord." Goodman Torquin took his notebook from his bag, extracted the page, and handed it over.

Lord Darcy scrutinized it carefully, then handed it back with a brief thanks. Then he wandered about the room, staring straight ahead as if he were looking at something others could not see. No one said anything. After a few minutes, he stopped suddenly and looked at Prince Richard. "I trust that the plumbing is functioning in this house, Your Highness?"

"I should think so. Like the gas, it's turned on from outside, and the servants would have made everything ready for him when they were told he was coming home."

"That's good. If you will pardon me, gentlemen?" He opened the door to the west of the fireplace and went into the front bedroom, closing the door behind him.

"He's a deep 'un, his lordship, eh, Master?" said Torquin the Locksman.

"Probably the most brilliant deductive reasoner on the face of the Earth," Master Sean said. "And possibly the most brilliant *in*ductive reasoner. I wonder what he saw in that sketch plan of yours? He saw something. I know him well."

"Let's take a look and see if we can spot it," Prince Richard said. "I think we have all the evidence he has. If he's come up with some kind of answer, we should be able to."

"As my friend Torquin, here, might say, 'Would ye care to put a gold sovereign on it?' " Master Sean said with a grin.

"No," said His Royal Highness.

The four men looked at the sketch plan.

They were still looking fruitlessly when Lord Darcy returned some minutes later. The smile on his face was beatific.

"Ah, Your Highness! You will be pleased to know that your worries are over! All is well! I predict—" He raised a forefinger histrionically. "I predict that very soon a man you have not seen for some time will appear in this very house, coming from the legendary direction of Hell itself, bearing with him that which you seek. He and his minions will come from the darkness into the light. I have spoken!"

The Duke stared at him. "How do you know all this?"

"Aha! I have heard voices, though I could not see the speakers," Lord Darcy said mysteriously.

"What's the matter with you, Darcy?" the Prince asked warily.

Lord Darcy spread his arms and bowed. "I am like the weather, Highness. When the weather is brisk, I am brisk; when the weather is cool, I am cool; when the weather is blustery, I am blustery. Have you noticed how balmy it is out tonight?"

"All right, my lord; you know something. What is it?" the Lord High Admiral said in quarterdeck tones.

"Indeed I do," Lord Darcy said, regaining some of his wonted composure. "Take a good look at that sketch plan, I beg you. And remember that Torquin the Locksman has stated unequivocally that Lord Vauxhall went through each and every one of the sixteen doors in this house—we're not counting bathroom doors—once and only once. Do I state the facts, my good Torquin?"

"Yea, my lord; ye do."

"Then the facts lead inescapably to one conclusion, which, in turn, leads us to the most likely place for the treaty to be. Don't you see?"

They didn't, none of them, for a minute or so.

Then Lord Darcy said quietly: "How did he get into the house?"

Torquin the Locksman looked at him in astonishment. "Through one of the outside doors, o' course. He had all the keys."

But Master Sean burst out with: "Good heavens, yes! Parity, me lord. *Parity!*"

"Exactly, me dear Sean! Parity!" Lord Darcy said.

"I don't get it," the Lord High Admiral said flatly. "What's 'parity'?"

"The ability to make pairs, yer lordship," said Master Sean. "In other words, is a number odd or even? The number of doors coming into this house is four—that's even. If he went through all four of those doors once and only once—it don't matter at all where he went between times—he'd have ended up back outside the house."

"In-out-in-out," said Prince Richard. "Why, of course he would! Then how—" He stopped and looked back at the paper.

"Would you give me a sheet of blank paper and a pencil?" Lord Darcy asked in a low aside to Torquin. The small man produced them from his bag.

"Is the route he took supposed to be of importance?" the Lord High Admiral asked.

"Not the route, no," Lord Darcy said. He had put the paper on the mantelpiece and was sketching rapidly. "There must be ten thousand different routes he could have taken and still gone through every door exactly once. No, the route's not important."

"Parity, again," said Master Sean. "It holds true for any room with an even number of doors. I see what his lordship is driving at."

"Certainly you do," Lord Darcy said. "Once I saw that he couldn't have entered from any of the outside doors, I knew that there had to be a secret entrance to this house. It fits in well with Vauxhall's romantic nature. And when I saw what the end-points of his route through this house were, I knew where to look for the hidden entrance. So I excused myself, and went to look. I didn't want to raise any false hopes in the rest of you, so I checked to make sure the treaty was there."

"You said you were going to the head," said the Lord High Admiral.

"I did not. I merely inquired after the plumbing. Your inferences were your own. At any rate, I checked, and I heard voices from—"

A voice from within the house said: "Halloo! Is someone up there?"

"Come along," Lord Darcy said. "That will be Chief Donal with good news. I left the treaty for him to find." They all went through the dining room to the service pantry. Chief Donal and two of his sergeants were climbing out of the little wine cellar.

The Chief Master-at-Arms was holding a heavy leather diplomatic case in his hands and a broad smile on his face. "We found it, Your Highness! There you are!" He had never looked less grim.

The Duke took the case and inspected its contents. "That's it, all right, Chief Donal. Congratulations. And thank you. Where was it?"

"Well, we got to looking for secret panels, Your Highness, since the first search of the house didn't yield anything. We found this old tunnel behind a dummy wine rack in the wine cellar. There used to be an old castle up on that hill, centuries ago, and the manor house was built on its foundations. This tunnel must have been an escape route for times of siege; it ended up down here, in what was woods, then. Lord Vauxhall must have deliberately built this house on top of the old tunnel exit. We followed it and came out here. The case, there, was on the floor of the tunnel, just behind another dummy wine rack that acted as a door."

"Well, thank you again, Chief Donal," the Prince said. "You can go call off your men now. We've got what we were looking for."

They all went back out to the receiving room again, and, after the Armsmen had left, Prince Richard speared Lord Darcy with an accusing eye. " 'A man I haven't seen in some time'," he quasi-quoted.

"A couple of hours, at least," Lord Darcy said tranquilly.

"May I ask what is on the piece of paper you were so assiduously working on?"

"Certainly, Your Highness. Here. As you see, it is merely one of the possible routes Vauxhall could have taken. There are thousands of possibilities, but every one of them has to either start in this room and end in the service pantry or vice versa. They are the only two rooms with an odd number of doors. Since he died in this room, he had to start his tour in the service pantry. And the only other way into that room had to be through the wine cellar."

"Simple, when you know how," the Duke said. "It's getting very late. I still have to tell Coronel Danvers to call off his dragoons. Let's shut off the lights and—if you would be so good, Journeyman Torquin—lock up those four outside doors."

"And the ones to the green room, Your Highness," the small man said firmly. "Lord Vauxhall wouldn't want no gard'ner prowlin' through the house."

"Of course."

The doors were locked and the lights put out.

As Lord Darcy turned the last gascock in the front room, he looked at the spot before the fireplace where Lord Vauxhall had died.

"Obit surfeit vanitatis," he said softly.

And the darkness came.

The Napoli Express

1

His Royal Highness, Prince Richard, Duke of Normandy, seated on the edge of his bed in the Ducal Palace at Rouen, had taken off one boot and started on the other when a discreet rap came at the door.

"Yes? What is it?" There was the sound of both weariness and irritation in his voice.

"Sir Leonard, Highness. I'm afraid it's important."

Sir Leonard was the Duke's private secretary and general factotum. If he said something was important, it was. Nevertheless—

"Come in, then, but damn it, man, it's five o'clock in the morning! I've had a hard day and no sleep."

Sir Leonard knew all that, so he ignored it. He came through the door and stopped. "There is a Commander Dhuglas downstairs, Highness, with a letter from His Majesty. It is marked *Most Urgent.*"

"Oh. Well, let's see it."

"The Commander was instructed to deliver it into your hands only, Highness."

"Bother," said His Highness without rancor, and put his boot back on.

By the time he got downstairs to the room where Commander Dhuglas was waiting, Prince Richard no longer looked either tired or disheveled. He was every inch a tall, blond, handsome Plantagenet, member of a proud family that had ruled the Anglo-French Empire for over eight centuries.

Commander Dhuglas, a spare man with graying hair, bowed when the Duke entered. "Your Highness."

"Good morning, Commander. I understand you have a letter from His Majesty."

"I do, Your Highness." The Naval officer handed over a large ornately-sealed envelope. "I am to wait for an answer, Your Highness."

His Highness took the letter and waved toward a nearby chair. "Sit down, Commander, while I see what this is all about."

He himself took another chair, broke the seal on the envelope and took out the letter.

At the top was the embossed seal of the Royal Arms, and, below that:

> My dear Richard,
>   There has been a slight change in plans. Due to unforseen events at this end, the package you have prepared for export must go by sea instead of over-land. The bearer of this letter, Commander Edwy Dhuglas, will take it and your courier to their des-tination aboard the vessel he commands, the *White Dolphin*. She's the fastest ship in the Navy, and will make the trip in plenty of time.
>   All my best,
>   Your loving brother,
>   John

Prince Richard stared at the words. The "package" to which His Majesty referred was a freshly-negotiated and signed Naval treaty between Kyril, the Emperor at Con-stantinople, and King John. If the treaty could be gotten to Athens in time, Kyril would take steps immediately to close the Sea of Marmara against certain Polish "merchant" vessels—actually disguised light cruisers—which King Casimir's Navy was building in Odessa. If those ships got out, Casimir of Poland would have Naval forces in the Mediterranean and the Atlantic for the first time in forty years. The treaty with the Scandinavians, at the end of the 1939 war, had stopped the Poles from getting out of the Baltic, but the treaty with the Greeks at that time had had holes in it.

The present treaty closed those holes, but Kyril would not act until the signed treaty was in his hands. There were three of the disguised cruisers in the Black Sea now; once they got past the Dardanelles, it would be too late. They had to be trapped in the Sea of Marmara, and that meant the treaty had to be in Athens within days.

Plans had been laid, timetables set and mathematically calculated to get that treaty there with all possible haste.

And now, His Imperial Majesty, John IV, by the Grace of God King of England, France, Scotland, and Ireland; Emperor of the Romans and Germans; Premier Chief of the Moqtessumid Clan; Son of the Sun; Lord and Protector of the Western Continents of New England and New France; Defender of the Faith, had changed those plans. He had every right to do so, of course; there was no question of that. But—

Prince Richard looked at his wristwatch and then at Commander Dhuglas. "I am afraid this message from the King my brother is a little late, Commander. The item to which he refers should be leaving Paris on the Napoli Express in five minutes."

2

The long, bright red cars of the Napoli Express seemed almost eager to get into motion; the two ten-inch-wide stripes along their length—one white and one blue—almost gave the impression that they were already in motion. Far down the track ahead, nearly outside the South Paris Station, the huge engine steamed with a distant hissing.

As usual, the Express was loaded nearly full. She only made the run from Paris to Naples twice a week, and she usually had all the passengers she could handle—plus a standby waiting list.

The trouble with being a standby is that when a reservation is cancelled at the last moment, the standbys, in order of precedence, have to take the accommodations offered or give them up to the next in line.

The poshest compartments on the Napoli Express are the eight double compartments on the last car of the train, the Observation Car, which is separated from the rest of the train by the dining car. All sixteen places had been reserved, but three of them had been cancelled at the last moment. Two of them had been filled by standbys who rather reluctantly parted with the extra fare required, but the sixteenth place remained empty. None of the other standbys could afford it.

The passengers were filing aboard. One of them—a short, stout, dark-haired, well-dressed Irishman carrying a symbol-decorated carpetbag in one hand and a suitcase in the other, and bearing papers which identified him as Seamus Kilpadraeg, Master Sorcerer—watched the other passengers carefully without seeming to do so. The man just ahead of him in line was a wide-shouldered, thick-set man with graying hair who announced himself as Sir Stanley Galbraith. He climbed aboard and did not look back as Master Seamus identified himself, put down his suitcase, surrendered his ticket and took back his stub.

The man behind him, the last in line, was a tall, lean gentleman with brown hair and a full, bushy brown beard. Master Seamus had previously watched him hurrying across the station toward the train. He carried a suitcase in one hand and a silver-headed walking stick in the other, and walked with a slight limp. The sorcerer heard him give his name to the ticket officer as Goodman John Peabody.

Master Seamus knew that the limp was phony and

that the walking stick concealed a sword, but he said nothing and did not look back as he picked up his suitcase and boarded the train.

The small lounge at the rear of the car already contained some five or six passengers. The rest were presumably in their compartments. His own compartment, according to his ticket, was Number Two, towards the front of the car. He headed toward it, suitcase in one hand, carpetbag in the other. He looked again at the ticket: Number Two Upper. The lower bed was now a day couch, the upper had been folded up into the wall and locked into place, but there were two lockers under the lower bed marked "Upper" and "Lower." The one marked "Upper" still had a key in its lock; the other did not, which meant that the man who shared his compartment had already put his luggage in, locked it and taken the key. Master Seamus stowed his own gear away, locked the locker and pocketed the key. Having nothing better to do, he went back to the lounge.

The bushy-bearded man named Peabody was seated by himself over in one corner reading the Paris *Standard*. After one glance, the sorcerer ignored him, found himself a seat, and looked casually around at the others.

They seemed a mixed lot, some tall, some short, some middle-aged, some not much over thirty. The youngest-appearing was a blond, pink-faced fellow who was standing by the bar as if impatiently awaiting a drink, although he must have known that liquor would not be served until the train was well under way.

The oldest-appearing was a white-haired gentleman in priest's garb; he had a small white moustache and beard, and smooth-shaven cheeks. He was quietly reading his breviary through a pair of gold-rimmed half-glasses.

Between those two, there seemed to be a sampling of every decade. There were only nine men in the lounge, including the sorcerer. Five others, for one reason or another, remained in their compartments. The last one almost didn't make it.

He was a plump man—not really fat, but definitely overweight—who came puffing up just as the ticket officer was about to close the door. He clutched his suitcase in one hand and his hat in the other. His sandy hair had been tousled by the warm spring wind.

"Quinte," he gasped. "Jason Quinte." He handed over his ticket, retaining the stub.

The ticket officer said, "Glad you made it, sir. That's all, then." And he closed the door.

Two minutes later, the train began to move.

3

Five minutes out of the station, a man in a bright red-and-blue uniform came into the car and asked those who were in their staterooms to please assemble in the after lounge. "The Trainmaster will be here in a moment," he informed everyone.

In due time, the Trainmaster made his appearance in the lounge. He was a man of medium height, with a fierce-looking black mustache, and when he doffed his hat, he revealed a vast expanse of bald head fringed by black hair. His red-and-blue uniform was distinguished from the other by four broad white stripes on each sleeve.

"Gentlemen," he said with a slight bow, "I am Edmund Norton, your Trainmaster. I see by the passenger manifest that all of you are going straight through to Napoli. The timetable is printed on the little cards inside the doors of your compartments, and another one—" he gestured "—is posted over there behind the bar. Our first stop will be Lyon, where we will arrive at 12:15 this afternoon, and there will be an hour stopover. There is an excellent restaurant at the station for your lunch. We arrive at Marsaille at 6:24 and will leave at 7:20. There will be a light supper served in the dining car at nine.

"At approximately half an hour after midnight, we will cross the border from the Duchy of Provence to the

Duchy of Liguria. The train will stop for ten minutes, but you need not bother yourselves with that, as no one will be allowed either on or off the train. We will arrive at Genova at 3:31 in the morning, and leave at 4:30. Breakfast will be served from 8 to 9 in the morning, and we arrive in Rome at four minutes before noon. We leave Rome at one o'clock, which will give you an hour for lunch. And we arrive at Napoli at 3:26 in the afternoon. The total time for the trip will be 34 hours and 14 minutes.

"For your convenience, the dining car will be open this morning at six. It is the next car ahead, toward the front of the train.

"Goodman Fred will take care of all of your needs, but feel free to call on me for anything at any time." Goodman Fred made a short bow.

"I must remind you, gentlemen, that smoking is not permitted in the compartments, in the corridor or in the lounge. Those of you who wish to smoke may use the observation platform at the rear of the car.

"If there are any questions, I will be glad to answer them at this time."

There were no questions. The Trainmaster bowed again. "Thank you, gentlemen. I hope you will all enjoy your trip." He replaced his hat, turned and left.

There were four tables reserved in the rear of the dining car for the occupants of the observation car. Master Sorcerer Seamus Kilpadraeg got into the dining car early, and one by one, three other men sat down with him at the table.

The tall, husky man with the receding white hair and the white, clipped, military mustache introduced himself first.

"Name's Martyn Boothroyd. Looks like we're going to be on the train together for a while, eh?" His attention was all on the sorcerer.

"So it would seem, Goodman Martyn," the stout little Irish sorcerer said affably. "Seamus Kilpadraeg I am, and pleased to meet you."

The blocky-faced man with the two-inch scar on his right cheek was Gavin Tailleur; the blond man with the big nose was Sidney Charpentier.

The waiter came, took orders, and went.

Charpentier rubbed a forefinger against the side of his imposing nose. "Pardon me, Goodman Seamus," he said in his deep, rumbling voice, "but when you came aboard, didn't I see you carrying a magician's bag?"

"You did, sir," said the sorcerer pleasantly.

Charpentier grinned, showing strong white teeth. "Thought so. Journeyman? Or should I have called you 'Master Seamus'?"

The Irishman smiled back. "Master it is, sir."

All of them were speaking rather loudly, and around them others were doing the same, trying to adjust their voice levels to compensate for the roar and rumble of the Napoli Express as she sped southwards towards Lyon.

"It's a pleasure to make your acquaintance, Master Seamus," Charpentier said. "I've always been interested in the field of magic. Sometimes wish I'd gone into it, myself. Never have made Master, though; math's way over my head."

"Oh? You've a touch of the Talent, then?" the sorcerer asked.

"A little. I've got my ticket as a Lay Healer."

The sorcerer nodded. A Lay Healer's License was good for first aid and emergency work or for assisting a qualified Healer.

The blocky-faced Tailleur tapped the scar on his cheek with his right forefinger and said, in a somewhat gravelly voice: "This would've been a damn sight worse than it is if it hadn't been for old Sharpy, here."

Boothroyd said suddenly: "There's a question I've always wanted to ask—oops, here's breakfast." While the waiter put plates of hot food on the table, Boothroyd began again. "There's a question I've always wanted to ask. I've noticed that Healers use only their hands, with perhaps a little oil or water, but sorcerers use all kinds of paraphernalia—wands, amulets, thuribles, that sort of thing. Why is that?"

"Well, sir, for one thing, they're slightly different uses of the Talent," the sorcerer said. "A Healer is assisting in a process that naturally tends in the direction he wants it to go. The body itself has a strong tendency to heal. Furthermore, the *patient* wants it to heal, except in certain cases of severe aberration, which a Healer can take care of in other ways."

"In other words," Charpentier said, "the Healer has the cooperation of both the body and the mind of the patient."

"Exactly so," the sorcerer agreed. "The Healer just greases the skids, so to speak."

"And how does that differ from what a sorcerer does?" Boothroyd asked.

"Well, most of a sorcerer's work is done with inanimate objects. No cooperation at all, d'ye see. So he has to use tools that a Healer doesn't need.

"I'll give you an analogy. Suppose you have two friends who weigh fourteen stone apiece. Suppose they're both very drunk and want to go home. But they are so drunk that they can't get home by themselves. You, who are perfectly sober, can take 'em both by the arm and lead 'em both home at the same time. It may be a bit o' trouble; it may require all your skill at handling 'em. But you can do it without help because, in the long run, they're cooperating with you. They *want* to get home.

"But suppose you had the same weight in two sandbags, and you want to get *them* to the same place at the same time. You'll get no cooperation from three hundred and ninety-two pounds of sand. So you have to use a tool to assist you. You have a great many tools, but you must pick the right one for the job. In this case, you'd use a wheelbarrow, not a screwdriver or a hammer."

"Oh, I see," said Boothroyd, "you'd say a healer's job was easier, then?"

"Not easier. Just different. Some men who could wheel twenty-eight stone of sand a mile in fifteen minutes might not be able to handle a couple of drunks at all without using physical force. It's a different approach, you see."

Master Seamus had let his eyes wander over the other men in the rear of the dining car as he talked. There were only fourteen men at breakfast. The white-haired priest was listening to two rather foppish-looking men discourse earnestly on church architecture at the next table. He couldn't hear any of the others because of the noise of the train. Only one man was missing. Apparently the bushy-bearded Goodman John Peabody had not wanted any breakfast.

4

The saba game started early.

An imposing man with a hawk nose and a full beard, completely white except for two narrow streaks of dark brown beginning at the corners of his mouth, came over to where Master Seamus was sitting in the lounge.

"Master Seamus, I'm Gwiliam Hauser. A few of us are getting up a little game and thought maybe you'd like to join us."

"I thank you for the offer, Goodman Gwiliam," the sorcerer said, "but I'm afraid I'm not much of a gambling man."

"Hardly gambling, sir. Twelfth-bit ante. Just a friendly game to pass the time."

"No, not even a friendly game of saba. But, again, I thank you."

Hauser's eyes narrowed. "May I ask why not?"

"Ah, that you may, sir, and I'll tell you. If a sorcerer gets in a saba game with men who don't have the Talent, he can only lose."

"And why is that?"

"Because if he wins, sir, there's sure to be someone at the table who will accuse him of using his Talent to cheat. Now you should see a saba game played among sorcerers, sir. That's something to watch, though likely you'd not see most of what was going on."

Hauser's eyes cleared, and a chuckle came from somewhere inside the heavy beard. "I see. Hadn't thought of it that way. Boothroyd said you might like to play, so I asked. I'll pass on your bit of wisdom to him."

Actually, it would never occur to most folk to distrust a magician, must less accuse one of cheating at cards. But a heavy loser, especially if he's been drinking, will quite often say things he regrets later. Sorcerers rarely gamble with un-Talented people unless they are close friends.

Eventually Hauser, Boothroyd, Charpentier, the plump, nearly late Jason Quinte, and one of the two fops —the tall one with the hairline mustache, who looked as though he had been pressed into his clothes—ended up at a corner table with a deck of cards and a round of drinks. The saba game was on.

The sorcerer watched the game for a while from across the room, then opened the copy of the *Journal of the Royal Thaumaturgical Society* and began to read.

At eight-fifteen, the Irish magician finished the article on "The Subjective Algebra of Kinetic Processes" and put the *Journal* down. He was tired, not having had enough sleep, and the swaying motion of the train made it difficult to keep his eyes focused on the lines of print. He closed his eyes and massaged the bridge of his nose between thumb and forefinger.

"Beg y'pardon, Master Seamus. Mind if I join you?"

The sorcerer opened his eyes and looked up.

"Not at all. Pray sit down."

The man had reddish hair, a bulbous nose, and sagging features that hung loosely on his facial bones. His smile was pleasant and his eyes sleepy-looking. "Zeisler's my name, Master Seamus. Maurice Zeisler." He extended his right hand; his left held a large glass of ouiskie and water—heavy on the ouiskie.

The two shook hands, and Zeisler eased himself into the chair to the sorcerer's left. He gestured toward the saba table.

"Damn silly game, saba. Have to remember all those cards. Miss one, play wrong, and you're down the drain for a sovereign at least. Remember 'em all, have all the luck, bluff all the others out, and you're four sovereigns ahead. I never get the luck, and I can't keep the cards straight. Vandepole can, every time. So I stand 'em all a round of drinks and let 'em play. Lose less that way."

"Very wise," murmured the sorcerer.

"Buy you a drink?"

"No, thank you, sir. It's a bit early for me. Later, perhaps."

"Certainly. Be a pleasure." He took a hefty swig from his glass and then leaned confidentially toward the sorcerer. "What I would really like to know is, *is* Vandepole cheating? He's the well-dressed chap with the hairline mustache. Is he using the Talent to influence the fall of the cards?"

The sorcerer didn't even glance at the saba table. "Are you consulting me professionally, sir?" he asked in a mild voice.

Zeisler blinked. "Well, I—"

"Because, if you are," Master Seamus continued relentlessly, "I must warn you that a Master's fees come quite high. I would suggest you consult a Journeyman Sorcerer for that sort of thing; his fees would be much lower than mine, and he'd give you the same information."

"Oh. Well. Thank you. I may do that. Thank you." He took another long pull at his drink. "Uh—by the bye, do you happen to know a Master Sorcerer named Sean O Lochlainn?"

The sorcerer nodded slowly. "I've met him," he said carefully.

"Fortunate. Never met him, myself, but I've heard a great deal about him. Forensic sorcerer, you know. Interesting work. Like to meet him sometime." His eyes had wandered away from the sorcerer as he spoke, and he was gazing out the window at the French countryside flowing by.

"You're interested in magic, then?" the Irishman asked.

Zeisler's eyes came back. "Magic? Oh, no. Got no Talent at all. No, what I'm interested in is investigative work. Criminal investigation." He blinked and frowned as though trying to remember something. Then his eyes brightened and he said: "Reason I brought up Master Sean was that I met the man he works for, Lord Darcy, who's the Chief Investigator for His Royal Highness, the Duke of Normandy." He leaned forward and lowered his voice. The ouiskie was strong on his breath. "Were you at the Healers and Sorcerers Convention in London some years back, when a sorcerer named Zwinge got murdered at the Royal Steward Hotel?"

"I was there," the sorcerer said. "I remember it well."

"I imagine so, yes. Well, I was attached to the Admiralty offices at the time. Met Darcy there." He winked an eye solemnly. "Helped him crack the case, actually, but I can't say anything more about it than that." His gaze went back out the window again. "Great investigator. Absolute genius in his field. Nobody else could crack that case, but he solved it in no time. Absolute genius. Wish I had his brains." He drained his glass. "Yes, sir, I wish I had his brains." He looked at his empty glass and stood up. "Time for a refill. Get you one?"

"Not yet. Later, perhaps."

"Be right back." Zeisler headed for the bar.

He did not come back. He got into a conversation with Fred, the attendant who was mixing drinks, and forgot about Master Seamus completely, for which the stout little Irish sorcerer was extremely grateful.

He noticed John Peabody, he of the full and bushy beard, was sitting alone at the far end of the long couch, apparently still reading his newspaper, and seemingly so thoroughly engrossed in it that it would be boorish for anyone to speak to him. But the sorcerer knew that the man was keeping at least a part of his attention on the long hallway that ran forward, past the compartments.

Master Seamus looked back at the saba game. The foppishly dressed man with the hairline mustache was raking in sizeable winnings.

If Vanderpole were cheating, he was doing it without the aid of the Talent, either latent or conscious; such usage of the Talent would have been easy for the sorcerer to pick up at this short range. It was possible, of course, that the man had a touch of the precognitive Talent, but that was something which the science of magic had, as yet, little data and no theory on. Someone, some day, might solve the problem of the asymmetry of time, but no one had done it yet, and even the relatively new mathematics of the subjective algebrae offered no clue.

The sorcerer shrugged and picked up his *Journal* again. What the hell, it was no business of his.

5

"Lyon, Gentlemen!" came Goodman Fred's voice across the lounge, fighting successfully against the noise of the train. *"Lyon in fifteen minutes! The bar will close in five minutes! Lunch will be served in the station restaurant, and we will leave at one-fifteen! It is now twelve noon!"*

Fred had everyone's attention now, so he repeated the message.

Not everyone was in the lounge. After the bar was closed—Zeisler had managed to get two more during the five minutes—Fred went forward along the passageway and knocked on each compartment door. "Lyon in ten minutes! Lunch will be served in the station restaurant. We will leave for Marsaille at 1:15."

The stout little Irish sorcerer turned in his couch to look out the window at the outskirts of Lyon. It was a pleasant place, he thought. The Rhone valley was famous for its viniculture, but now the grape arbors were giving way to cottages more and more densely packed, and finally the train was in the city itself. The houses were old, most of them, but neat and well-tended. Technically, the County of Lyonnais was a part of the Duchy of Burgundy, but the folk never thought of themselves as Burgundians. The Count de Lyonnais commanded their respect far more than the Duke of Burgundy did. His Grace respected those feelings, and allowed My Lord Count as free a hand as the King's Law would permit. From the looks of the countryside, it appeared My Lord Count did a pretty good job.

"Excuse me, Master Sorcerer," said a soft, pleasant voice.

He turned away from the window. It was the elderly-looking gentleman in clerical garb. "How may I help you, Father?"

"Allow me to introduce myself; I am the Reverend Father Armand Brun. I noticed you sitting here by yourself, and I wondered if you would care to join me and some other gentlemen for lunch."

"Master Seamus Kilpadraeg at your service, Reverend Sir. I'd be most happy to join you for lunch. We have an hour, it seems."

The "other gentlemen" were standing near the bar, and were introduced in that quiet, smooth voice. Simon Lamar had thinning dark hair that one could see his scalp through, a long face and lips that were drawn into a thin line. His voice was flat, with just a touch of

Yorkshire in it as he said: "I'm pleased to meet you, Master Seamus."

Arthur Mac Kay's accent was both Oxford and Oxfordshire, and was smooth and well-modulated, like an actor's. He was the other foppishly dressed man—immaculate, as though his clothes had been pressed seconds before. He had dark, thick, slightly wavy hair, luminous brown eyes surrounded by long, dark lashes, and a handsome face that matched. He was almost too pretty.

Valentine Herrick had flaming red hair, an excessively toothy smile, and a body that seemed to radiate health and strength as he shook the sorcerer's hand. "Hate to see a man eat alone, by S'n George! A meal's not a meal without company, is it?"

"Not really," the sorcerer agreed.

"Especially at these train station restaurants," said Lamar in his flat voice. "Company keeps your mind off the tasteless food."

Mac Kay smiled angelically. "Oh, come; it's not as bad as all that. Come along; you'll see."

The *Heart of Lyon* restaurant was a fairly comfortable-looking place, not more than fifty years old, but designed in the King Gwiliam IV style of the late Eighteenth Century to give it an air of stability. The decor, however, reflected a mild pun on the restaurant's name—which had probably been carefully chosen for just that reason. Over the door, three-quarters life size, legs braced apart, right hand on the pommel of a great naked sword whose point touched the lintel, left arm holding a shield bearing the lions of England, stood the helmed, mail-clad figure of King Richard the Lion-Hearted in polychromed bas-relief. The interior, too, was decorated with knights and ladies of the time of Richard I.

It was fitting. Although most of the first ten years of his reign had been spent in the noble and heroic', but foolish and expensive, fighting of the Third Crusade, he had settled down after his near-fatal wound at the seige of Chaluz to become a really effective ruler. There were some historians who claimed that if Richard had died at Chaluz, a Capet would now be sitting on the throne of the Anglo-French Empire instead of a Plantagenet. But the Capets had died out long ago, as had the unstable cadet branch of the Plantagenets descended from the exiled Prince John, Richard's younger brother. It was Richard and Arthur, the nephew who had succeeded him in 1219, who had held the Anglo-French nation together during those troubled times, and it had been the descendants of King Arthur who had kept it stable through seven and a half centuries.

Old Richard may have had his faults, but he had been a fine king.

"Interesting motif for the decorations," Father Armand said as the waiter led the five men to a table. "And very well done, too."

"Not period, though," Lamar said flatly. "Too realistic."

"Oh, true, true," Father Armand said agreeably. "Not early Thirteenth Century style at all." He seated himself as the waiter pulled out a chair for him. "It's the painstakingly detailed realism of the late Seventeenth, which fits in very well with the style of the rest of the interior. It must have been expensive; there are very few artists nowadays who can or will do that sort of work."

"Agreed, Father," said Lamar. "Workmanship in general isn't what it used to be."

Father Armand chose to ignore that remark. "Now, you take a look up there, at Gwiliam the Marshal—at least I presume it's he; he's wearing the Marshal arms on his surcoat. I'll wager that if you climbed up there on a stepladder and looked closely, you could see the tiny rivets in every link of his mail."

Lamar raised a finger. "And that's not period, either."

Father Armand looked astonished. "Riveted link mail not period for the Thirteenth Century? Surely, sir—"

"No, no," Lamar interrupted hastily. "I meant the surcoat with the Marshal arms. Armorial bearings of that sort didn't come in till about a century later."

"You know," said Arthur Mac Kay suddenly, "I've always wondered what I'd look like in one of those outfits. Rather dashing, I think." His actor's voice contrasted strongly with Lamar's flat tones.

Valentine Herrick looked at him, smiling toothily. "Hey! Wouldn't that be great? Imagine! Charging into combat with a broadsword like that! Or rescuing a fair princess! Or slaying a dragon! Or a wicked magician!" He stopped suddenly and actually blushed. "Oops. Sorry, Master Sorcerer."

"That's all right," said Master Seamus mildly. "You may slay all the *wicked* magicians you like. Just don't make any mistakes."

That got a chuckle from everyone, even Herrick.

They looked over their menus, chose and ordered. The food, which the sorcerer thought quite good, came very quickly. Father Armand said grace, and more small talk ensued. Lamar said little about the food, but the wine was not to his exact taste.

"It's a Delacey '69, from just south of Givors. Not a bad year for the reds, but it can't compare with the Monet '69, from a lovely little place a few miles southeast of Beaune."

Mac Kay lifted his glass and seemed to address his remarks to it. "You know, I have always contended that the true connoisseur is to be pitied, for he has trained his taste to such perfection that he enjoys almost nothing. It is, I believe, a corollary of Acipenser's Law, or perhaps a theorem derived therefrom."

Herrick blinked bright blue eyes at him. "What? I don't know what you're talking about, but, by S'n

George, *I* think it's damn good wine." He emphasized his point by draining his glass and refilling it from the carafe.

Almost as if he had heard the pouring as a summons, Maurice Zeisler came wandering over to the table. He did not stagger, but there was a controlled precision about his walking and about his speech that indicated a necessity to concentrate in order to do either one properly. He did not sit down.

"Hullo, fellows," he said very carefully. "Did you see who's over in the corner?" There were, of course, four corners to the big room, but a slight motion of his head indicated which one he meant.

It was bushy-bearded John Peabody, eating by himself, his suitcase on the floor beside his chair.

"What about him?" asked Lamar sourly.

"Know him?"

"No. Kept pretty much to himself. Why?"

"I dunno. Seems familiar, somehow. Like I ought to know him. Can't exactly place him, though. Oh, well." And he wandered off again, back towards the bar, whence he had come.

"Condition he's in, he wouldn't recognize his own mother," muttered Lamar. "Pass the wine, please."

6

The Napoli Express crossed the Rhone at Lyon and headed southwards through the Duchy of Dauphine, toward the Duchy of Provence, following the river valley. At Avignon, it would angle away from the river, southeast toward Marsaille, but that wouldn't be until nearly five o'clock.

The Napoli Express was not a high speed train; it was too long and too heavy. But it made up for that by making only four stops between Paris and Napoli. Five, if you counted the very short stop at the Provence-Liguria border.

In order to avoid having to cross the Maritime Alps, the train ran along the coast of the Mediterranean after leaving Marsaille, past Toulon, Canne, Nice, and Monaco to the Ligurian coast. It looped around the Gulf of Genova to the city of Genova, then stayed with the seacoast all the way to the Tiber, where it turned east to make the short side trip to Rome. There, it crossed the Tiber and headed back toward the sea, staying with the coast all the way to arrive at last at Napoli.

But that would be tomorrow afternoon. There were hundreds of miles and hours of time ahead of her yet.

Master Seamus sat on one of the chairs on the observation deck at the rear of the car and watched the Rhone Valley retreat into the distance. There were four seats on the semicircular observation deck, two on each side of the central door that led into the lounge. The two on the starbord side were occupied by the plump, sandy-haired man who had almost missed the train—Jason Quinte—and the blond, pink-faced young man whose name the sorcerer did not know. Both were smoking cigars and talking in voices that could be heard but not understood above the rush of the wind and the rumble of the wheels over the steel tracks.

Master Seamus had taken the outer of the two remaining chairs, and Father Armand, who was trying valiantly to light his pipe in the gusts that eddied about him, had taken the other. When at last the pipe was burning properly, Father Armand leaned back and relaxed.

The door slid open and a fifth man came out, thumbing tobacco into his own pipe, a stubby briar. It was Sir Stanley Galbraith, the wide-shouldered, muscular, graying man who had preceded the sorcerer aboard the train. He ignored the others and went to the high railing that surrounded the observation deck and looked into the distance. Having packed his pipe to his satisfaction, he put away his tobacco pouch and then proceeded to search himself. Finally, he turned around, scowling. The scowl vanished when he saw Father Armand's pipe.

"Ah. Begging your pardon, Reverend Sir, but could I borrow your pipe lighter? Seem to have left my own in my compartment."

"Certainly." Father Armand proffered his lighter, which Sir Stanley promptly made use of. He succeeded in an astonishingly short time and handed the lighter back. "Thank you. My name's Galbraith, Sir Stanley Galbraith."

"Father Armand Brun. I am pleased to meet you, Sir Stanley. This is Master Sorcerer Seamus Kilpadraeg."

"A pleasure, gentlemen, a pleasure." He puffed vigorously at his pipe. "There. She'll stay lit now. Good thing it isn't raining; left my weather pipe at home."

"If you need one, Sir Stanley, let me know." It was the plump Jason Quinte. He and the pink-faced youngster had stopped talking when Sir Stanley had appeared and had been listening. Sir Stanley's voice was not overly loud, but it carried well. "I have a couple of them," Quinte went on. "One of 'em never used. Glad to make you a present of it if you want it."

"No, no. Thanks all the same, but there's no bad weather predicted between here and Napoli." He looked at the sorcerer. "Isn't that right, Master Seamus?"

The sorcerer grinned. "That's what the report said, Sir Stanley, but I couldn't tell you of my own knowledge. Weather magic isn't my field."

"Oh. Sorry. You chaps do all specialize, don't you? What is your specialty, if I may ask?"

"I teach forensic sorcery."

"Ah, I see. Interesting field, no doubt." He shifted his attention as a whiff of cigar smoke came his way. "Jamieson."

The pink-faced youth took the cigar from his mouth and looked alert. "Sir?"

"What the devil is that you're smoking?"

Jamieson looked down at the cigar in his hand as though he were wondering where the thing had come from and how it had got there. "A Hashtpar, sir."

"Persian tobacco; I thought so." A smile came over his tanned face. "Good Persian is very good; bad Persian—which that is—will probably rot your lungs, my boy. That particular type is cured with some sort of perfume or incense. Reminds me of a whorehouse in Abadan."

There was a sudden awkward pause as it came to the minds of all of them that there was a man of the cloth present.

"Toss it overboard, Jamie," Quinte said in a rather too-loud voice. "Here, have one of mine."

Jamieson looked at the three-quarters-smoked cigar again, then flipped it over the rail. "No, thanks, Jason. I was through with it anyway. Just thought I'd try one." He looked up at Sir Stanley with a rather sheepish grin. "They were expensive, sir, so I bought one. Just to try it, you see. But you're right—they do smell like the inside of a—uh—Daoist temple."

Sir Stanley chuckled. "Some of the worst habits are the most expensive, son. But, then, so are some of the best."

"What are you smoking, Sir Stanley?" Father Armand asked quietly.

"This? It's a blend of Balik and Robertian."

"I favor a similar blend, myself. I find Balik the best of Turkish. I alternate with another blend: Balik and Couban."

Sir Stanley shook his head slowly. "Tobacco from the Duchy of Couba is much better suited for cigars, Reverend Sir. The Duchy of Robertia produces the finer pipe tobacco, I find. Of course, I'll admit it's all a matter of taste."

"Never seen Couba," said Quinte, "but I've seen the tobacco fields in Robertia. Don't know if you've ever seen the stuff grow, Father?" It was only half a question.

"Tell me about it," said Father Armand.

Robertia was a duchy on the southern coast of the

northern continent of the Western Hemisphere, New England, with a seacoast on the Gulf of Mechicoe. It had been named after Robert II, since it had been founded during his reign in the early Eighteenth Century.

"It grows about so high," Quinte said, holding his hand about thirty inches off the deck. "Big, wide leaves. I don't know how it's cured; I only saw it in the fields."

He may have been going to say more, but the door leading into the lounge slid open and Trainmaster Edmund Norton stepped out, his red-and-blue uniform gleaming in the afternoon sun.

"Good afternoon, gentlemen," he said with a smile. "I hope I'm not interrupting."

"Oh, no," said Sir Stanley. "Not at all. Just chit-chat."

"I hope you gentlemen have all been comfortable, enjoying the trip, eh?"

"No complaints at all, Trainmaster. Eh, Father?"

"Oh, none at all, none at all," said Father Armand. "A very enjoyable trip so far. You run an excellent train, Trainmaster."

"Thank you, Reverend Sir." The Trainmaster cleared his throat. "Gentlemen, it is my custom at this hour to invite all my special passengers to join me in a drink—of whatever kind you prefer. Will you join me, gentlemen?"

There could, of course, be no argument with an invitation like that. The five passengers followed the Trainmaster into the lounge.

"One thing I'll say," Father Armand murmured to the sorcerer, "It's certainly quieter in here than out there."

The Trainmaster went quietly over to the table where the saba game had resumed after lunch. He had judged his time accurately.

Vanderpole raked in his winnings with one hand,

while he ran the forefinger of the other across his hair-line mustache.

The Trainmaster said a few words, which the sorcerer did not hear over the rumble of the train. It was quieter in here, yes, but not exactly silent.

Then Trainmaster Edmund went over to the bar, where Goodman Fred stood waiting, turned to the passengers and said in a loud voice: "Gentlemen, step up and order your pleasure. Fred, I'll see what the gentlemen at the saba table will have."

A few minutes later, the Irish sorcerer was seated at the bar watching the foam on a glass of beer slosh gently from side to side with the swaying of the train. Maurice Zeisler, he thought, was going to hate himself later. The scar-faced Gavin Tailleur had gone back to his compartment to tell him that the Trainmaster was treating, but had been unable to rouse him from his—er—nap.

Master Seamus was seated at the end of the bar, near the passageway. The Trainmaster came over and stood at the end of the bar after making sure everyone who wanted one had been served a drink.

"I'll have a beer, Fred," he said to the attendant.

"Comin' right up, Trainmaster."

"I see beer's your tipple, too, Master Sorcerer," Trainmaster Edmund said as Fred put a foaming brew before him.

"Aye, Trainmaster, that it is. Wine's good with a meal, and a brandy for special occasions is fine, but for casual or even serious drinkin', I'll take beer every time."

"Well spoken. Do you like this particular brew?"

"Very much," said the sorcerer. "Norman, isn't it?"

"Yes. There's a little area in the Duchy of Normandy, up in the highlands where the Orne, the Sarthe, the Eure, the Risle, and the Mayenne all have their sources, that has the best water in all of France. There's good beer comes from Ireland, and there are those who prefer

English beer, but to my taste, Norman is the best, which is why I always order it for my train."

Master Seamus, who *did* prefer English beer, but by the merest hair, merely said: "It's very fine stuff. Very fine, indeed." He suspected that the Trainmaster's preference might be shaded just a little by the fact that Norman beer was cheaper in Paris than English beer.

"Have you been getting along well with your compartment mate?" the Trainmaster asked.

"I haven't been informed who my compartment mate is," the sorcerer replied.

"Oh? Sorry. It's Father Armand Brun."

7

By half past four that afternoon, Master Seamus Kilpadraeg was dozing on the rearward couch, leaning back in the corner, his arms folded across his chest and his chin nearly touching his sternum. Since he did not snore, he offended no one. Father Armand had gone back to Compartment Number Two at a quarter after three, and, suspecting that the gentleman was tired, the sorcerer had decided to let him have the day couch there to himself.

The train and the saba game went on. Jason Quinte had dropped out of the game, but his place had been taken by the red-haired Valentine Herrick. Gavin Tailleur had taken Sidney Charpentier's place, and now Charpentier was sitting on the forward couch, his large nose buried in a book entitled *The Infernal Device,* an adventure novel. Sir Stanley Galbraith and Arthur Mac Kay were at the bar with a dice cup, playing for drinks.

Quinte and young Jamieson were back out on the observation deck with more cigars—presumably not Hashtpars this time.

Zeisler was still snoozing, and Lamar had apparently retired to his own compartment.

At Avignon, the train crossed the bridge that spanned

the River Durance and curved away from the Rhone toward Marsaille.

Master Seamus was roused from his doze by the sound of Simon Lamar's flat voice, but he neither opened his eyes nor lifted his head.

"Sidney," he said to Charpentier, "I need your Healing Talent."

"What's the matter? Got a headache?"

"I don't mean *I* need it. Maurice does. He's got one hell of a hangover. I've ordered some caffe from Fred, but I'd like your help. He hasn't eaten all day, and he has a headache."

"Right. I'll come along. We'll have to get some food in him at Marsaille." He rose and left with Lamar.

The sorcerer dozed off again.

8

When the Napoli Express pulled into Marsaille at twenty-four minutes after six that evening, Master Seamus had already decided that he needed exercise before he needed food. He got off the train, went through the depot, and out into the street beyond. A brisk fifteen-minute walk got his blood going again, made him feel less drowsy, and whetted his appetite. The tangy air of the Duchy of Provence, given a touch of piquancy by the breeze from the Mediterranean, was an aperitif in itself.

The *Cannebiere* restaurant—which was nowhere near the street of the same name name—was crowded by the time the sorcerer got back. With apologies to both sides, the waiter seated him at a table with a middle-aged couple named Duprey. Since he was not carrying his symbol-decorated carpetbag, there was no way for them to know that he was a magician, and he saw no reason to enlighten them.

He ordered the specialty of the house, which turned out to be a delicious thick whitefish stew with lots of garlic. It went fine with a dry white wine of rather pronounced character.

The Dupreys, as the conversation brought out, were the owners of a small leather-goods shop in Versaille who had carefully saved their money to make a trip to Rome, where they would spend a week, leaving the business in the hands of their two sons, each of whom was married to a delightful wife, and one of them had two daughters and the other a son, and . . .

And so on.

The sorcerer was not bored. He liked people, and the Dupreys were a very pleasant couple. He didn't have to talk much, and they asked him no questions. Not, that is, until the caffe was served. Then: "Tell me, Goodman Seamus," said the man, "why is it that we must stop at the Ligurian border tonight?"

"To check the bill-of-lading for the freight cars, I believe," the sorcerer said. "Some Italian law about certain imports."

"You see, John-Paul," said the woman, "it is as I told you."

"Yes, Martine, but I do not see why it should be. We are not stopped at the border of Champagne or Burgundy or Dauphine or Provence. Why Liguria?" He looked back at the magician. "Are we not all a part of the same Empire?"

"Well, yes—and no," Master Seamus said thoughtfully.

"What can you mean by that, sir?" John-Paul said, looking puzzled.

"Well, the Duchies of Italy, like the Duchies of Germany, are a part of the *Holy Roman* Empire, d'ye see, which was established in A.D. 862, and King John IV is Emperor. But they are *not* a part of what is unofficially called the *Anglo-French* Empire, which technically includes only France, England, Scotland, and Ireland."

"But we all have the same Emperor, don't we?" Martine asked.

"Yes, but His Majesty's duties are different, d'ye see. The Italian States have their own Parliament, which meets in Rome, and the laws they have passed are slightly different than those of the Anglo-French Empire. Its acts are ratified, not by the Emperor directly, but by the Imperial Viceroy, Prince Roberto VII. In Italy, the Emperor reigns, but does not rule, d'ye see."

"I—I think so," John-Paul said hesitantly. "Is it the same in the Germanies? I mean, they're part of the Empire, too."

"Not quite the same. They're not as unified as the Duchies of Italy. Some of them take the title of Prince, and some would like to take the title of King, though that's forbidden by the Concordat of Magdeburg. But the general idea's the same. You might say that we're all different states, but with the same goals, under the same Emperor. We all want individual freedom, peace, prosperity, and happy homes. And the Emperor is the living symbol of those goals for all of us."

After a moment's silence, Martine said: "Goodness! That's very poetic, Goodman Seamus!"

"It still seems silly," John-Paul said doggedly, "to have to stop a train at the border between two Imperial Duchies."

Master Seamus sighed. "You should try visiting the Poles—or even the Magyars," he said. "The delay might be as much as two hours. You would have to have a passport. The train would be searched. Your luggage would be searched. Even *you* might be searched. And the Poles do that even when their own people are crossing their own internal borders."

"Well!" said Martine, "I certainly shan't ever go *there!*"

"No need to worry about that," said John-Paul. "Will you have more caffe, my dear?"

Master Seamus went back to the train feeling very relaxed, thankful that two very ordinary people had taken his mind off his troubles. He never saw nor heard of either of them again.

9

By eight o'clock that evening, the *Napoli Express* was nearly twenty-five miles out of Marseille, headed for a rendezvous with the Ligurian border.

The saba game was in full swing again, and Master Seamus had the private feeling that, if it weren't for the fact that no one was permitted in the lounge while the train was in the station, three or four of the die-hards would never have bothered to eat.

By that time, the sorcerer found his eyelids getting heavy again. Since Father Armand was in deep conversation with two other passengers, Master Seamus decided he might as well go back to the compartment and take his turn on the day couch. He dropped off to sleep almost immediately.

The sorcerer's inward clock told him that it was ten minutes of nine when a rap sounded at the door.

"Yes? Who is it?"

"Fred, sir. Time to make up the bed, sir."

Wake up, it's time to go to sleep, the sorcerer thought glumly as he got his feet on the floor. "Certainly, Fred; come in."

"Sorry, sir, but the beds have to be made before I go off at nine. The night man doesn't have the keys, you see."

"Certainly; that's all right. I had me little nap, and I feel much better. I'll go on out to the lounge and let you work; there's hardly room in here for two of us."

"That's true, sir; thank you, sir."

There was a new man on behind the bar. As the sorcerer sat down, he put down the glass he was polishing and came over.

"May I serve you, sir?"

"Indeed you may, me lad. A beer, if you please."

"One beer; yes, sir." He took a pint mug, filled it, and served it.

There was no one else at the bar. The saba game, like the constellations in the sky, seemed unchanged. Master Seamus entertained a brief fantasy of taking this same trip a hundred years hence and seeing nothing re-markably different about that saba game. (Young Jamieson had replaced Boothroyd, but Hauser, Tailleur, Herrick and Vandepole were still at it.) Master Seamus drank his beer slowly and looked around the lounge.

Sir Stanley Galbraith and Father Armand were seated on the rearward couch, not talking to each other, but reading newspapers which they had evidently picked up in Marsaille.

Apparently, Charpentier had managed to cure Zeisler's hangover and get some food in him, for the two of them were sitting at the near table with Boothroyd and Lamar, talking in low tones. Zeisler was drinking caffe.

Mac Kay, Quinte, and Peabody were nowhere in sight.

Then Peabody, with his silver-handled stick, limped in from the passageway. He ordered ouiskie-and-splash and took it to the forward couch to sit by himself. He, too, had a newspaper, and began reading it with his touch-me-not attitude.

The sorcerer finished his beer and ordered another.

After a few minutes, Fred came back from his final duties for the day and said to the night man: "It's all yours, Tonio. Take over." And promptly left.

"No, no; I can get it. I'm closer." It was Zeisler's voice, raised just high enough for the sorcerer to hear it. His chair was nearest the bar. He got up, caffe cup in hand, and brought it over to the bar. "Another cup of caffe, Tonio."

"Yes, sir."

Zeisler smiled and nodded at Master Seamus, but said nothing. The sorcerer returned the greeting.

And then pretended not to notice what Tonio was doing. He set the cup down behind the bar, carefully poured in a good ounce of ouiskie, then filled the cup from the carafe that sat over a small alcohol lamp. It was done in such a way that the men at the table could not possibly have told that there was anything but caffe in the cup.

Zeisler had obviously tipped him well for that bit of legerdemain long before Master Seamus had come into the lounge.

Mentally, the sorcerer allowed himself a sad chuckle. Boothroyd, Lamar, and Charpentier thought they were dutifully keeping Zeisler sober, and here he was getting blotto before their very eyes. Ah, well.

Peabody put down his newspaper and came over to the bar, glass in hand. "Another ouiskie-and-splash, if you please," he said in a very low voice.

It was brought, and he returned to his seat and his newspaper. Tonio went back to polishing glasses.

Master Seamus was well into his third beer when the Trainmaster showed up. He went around and nodded and spoke to everyone, including the sorcerer. He went back to the observation deck, and Master Seamus concluded that Quinte and Mac Kay must be back there.

Trainmaster Edmund came back to the bar, took off his hat, and wiped his balding head with a handkerchief. "Warm evening. Tonio, how are your supplies holding out?"

"We'll have plenty for the rest of the evening, Trainmaster."

"Good; good. But I just checked the utility room, and we're short of towels. These men will be wanting to bathe in the morning, and we're way short. Run up to supply and get a full set. I'll watch the bar for you."

"Right away, Trainmaster." Tonio hurried without seeming to.

The Trainmaster left his cap off and stood behind the

bar. He did not polish any glasses. "Another beer, Master Sorcerer?" he asked.

"No, thanks, Trainmaster. I've had me limit for a while. I think I'll stretch me legs." He got up off the barchair and turned toward the observation deck.

"How about you, sir?" the Trainmaster called to Peabody, a few feet away, in the forward couch.

Peabody nodded, got up, and brought his glass over.

As Master Seamus passed the table where Zeisler and the other three were sitting, he heard Zeisler say: "You chaps know who that bearded chap at the bar is? I do."

"Morrie, will you shut up?" said Boothroyd coldly.

Zeisler said no more.

10

"What is going on out there? A convention?" came the voice of the sorcerer's companion from the lower berth. It was a rhetorical question, so the Master Sorcerer didn't bother to answer.

It is not the loudness of a noise, nor even its unexpectedness, wakes one up. It is the *unusual* noise that does that. And when the noise becomes *interesting,* it is difficult to go back to sleep.

The rumble and roar of the train as it moved toward Italy was actually soothing, once one got used to it. If it had only drowned out these other noises, all would have been well. But it didn't; it merely muffled them somewhat.

The sorcerer had been one of the last few to retire; only Boothroyd and Charpentier had still been in the lounge when he left to go to his compartment.

The hooded lamp had been burning low, and the gentle snores from the lower berth told him that his compartment-mate was already asleep.

He had prepared for bed and climbed in, only to find that the other man had left his newspaper on the other berth. It had been folded so that one article was uppermost, but in the dim light all he could read was the headline: NICHOLAS JOURDAN RITES TO BE HELD IN NAPOLI. It was an obituary notice.

He put the paper on the nearby shelf and began to doze off.

Then he heard a door open and close, and footsteps moving down the passageway. *Someone going to the toilet,* he thought drowsily. No, for the footsteps went right by his own door to Compartment Number One. He heard a light rap. *Hell of a time of night to go visiting,* he thought. Actually, it wasn't all that late—only a little after ten. But everyone aboard had been up since at least four that morning, some even longer. Oh, well; no business of his.

But there were other footsteps, farther down the corridor, other doors opening and closing.

He tried to get to sleep and couldn't. Things would get quiet for a minute or two, then they would start up again. From Compartment Three, he could hear voices, but only because the partition was next to his berth. There was only the sound; he couldn't distinguish any words. Being a curious man, he shamelessly put his ear to the wall, but could still make out no words.

He tried very hard to go to sleep, but the intermittent noises continued. Footsteps. Every five minutes or so, they would go to Number One or return from there, and, of course, these were the loudest. But there were others, up and down the passageway.

There was little he could do about it. He couldn't really say they were noisy. Just irritating.

He lay there, dozing intermittently, coming up out of it every time he heard something, drifting off each time there was a lull.

After what seemed like hours, he decided there *was* something he could do about it. He could at least get up and see what was going on.

That was when his companion had said: "What's going *on* out there? A convention?"

The sorcerer made no reply, but climbed down the short ladder and grabbed his dressing gown. "I feel the call of nature," he said abruptly. He went out.

There was no one in the passageway. He walked slowly down to the toilet. No one appeared. No one stuck his head out of a door. No one even opened it a crack to peek. Nothing.

He took his time in the toilet. Five minutes. Ten.

He went back to his compartment. His slippers on the floor had been almost inaudible, and he'd been very careful about making any noise. They couldn't have heard him.

He reported what he had found to his compartment-mate.

"Well, whatever they were up to," said the other, "I am thoroughly awake now. I think I'll have a pipe before I go back to bed. Care to join me?"

When they came into the lounge, Tonio was seated on a stool behind the bar. He looked up. "Good evening, Father; good evening, Master Sorcerer. May I help you?"

"No, we're just going out for a smoke," said the sorcerer. "But I guess you've had a pretty busy evening, eh?"

"Me? Oh, no, sir. Nobody been in here for an hour and a half."

The two men went on out to the observation deck. Their conversation was interrupted a few minutes later by Tonio, who slid open the door and said: "Are you sure there's nothing I can get you gentlemen? I have to go forward to the supply car to fetch a few things for tomorrow, but I wouldn't want you to be needing anything."

"No, thanks. That'll be all right. As soon as the good father finishes his pipe, we'll be goin' back to bed."

Twenty minutes later, they did just that, and fell asleep immediately. It was twenty minutes after midnight.

11

At 12:25, Tonio returned with his first load. During the daytime, when people were awake, it was permissible to use a handcart to trundle things through the aisles of the long train. But a sudden lurch of the train could upset a handcart and wake people up. Besides, there was much less to carry at night.

He carefully put his load of stuff away in the cabinets behind the bar, then went back to check the observation deck to see if his two gentlemen were still there. They were not. Good; everyone was asleep.

About time, too, he thought as he headed back up-train for his second and last load. The gentlemen had certainly been having themselves some sort of party, going from one compartment to another like that. Though they hadn't made much noise, of course.

Tonio Bracelli was not a curious young man by nature, and if his gentlemen and ladies gave him no problems on the night run, he was content to leave them alone.

The train began to slow, and at thirty minutes after midnight, it came to an easy stop at the check station on the Ligurian border. The stop was only a formality, really. The Ligurian authorities had to check the bills of lading for the cargo in the freight cars at the front of the train, but there was no search or actual checking of the cargo itself. It was all bookkeeping.

Tonio picked out what he needed for the second load, and then stood talking to the Supply Master while the train was stopped. The locomotive braked easily enough to a smooth stop, but getting started again was sometimes a little jerky, and Tonio didn't want to be walking with his arms full when that happened. He'd wait until the train picked up speed.

He reached the rearmost car at 12:50, took his load of goods to the bar and stashed them as before. Then he went to do his last duty until the morning: cleaning out the bathroom.

It was a touchy job—not because it was hard work, or even unpleasant, but because one had to be so infernally *quiet!* The day man could bang around all he liked, but if the night man did so, the gentlefolk in Four and Five, on each side of the bathroom, might complain.

He went up to the utility compartment, just forward of Number One, got his equipment, went back to the bathroom, and went to work.

When he was finished, he took a final look around to make sure. All looked fine until he came to the last check.

He looked at the floor.

Strange. What were those red stains?

He had just mopped down the floor. It was still damp, but . . .

He stepped to one side and looked down.

The stains were coming from his right boot.

He sat down on the necessary, lifted his right foot, and looked at the bootsole. Red stains, almost gone, now.

Where the devil had they come from?

Tonio Bracelli, if not curious, was conscientious. After wiping the stains from his boot and checking the other to make sure there were none, he wiped the floor and went out to track down the source of those stains.

"Track" was certainly the word. He had left footprints of the stuff, whatever it was, up and down on the tan floor of the passageway. The darker tracks led up-train. He followed them.

When he found their source, he lost his composure.

A great pool of what was obviously blood had seeped out from beneath the door of Compartment Number One.

12

The Irish sorcerer was brought out of his sleep by a banging that almost slammed him awake, and a voice that was screaming: *"Sir! Sir! Open the door! Sir! Are you all right? Sir!"*

Both of the men in Compartment Number Two were on their feet and at the door within two seconds.

But the banging was not at their door, but at the one to their right—Number One. The two men grabbed their robes and went out.

Tonio was pounding his fists on the door of Number One and shouting—almost screaming—at the top of his voice. Down the passageway, other doors were opening.

An arm reached out and a hand grabbed Tonio's shoulder. "Now, calm down, my son! What's the trouble?"

Tonio suddenly gasped and looked at the man who had laid such a firm hand on his shoulder. "Oh, Father! Look! Look at this!" He stepped back and pointed at the blood at his feet. "He doesn't answer! What should I do, Father?"

"The first thing to do, my son, is go get the Trainmaster. You don't have the key to this door, do you? No. Then go fetch Trainmaster Edmund immediately. But mind! No noise, no shouting. Don't alarm the passengers in the other cars. This is for the Trainmaster only. Do you understand?"

"Yes, Father. Certainly." His voice was much calmer.

"Very well. Now, quickly." Then, and only then, did that strong hand release the young man's shoulder. Tonio left—hurriedly, but now obviously under control.

"Now, Master Seamus, Sir Stanley, we must be careful not to crowd round here any more than necessary."

Sir Stanley, who had come boiling out of Number Eight only half a second later than the sorcerer and his companion had come out of Number Two, turned to block the passageway.

His voice seemed to fill the car. "All right, now Stand away, all of you! You men get back to your quarters! Move!"

Within half a minute, the passageway was empty, except for three men. Then Sir Stanley said: "What's happened here, Father?"

"I know no more than you do, Sir Stanley. We must wait for the Trainmaster."

"I think we ought to—" Whatever it was that Sir Stanley thought they ought to do was cut off forever by the appearance of Trainmaster Edmund, who came running in from the dining car ahead, followed by Tonio, and asked almost the same question.

"What's happened here?"

The magician stepped forward. "We don't know, Trainmaster, but that looks like blood, and I suggest you open that door."

"Certainly, certainly." The Trainmaster keyed back the bolt of Number One.

On Lower One, Goodman John Peabody lay with his smashed head hanging over the edge, his scalp a mass of clotted blood. He was very obviously quite dead.

"I wouldn't go in there if I were you, Trainmaster," said the sorcerer, putting an arm in front of Trainmaster Edmund as he started to enter.

"What? On my own train? Why not?" He sounded indignant.

"With all due apologies, Trainmaster, have you ever had a murder on your train before?"

"Well, no, but—"

"Have you ever been involved in a murder investigation?"

"No, but—"

"Well, again with apologies, Trainmaster, I have. I'm a trained forensic sorcerer. The investigators aren't going to like it if we go tramping in there, destroying clues. Do you have a chirurgeon on board?"

"Yes; the train chirurgeon, Dr. Vonner. But how do

you know it's murder?"

"It's not suicide," the sorcerer said flatly. "His head was beaten repeatedly by that heavy, silver-headed walking-stick there on the floor. A man doesn't kill himself that way, and he doesn't do it accidentally. Send Tonio for the chirurgeon."

Dr. Vonner, it turned out, had had some experience with legal cases and knew what to do—and, more important, what *not* to do. He said, after examination, that not only was Peabody dead but, in his opinion, had been dead for at least an hour. Then he said that if he was needed no further, he was going back to bed. The Trainmaster let him go.

"It's nearly two hours yet to Genova," the sorcerer said. "We won't be able to notify the authorities until then. But that's all right; nobody can get off the train while it's at speed, and I can put a preservative spell over the body and an avoidance spell on the compartment."

A voice from behind the sorcerer said: "Should I not give the poor fellow the Last Rites of Holy Mother Church?"

The Irishman turned and shook his head. "No, Father. He's quite dead now, and that can wait. If there's any Black Magic involved in this killing, your work could dissipate all trace of it, destroying what might be a valuable clue."

"I see. Very well. Shall I fetch you your bag?"

"If you would be so good, Reverend Sir."

The bag was brought, and the sorcerer went about his work. The preservative spell, cast with a night-black wand, was quickly done; the body would remain in stasis until the authorities finished their investigation. The sorcerer noted down the time carefully, checking his wristwatch against that of the Trainmaster.

The avoidance spell was somewhat more involved, requiring the use of a smoking thurible and two wands, but when it was finished, no one would enter that room, or even look into it of his own free will. "You'd best relock that door, Trainmaster," said the Irish sorcerer. He looked down at the floor. "As for that stain, Tonio has already walked through it, but we'd best not have any more people do so. Would you be so good as to tell the others to stay away from this area until we get to Genova, Sir Stanley?"

"Certainly, Master Sorcerer."

"Thank you. I'll put me bag away now."

13

The sorcerer put his symbol-decorated carpetbag down on the floor while his compartment-mate closed the door behind them.

"Now that's what I call stayin' in character, me lord," said Sean O Lochlainn, Chief Forensic Sorcerer for His Royal Highness, the Duke of Normandy.

"What? Oh, you mean offering to perform the Last Rites?" Lord Darcy, the Duke's Chief Investigator, smiled. "It's what any real priest would have done, and I knew you'd get me off the hook." When he did come up out of character, he looked much younger, in spite of the disguising white hair and beard.

"Well, I did what I could, me lord. Now I suppose there's nothing for us to do but wait until we get to Genova, where the Italian authorities can straighten this out."

His lordship frowned. "I am afraid we shall have to do more than that, my dear Sean. Time is precious. We absolutely *must* get that Naval treaty to Athens in time. That means we have to be in Brindisi by ten o'clock tonight. And that means we *have* to catch that Napoli-Brindisi local, which leaves fifteen minutes after the Napoli Express gets into the station. I don't know what the Genovese authorities will do, but if they don't hold us up in Genova, they most certainly will when we reach Rome. They'll cut the car off and hold the whole lot of us until they *do* solve it. Even if we were to go through all the proper channels and prove who we are and what we're up to, it would take so long that we'd miss that train."

Now Master Sean looked worried. "What do we do if it *isn't* solved by then, in spite of everything we do?"

Lord Darcy's face became impassive. "In that case, I shall be forced to leave you. 'Father Armand Brun' would perforce disappear, evading the Roman Armsmen and becoming a fugitive—undoubtedly accused of the murder of one John Peabody. I would have to get to Brindisi by myself, under cover. It would be difficult in the extreme, for the Italians are very sharp indeed at that sort of work."

"I would be with you, me lord," Master Sean said stoutly.

Lord Darcy shook his head. "No. What would be difficult for one man would be impossible for two—especially two who had been known to have escaped together. 'Master Seamus Kilpadraeg' is a bona fide sorcerer, with bona fide papers from the Duke of Normandy and, ultimately, from the King himself. 'Father Armand' is a total phony. You can stick it out; I can't. Unless, of course, I want to explode our whole mission."

"Then me lord, we must solve the case," the magician said simply. "Where do we start?"

His lordship smiled, sighed, and sat down on the lower bed. "Now, that's more like it, my dear Sean. We start with everything we know about Peabody. When did you first notice him?"

"As I came aboard the train, me lord. I saw the walking-stick he carried. On an ordinary stick there is a decorative silver ring about two inches down from the handle. The ring on his stick was a good four inches below the silver head, the perfect length for the hilt on a sword stick. Just above the ring is an inconspicuous black stud that you press with your thumb to release the hilt from the scabbard."

Lord Darcy nodded silently. He had noticed the weapon.

"Then there was his limp," Master Sean continued. "A man with a real limp walks with the same limp all the time. He doesn't exaggerate it when he's walking slowly, then practically lose it when he's in a hurry."

"Ah! I hadn't noticed that," his lordship admitted. "It is difficult to judge the quality of a man's limp when he is trying to move about on a lurching train car, and I observed him at no other time. Very good! And what did you deduce from that?"

"That the limp was an excuse to carry the stick."

"And I dare say you are right. That he needed that stick as a weapon, or thought he would, and was not used to carrying it."

Master Sean frowned. "How so, me lord?"

"Otherwise, he would either have perfected his limp or not used a limp at all." Lord Darcy paused, then: "Anything else?"

"Only that he carried his small suitcase to lunch with him, and that he always sat in the lounge on the first couch, where he could watch the door of his compartment," Master Sean said. "I think he was afraid someone would steal his suitcase, me lord."

"Or something in it," Lord Darcy amended.

"What would that be, me lord?"

"If we knew that, my dear Sean, we'd be a great deal closer to solving this problem than we are at this moment. We—" He stopped suddenly and put his finger to his lips. There were footsteps in the passageway again. Not as loud this time, for the men were wearing slippers instead of boots, but the doors could be heard opening and closing.

"I think the convention has started again," Lord Darcy said quietly. He walked over to the door. By the time he was easing it open, he had again donned the character of an elderly priest. He opened the door almost noiselessly.

Sir Stanley, facing down the car toward the lounge, had his back to Lord Darcy. Through the windows beyond him, the Ligurian countryside rushed by in the darkness.

"Standing guard, Sir Stanley?" Lord Darcy asked mildly.

Sir Stanley turned. "Guard? Oh, no, Father. The rest of us are going into the lounge to discuss this. Would you and Master Seamus join us?"

"I would be glad to. You, Master Sorcerer?"

Master Sean blinked, and, after a moment, said: "Certainly, Father."

14

"Are you absolutely *certain it was murder?"* Gwiliam Hauser's voice was harsh.

Master Sean O Lochlainn leaned back in the couch and narrowed his eyes at Hauser. *"Absolutely* certain? No, sir. Can you tell me, sir, how a man can have the whole front of his head smashed in while lying on a lower berth? *Unless* it is murder? If so, then I may reconsider my statement that I am *reasonably* certain that it was murder."

Hauser stroked his dark-streaked white beard. "I see. Thank you, Master Sorcerer." His sharp eyes looked round at the others in the lounge. "Did any of you—*any* of you—see anything at all that looked suspicious last night?"

"Or *hear* anything?" Lord Darcy added.

Hauser gave him a quick glance. "Yes. Or hear anything."

The others all looked at each other. Nobody said a word.

Finally, the too-handsome Mac Kay leaned back in his chair at the table near the bar and said: "Uh, Father, you and the Master Sorcerer had the compartment next to Peabody's. Didn't either of you hear anything?"

"Why, yes, we did," Lord Darcy said mildly. "We both remarked upon it."

All eyes in the lounge were focused on him now, with the exception of Master Sean's. The sorcerer was watching the others.

"Beginning at about twenty minutes after ten last night," Lord Darcy continued in the same mild voice, "and continuing for about an hour and a half, there was an absolute parade of footsteps up and down that passageway. There was much conversation and soft rappings at door. There were knockings on the door of Peabody's compartment more than a dozen times. Other than that, I heard nothing out of the usual."

The three second silence was broken by Sir Stanley. "We were just walking around, talking. Visiting, you know."

Zeisler was over at the bar, drinking caffe. Master Sean hadn't seen it this time, but he was certain Tonio had spiked the cup again. "That's right," Zeisler said in a sudden voice. "Talking. I couldn't sleep, myself. Had a nap this afternoon. Went visiting. Seems nobody else could sleep, either."

Boothroyd nodded. "I couldn't sleep, either. Noisy damn train."

At that point all the others joined in—the words were different, but the agreement was there.

"And Peabody couldn't sleep either?" Lord Darcy's voice was bland.

"No, he couldn't," said Sir Stanley gruffly.

"I didn't know any of you knew the gentleman." Lord Darcy's voice was soft, his eyes mild, his manner gentle. "I did notice none of you spoke to him during the day."

"I recognized him," Zeisler said. The ouiskie wasn't slowing his brain down much. "Chap I used to know. Didn't get his name, and didn't recognize him at first, what with the beard. Didn't used to wear a beard, you see. So I went to talk to him—renew old acquaintance, you know. Bit shy at first, but we got along. He wanted to talk to the other chaps, so—" He gestured with one hand, leaving the sentence unfinished.

"I see." His Lordship smiled benevolently. "Then which of you was the last to see him alive?"

Hauser looked at Jason Quinte. "Was that you, Quinte?"

"Me? No, I think it was Val."

"No, Mac talked to him after I did."

"But then Sharpie went back in, didn't you, Sharpie?"

"Yes, but I thought Simon—"

And so it went. Lord Darcy listened with a sad but benevolent smile on his face. After five minutes, it was obvious that they could not agree on who had seen Peabody last, and that not one of them wanted to own up to it.

Finally, Gavin Tailleur stood up from his seat in the rearward couch. His face was paler than usual, making the scar more conspicuous. "I don't know about the rest of you, but it's obvious *I* am not going to get any more sleep tonight. I am tired of wandering about in my nightclothes. I'm going back and put some clothes on."

Valentine Herrick, his bright red hair looking badly mussed, said: "Well, I'd like to get some sleep, myself, but . . ."

Lord Darcy, in a voice that seemed soft but still carried, said: "It doesn't much matter what we do now; we won't get any sleep after we reach Genova, and we might as well be prepared for it."

15

Master Sean wanted to talk privately with Lord Darcy. For one thing, he wanted to know why his lordship had permitted all the passengers in the car to get together to compare stories when the proper procedure would be to get them alone and ask them questions separately. Granted, here in Italy Lord Darcy had no authority to question them, and, granted, he was playing the part of a priest, but—damn it!—he should have done *something*.

But no, he just sat there on the forward sofa, smiling, watching, listening, and saying very little, while the other passengers sat around and talked or drank or both.

There was quite a bit of caffe consumed, but the ouiskie, brandy, wine, and beer were not neglected, either. Master Sean and Lord Darcy stuck to caffe.

Tonio didn't seem to mind. He had to stay up all night, anyway, and at least he wasn't bored.

Just before the train reached Genova, the Trainmaster returned. He took off his hat and asked for the gentlemen's attention.

"Gentlemen, we are approaching Genova. Normally, if you happened to be awake, you could take advantage of the hour stopover to go to the restaurant or tavern, although most people sleep through this stop.

"I am afraid, however, that I shall have to insist that you all remain aboard until the authorities arrive. The doors will not be opened until they get here. I am sorry to inconvenience you in this way, but such is my duty."

There were some low mutterings among the men, but nobody said anything to contradict Trainmaster Edmund.

"Thank you, gentlemen," the Trainmaster said. "I shall do my best to see that the authorities get their work over with as promptly as possible." He returned his hat to his head and departed.

"Technically," Boothroyd said, "I suppose we're all under arrest."

"No," Hauser growled. "We are being detained for questioning. Not quite the same thing. We're only here as witnesses."

One of us isn't, Master Sean thought. And wondered how many others were thinking the same thing. But nobody said anything.

The Genovese Armsmen were surprisingly prompt. Within fifteen minutes after the train's brakes had made their last hissing sigh, a Master-at-Arms, two Sergeants-at-Arms, and four Armsmen had come aboard. All were in uniform.

This was merely the preliminary investigation. Names were taken and brief statements were written down by the Master and one of the Sergeants, apparently the only ones of the seven who spoke Anglo-French with any fluency. Master Sean and Lord Darcy both spoke Italian, but neither said anything about it. No need to volunteer information that wasn't asked for.

It was while the preliminary investigation was going on that the two Norman law officers found where each of the other twelve were billeted.

Compartment No. 3—Maurice Zeisler; Sidney Charpentier

Compartment No. 4—Martyn Boothroyd; Gavin Tailleur

Compartment No. 5—Simon Lamar; Arthur Mac Kay

Compartment No. 6—Valentine Merrick; Charles Jamieson

Compartment No. 7—Jason Quinte; Lyman Vandepole

Compartment No. 8—Sir Stanley Galbraith; Gwiliam Hauser

Number Two, of course, contained "Armand Brun" and "Seamus Kilpadraeg" and John Peabody had been alone in Number One.

The uniformed Master-at-Arms made a short, polite bow to Master Sean. Since he was armed by the sword at his side, he did not remove his hat. "Master Sorcerer, I believe it was you who so kindly put the avoidance spell and the preservation spell on the deceased one?"

"Aye, Master Armsman, I am."

"I must ask you to remove the avoidance spell, if you please. It is necessary that I inspect the body in order to determine that death has, indeed, taken place."

"Oh, certainly. Certainly. Me bag is in me compartment. Won't take but a minute."

As they went down the passageway, Master Sean saw Trainmaster Edmund standing patiently by the door of Number One, holding the key in his hand. The sorcerer knew what the Armsman's problem was. A death had been reported, but, so far, he hadn't seen any real evidence of it. Even if the Trainmaster had unlocked the door, the spell would have kept both men out, and, indeed, kept them from even looking into the compartment.

Master Sean got his symbol-decorated carpetbag out of Number Two, and told Trainmaster Edmund: "Unlock it, Trainmaster—and then let me have a little room to work."

The Trainmaster unlocked the door, but did not open it. He and the Master-at-Arms stood well back, in front of Number Three. Master Sean noticed with approval that a Man-at-Arms was standing at the far end of the passageway, in front of Number Eight, facing the lounge, blocking the way.

Himself being immune to his own avoidance spell, Master Sean looked all around the compartment. Everything was as he had left it. He looked down at the body. The blood still looked fresh, so the preservative spell had been well cast—not that the stout little Irish sorcerer had ever doubted it, but it was always best to check.

He looked down at the floor near his feet. The blood which had leaked out into the passageway was dark and dried. It had not, he noticed, been disturbed since Tonio had tromped through it. Good.

Master Sean placed his carpetbag carefully on the floor and took from it a small bronzen brazier with tripod legs. He put three lumps of willow charcoal in it, set it on the floor in the doorway, and carefully lit the charcoal. When it was hot and glowing, he took a pinch of powder from a small glass phial and dropped it on the coals. A spiral of aromatic smoke curled upwards. The magician's lips moved silently.

Then he took a four-by-four inch square of white paper from his bag and folded it in a curious and intricate manner. Murmuring softly, he dropped it on the coals, where it flared into orange flame and subsided into gray ash.

After a moment, he took a bronze lid from among his paraphernalia and fitted it to the brazier to smother the coals. He picked up the brazier by one leg and moved it aside. Then he stood up and looked at the Armsman. "There you are, Master Armsman; it's all yours." Then he gestured. "Watch the bloodstain, here, and watch that brazier. It's still hot."

The Master-at-Arms went in, looked at the remains of John Peabody and touched one wrist. He wrote in a notebook. Then he came out. "Lock it up again, Trainmaster. I can now state that a man identified as one John Peabody is dead, and that there is reason to believe that a felony has been committed."

Trainmaster Edmund looked surprised. "Is that all?"

"For now," the Armsmaster said. "Lock it up, and give me the key."

The Trainmaster locked the compartment, saying as he did so: "I can't give you a duplicate. We don't keep them around for security reasons. If a passenger loses one—" He took the key from the lock. "—we get a duplicate either from the Paris office or the Napoli office. I'll have to give you one of my master keys. And I'll want a receipt for it."

"Certainly. How many master keys do you have?"

"For this car? Two. This one, here, and one that's locked in my office forward for emergencies."

"See that it stays locked up. This key, then, is a master for this car only?"

"Oh, yes. Each car has separate lock sets. What are you doing, Master Sorcerer?" The Trainmaster looked puzzled.

Master Sean was kneeling by the door, the fingers of his right hand touching the lock, his eyes closed. "Just checking." The sorcerer stood up. "I noticed your lock spell on my own lock when I first used my key. Commercial, but very tight and well-knit. No wonder you don't keep duplicates aboard. Even an exact duplicate wouldn't work unless it was attuned to the spell. May I see that master key, Armsmaster? Thank you. Mmmmm. Yes. Thank you again." He handed the key back.

"What were you checking just now?" the Trainmaster asked.

"I wanted to see if the spell had been tampered with," Master Sean explained. "It hasn't been."

"Thank you, Master Sorcerer," the Master-at-Arms said, making a note in his notebook. "And thank you, Trainmaster. That will be all for now."

The three of them went on back to the lounge.

There was an empty space on the sofa next to Lord Darcy—who was still playing "Father Armand" to the hilt—so Master Sean walked over and sat beside him.

"How are things going, Father?" he asked in a low, conversational tone. In the relative quiet of the stationary car, it was easier to talk in soft voices without seeming to whisper.

"Interestingly," Lord Darcy murmured. "I haven't heard everything, of course, but I've been listening. They seem to be finished now."

At that moment, one of the Sergeants-at-Arms said, in Italian: "Master Armsman, here comes the Praefect."

Master Sean, like the Armsmaster, turned his head to look out the window. Then he looked quickly away.

"Our goose is cooked," he said very softly to Lord Darcy. "Look who's coming."

"I did. I don't know him."

"I do. It's Cesare Sarto. And *he* knows *me.*"

16

The Roman Praefecture of Police has no exact counterpart in any other unit of the Empire. As elsewhere, every Duchy in Italy has its own organization of

Armsmen which enforces the law within the boundaries of that Duchy. The Roman Praefecture is an instrumentality of the Italian Parliament to coordinate the efforts of these organizations.

The Praefects' powers are limited. Even in the Principality of Latium, where Rome is located, they have no police powers unless they have been called in by the local authorities. (Although a "citizen's arrest" by a Roman Praefect carries a great deal more weight than such an arrest by an ordinary civilian.)

They wear no uniforms; their only official identification is a card and a small golden shield with the letters SPQR above a bas-relief of the Capitoline Wolf, with a serial number and the words *Praefecture of Police* below her.

Their record for cases solved and convictions obtained is high, their record for violence low. These facts, plus the always gentlemanly or ladylike behavior of every Praefect, has made the Roman Praefecture of Police one of the most prestigious and honored bodies of criminal investigators on the face of the Earth.

In the gaslight of the train platform, Cesare Sarto waited as the Master-at-Arms came out of the car to greet him. Master Sean kept his face averted, but Lord Darcy watched carefully.

Sarto was a man of medium height with dark hair and eyes and a neatly-trimmed mustache. He was of average build, but carried himself like an athlete. There was power and speed in that well-muscled body. His face, while not exactly handsome, was strong and showed character and intelligence.

After a few minutes, he came into the car. He had a suitcase in one hand and a notebook in the other. He put the suitcase on the floor and looked around at the fourteen passengers assembled in the lounge. They all watched him, waiting.

His eyes betrayed no flicker of recognition as they passed over Master Sean's face.

Then he said: "Gentlemen, I am Cesare Sarto, an

agent of the Roman Praefecture of Police. The Chief Master-at-Arms of the city of Genova has asked me to take charge of this case—at least until we get to Rome." His Anglo-French was almost without accent.

"Technically," he continued, "this is the only way it can be handled. John Peabody was apparently murdered, but we do not yet know whether he was killed in Provence or in Liguria, and until we do, we won't know who has jurisdiction over the case.

"As of now, we must act on the assumption that Peabody died *after* this train crossed the Italian border. Therefore, this train will proceed to Rome. If we have not determined exactly what happened by then, this car will be detached and the investigation will continue. Those of you who can be exonerated beyond doubt will be allowed to go on to Napoli. The others, I fear, will have to be detained."

"Do you mean," Sir Stanley interrupted, "that you suspect one of *us?*"

"No one of you individually, sir. Not yet. But all of you collectively, yes. It surely must be obvious, sir, that since Peabody was killed in this car, someone in this car must have killed him. May I ask your name, sir?"

"Sir Stanley Galbraith," the gray-haired man said rather curtly.

Praefect Cesare looked at his notebook. "Ah, yes. Thank you, Sir Stanley." He looked around at the others. "I have here a list of your names as procured by the Master-at-Arms. In order that I may know you better, I will ask that each of you raise his hand when his name is called."

As he called off the names, it was obvious that each man's name and face were linked permanently in his memory when the hand was raised.

When he came to "Seamus Kilpadraeg," he looked the sorcerer over exactly as he had the others, then went on to the next name.

When he had finished, he said: "Now, gentlemen, I will ask you to go to your compartments and remain there until I call for you. The train will be leaving for Rome in—" He glanced at his wristwatch. "—eighteen minutes. Thank you."

Master Sean and Lord Darcy dutifully returned to their compartment.

"Praefect Cesare," Lord Darcy said, "is not only highly intelligent, but very quick-minded."

"How do you deduce that, me lord?"

"You said he knew you, and yet he showed no sign of it. Obviously, he perceived that if you were traveling under an alias, you must have a good reason for it. And, you being who you are, that the reason was probably a legitimate one. Rather than betray you in public, he decided to wait until he could talk to you privately. When he does, tell him that Father Armand is your confidant and close friend. Vouch for me, but don't reveal my identity."

"I expect him to be here within minutes."

There came a knock on the door.

Master Sean slid it open to reveal Praefect Cesare Sarto. "Come in, Praefect," the sorcerer said. "We've been expecting you."

"Oh?" Sarto raised an eyebrow. "I would like to talk to you privately, Master Seamus."

Master Sean lowered his voice almost to a whisper. "Come in, Cesare. Father Armand knows who I am."

The Praefect came in, and Master Sean slid the door shut. "Sean O Lochlainn at your service, Praefect Cesare," he said with a grin.

"Sean!" the Praefect grabbed him by both shoulders. "It's been a long time! You should write more often." He turned to Lord Darcy. "Pardon me, Padre, but I haven't seen my friend here since we took a course together at the University of Milano, five years ago. 'The Admissibility of Certain Magically Derived Evidence in Criminal Jurisprudence' it was."

"That's all right," Lord Darcy said. "I'm glad for both of you."

The Praefect looked for a moment at the slack-shouldered, white-haired, white-bearded man who peered benignly at him over gold-rimmed half-glasses. Then he looked back at Master Sean. "You say you know the Padre?"

"Intimately, for many years," Master Sean said. "Anything you have to say to me can be said in front of Father Armand in perfect confidence. You can trust him as you trust me."

"I didn't mean—" Sarto cut himself off and turned to Lord Darcy. "Reverend Sir, I did not intend to imply that one of the Sacred Clergy was not to be trusted. But this is a murder case, and they're touchy to handle. Do you know anything about criminology?"

"I have worked with criminals, and I have heard their confessions many times," Lord Darcy said with a straight face. "I think I can say I have some insight into the criminal mind."

Master Sean, with an equally straight face, said: "I think I can safely say that there are several cases that Lord Darcy might not have solved without the aid of this man here."

Pracfect Cesare relaxed. "Well! That's fine, then. Sean, is it any of my business why you're traveling under an alias?"

"I'm doing a little errand for Prince Richard. It has nothing whatever to do with John Peabody, so, strictly speaking, it is none of your business. I imagine, though, that if you really had to know, His Highness would give me permission to tell you before any case came to trial."

"All right; let that rest for now. There are some other questions I must ask you."

The questions elicited the facts that neither Master Sean nor "Father Armand" had ever seen or heard of Peabody before, that neither had ever spoken to him, and that each could account for his time during the night. On being put the direct question, each gave his solemn word that he had not killed Peabody.

"Very well," the Praefect said at last, "I'll accept it as a working hypothesis that you two are innocent. Now, I have a little problem I want you to help me with."

"The murder, you mean?" Master Sean asked.

"In a way, yes. You see, it's like this: I have never handled a murder case before. My field is fraud and embezzlement. I'm an accountant, not, strictly speaking, an Armsman at all. I just happened to be in Genova, finishing up another case. I was going to go back to Rome on this train, anyway. So I got a teleson call from Rome, telling me to take over until we get there. Rome doesn't expect me to solve the case; Rome just wants me as a caretaker until the experts can take over."

He was silent for a moment, then, suddenly, a white-toothed, almost impish grin came over his face. "But the minute I recognized you, an idea occurred to me. With your experience, we just might be able to clear this up before we get to Rome! It would look good on my record if I succeed, but no black mark if I don't. I can't lose, you see. The head of the homicide division, Angelo Ratti, will be waiting for us at the station in Rome, and I'd give half a year's pay to see the look on his face if I could hand him the killer when I step off."

Master Sean gawped. Then he found words. "You mean you want us to help you nail the murderer *before* we get to Rome?"

"Exactly."

"I think that's a capital idea," said Lord Darcy.

17

The *Napoli Express* moved toward Rapello, on its way to Rome. In a little over an hour, it would be dawn. At four minutes of noon, the train would arrive in Rome.

First on the agenda was a search of the body and the compartment in which it lay. Peabody's suitcase was in the locker reserved for Lower One, but the key was in the lock, so there was no trouble getting it. It contained nothing extraordinary—only clothes and toilet articles.

Peabody himself had been carrying nothing unusual, either—if one excepted the sword-stick. He had some loose change, a gold sovereign, two silver sovereigns, and five gold-sovereign notes. He carried some keys that probably fit his home locks or office locks. A card identified him as Commander John Wycliffe Peabody, Imperial Navy, Retired.

"I see nothing of interest there," Praefect Cesare commented.

"It's what *isn't* there that's of interest," Lord Darcy said.

The Praefect nodded. "Exactly. Where is the key to his compartment?"

"It appears to me," Lord Darcy said, "that the killer went in, killed Peabody, took the key, and locked the compartment so that the body wouldn't be found for a while."

"I agree," Cesare said.

"Then the murderer might still have the key on him," Master Sean said.

"It's possible." Praefect Cesare looked glum. "But it's far more likely that it's on or near the railroad tracks somewhere between here and Provence."

"That would certainly be the intelligent thing to do," Lord Darcy said. "Should we search for it anyway?"

"Not just yet, I think. If he kept it, he won't throw it away now. If not, we won't find it."

Lord Darcy was rather pleased with the Praefect's answer. It was the one he would have given, had he been in charge. It was rather irksome not to be in charge of the case, but at least Cesare Sarto knew what he was doing.

"The killer," the Praefect went on, "had no way of knowing that the blood from Peabody's scalp would run under the door and into the passageway. Let's assume it hadn't. When would the body have been discovered?"

"Probably not until ten o'clock this morning," Master Sean said firmly. "I've taken this train before, though not with the same crew. The day man—that's

Fred, this trip—comes on at nine. He makes up the beds of those who are already awake, but he doesn't start waking people up until about ten. It might have been as late as half past ten before Peabody was found."

"I see," said Praefect Cesare. "I don't see that that gets us any forwarder just yet, but we'll keep it in mind. Now, we cannot do an autopsy on the body, of course, but I'd like a little more information on those blows and the weapon."

"I think I can oblige you, Praefect," said Master Sean.

The sorcerer carefully inspected the walking-stick with its concealed blade. "We'll do this first; it's the easier job and may give us some clue that will tell us what to do next."

From his bag, he took a neatly-folded white cerecloth and spread it over the small nearby table. "First time I've done this on a train," he muttered, half to himself. "Have to watch me balance."

The other two said nothing.

He took out a thin, three-inch, slightly concave golden disk, a pair of tweezers, a small insufflator, and an eight-inch, metallic-looking, blue-gray wand with crystalline sapphire tips.

With the tweezers, he selected two hairs, one from the dead man and one from the silver head of the stick. He carefully laid them parallel, an inch and a half apart, on the cerecloth. Then he touched each with the wand, murmuring solemn spondees of power under his breath. Then he stood up, well away from the hairs, not breathing.

Slowly, like two tiny logs rolling toward each other, the hairs came together, still parallel.

"His hair on the stick, all right," Master Sean said. "We'll see about the blood."

The only sound in the room except the rumbling of the train was the almost inaudible movement of Sarto's pen on his notebook.

A similar incantation, this time using the little golden saucer, showed the blood to be the same.

"This one's a little more complex," Master Sean said. "Since the wounds are mostly on the forward part of the head, I'll have to turn him over and put him flat on his back. Will that be all right?" He directed the question to the Praefect.

"Certainly," Praefect Cesare said. "I have all the notes and sketches of the body's position when found. Here, I'll give you a hand."

Moving a two-hundred-pound dead body is not easy in the confines of a small compartment, but it would have been much more difficult if Master Sean's preservative spell had not prevented *rigor mortis* from setting in.

"There; that'll do. Thank you," the stout little sorcerer said. "Would either of you care to check the wounds visually?"

They would. Master Sean's powerful magnifying glass was passed from hand to hand.

"Bashed in right proper," Sarto muttered.

"Thorough job," Lord Darcy agreed. "But not efficient. Only two or three of those blows were hard enough to kill, and there must be a dozen of them. Peculiar."

"Now gentlemen," the sorcerer said, "we'll see if that stick actually was the murder weapon."

It was a crucial test. Hair and blood had been planted before on innocent weapons. The thaumaturgical science would tell them whether or not it had happened this time.

Master Sean used the insufflator to blow a cloud of powder over both the area of the wounds and the silver knob on the stick. There was very little of the powder, and it was so fine that the excess floated away like smoke.

"Now, if you'll turn that lamp down . . ."

In the dim yellow glow of the turned-down wall lamp,

almost no details could be seen. All was in shadow. Only the glittering tips of Master Sean's rapidly moving wand could be seen, glowing with a blue light of their own.

Then, abruptly, there seemed to be thousands of tiny white fireflies moving over the upper part of the dead man's face—and over the knob of the stick. There were several thin, twinkling threads of the minute sparks between face and knob.

After several seconds, Master Sean gave his wand a final snap with his wrist, and the tiny sparks vanished.

"That's it. Turn up the lights, if you please. The stick was definitely the murder weapon."

Praefect Cesare Sarto nodded slowly, looking thoughtful. "Very well. What's our next step?" He paused. "What would Lord Darcy do next?"

His lordship was standing behind and a little to the left of the Italian, and, as Master Sean looked at both of them, Darcy traced an interrogation point in the air with a forefinger.

"Why, me lord's next step," said the sorcerer as if he had known all along, "would be to question the suspects again. More thoroughly, this time." Lord Darcy held up the forefinger, and Master Sean added: "One at a time, of course."

"That sounds sensible," Sarto agreed. "And I can get away with having you two present by saying that you are Acting Forensic Sorcerer on this case and that you, Reverend Sir, are *amicus curia* as a representative of Holy Mother Church. By the way, are you a Sensitive, Father?"

"No, unfortunately, I am not."

"Pity. Well, we needn't tell them that. Let them worry. Now, what sort of questions do we ask? Give me a case of tax fraud, and I have an impressive roster of questions to ask the people involved, but I'm a little out of my element here."

"Why, as to that," Lord Darcy began . . .

18

"They are lying," Praefect Cesare said flatly, three hours later. "Each and severally, every single one of the bastards is lying."

"And not very well, either," added Master Sean.

"Well, let us see what we have here," Lord Darcy said, picking up his notes.

They were seated at the rear table in the lounge; there was no one else in the car. Segregation of the suspects had not been difficult; the Trainmaster had opened up the dining car early, and the Genovese Master-at-Arms that Sarto had brought with him was watching over it. The men had been taken from their compartments one at a time, questioned, then taken back to the dining car. That kept them from discussing the questioning with those who hadn't been questioned yet.

Tonio, the night man, had been questioned first, then told to get out of the car and stay out. He didn't mind; he knew there would be no business and no tips that morning.

The Trainmaster had arranged for caffe to be served early in the rear of the dining car, and Lord Darcy had prepared the three interrogators a pot from behind the bar.

At eight o'clock, the stewards had begun serving breakfast in the dining car. It was now nearly nine.

Rome was some three hours away.

Lord Darcy was looking over his transcript of the questioning when the Roman Praefect said: "Do you see the odd thing about this group? That they know each other?"

"Well, some of 'em know each other," Master Sean said.

"No, the Praefect is perfectly right," Lord Darcy said without looking up. "They *all* know each other—and well."

"And yet," Cesare Sarto continued, "they seem anxious that we should not know that. They are together for a purpose, and yet they say nothing about that purpose."

"Master Sean," Lord Darcy said, "obviously you did not read the Marsaille newspaper I left on your berth last night."

"No, Father. I was tired. Come to think of it, I still am. You refer to the obituary?"

"I do." Lord Darcy looked at Sarto. "Perhaps it was in the Genova papers. The funeral of a certain Nicholas Jourdan is to be held in Napoli on the morrow."

"I heard of it," Praefect Cesare said. "And I got more from the talk of my fellow officers than was in the paper. Captain Nicholas Jourdan, Imperial Navy, Retired, was supposed to have died of food poisoning, but there's evidence that it was a very cleverly arranged suicide. If it *was* suicide, it was probably dropped by the Neapolitan officials. We don't like to push that sort of thing if there's no crime involved because there's such a fuss afterwards about the funeral. As you well know."

"Hmm," said Lord Darcy. "I didn't know the suicide angle. Is there evidence that he was depressed?"

"I heard there was, but nobody mentioned any reason for it. Health reasons, perhaps."

"I know of another reason," Lord Darcy said. "Or, at least, a possible reason. About three years ago, Captain Jourdan retired from the Navy. It was an early retirement; he was still a young man for a Captain. Health reasons were given.

"Actually, he had a choice between forced retirement or a rather nasty court-martial.

"Apparently, he had been having a rather torrid love affair with a young Sicilian woman from Messina, and was keeping her in an apartment in Napoli. Normally, that sort of thing doesn't bother the Navy too much, but this particular young person turned out to be an agent of His Slavonic Majesty, Casimir of Poland."

"Ah*ha*!" Espionage rears its ugly head," the Praefect said.

"Precisely. At the time, Captain Jourdan was commanding *H.I.M.S. Helgoland Bay* and was a very popular commander, both with his officers and his men. Obviously, the Admiralty thought well of him, too, or they shouldn't have put him in command of one of the most important battleships of the line.

"But the discovery that his mistress was a spy cast a different light on things. It turned out that they could not prove he knew she was a spy, nor that he had ever told her any Naval secrets. But the suspicion remained. He was given his choice.

"A court-martial would have ruined his career with the Navy forever, of course. They'd have found him innocent, then shipped him off to some cold little island off the southern coast of New France and left him there with nothing to do but count penguins. So, naturally, he retired.

"If, as you suggest, it was suicide, it might have been three years of despondency that accounted for it."

Praefect Cesare nodded slowly, a look of satisfaction on his face. "I should have seen it. The way these twelve men deport themselves, the way certain of them show deference to certain others . . . They are some of the officers of the *Helgoland Bay*. And so, obviously, was Peabody."

"I should say so, yes," Lord Darcy agreed.

"The trouble is," Sarto said, "we still have no motive. What we have to do is get one of them to crack. Both of you know them better than I do; which would you suggest?"

Master Sean said: "I would suggest young Jamieson. Father?"

"I agree, Master Sean. He admitted that he went back to talk to Peabody, but I had the feeling that he didn't want to, that he didn't like Peabody. Perhaps you could put some pressure on him, my dear Praefect."

Blond, pink-faced young Charles Jamieson was called in forthwith.

He sat down nervously. It is not easy for a young man to be other than nervous when faced by three older, stern-faced men—a priest, a powerful sorcerer, and an agent of the dread Roman Praefecture of Police. It is worse when one is involved in a murder case.

Cesare Sarto looked grim, his mouth hard, his eyes cold. The man he had been named for, Caius Iulius, must have looked similar when faced by some badly erring young centurion more than two millenia before.

"Young man, are you aware that impeding the investigation of a major felony by lying to the investigating officer is not only punishable by civilian law, but that I can have you court-martialed by the Imperial Navy, and that you may possibly lose your commission in disgrace?"

Jamieson's pink face turned almost white. His mouth opened, but nothing came out.

"I am aware," the Praefect continued remorselessly, "that one or more of your superiors now in the dining car may have given you orders to do what you have done, but such orders are unlawful, and, in themselves, constitute a court-martial offense."

The young man was still trying to find his voice when kindly old Father Armand broke in. "Now, Praefect, let us not be too hard on the lad. I am sure that he now sees the seriousness of his crime. Why don't you tell us all about it, my son? I'm sure the Praefect will not press charges if you help us now."

Sarto nodded slowly, but his face didn't change, as though he were yielding the point reluctantly.

"Now, my son, let's begin again. Tell us your name and rank, and about what you and your fellow officers did last night."

Janieson's color had come back. He took a breath. "Charles James Jamieson, Lieutenant, Imperial Navy, British Royal Fleet, at present Third Supply Officer

aboard His Imperial Majesty's Ship *Helgoland Bay,* sir!
Uh—that is, *Father."* He had almost saluted.

"Relax, my son; I am not a Naval Officer. Go on.
Begin with why you and the others are aboard this train
and not at your stations."

"Well, sir, the *Hellbay* is in drydock just now, and we
were all more or less on leave, you see, but we had to
stay around Portsmouth. Then, a week ago, we got the
news that our old Captain, who retired three years ago,
had died and was being buried in Napoli, so we all got
together and decided to form a party to go pay our re-
spects. That's all there is to it, really, Father."

"Was Commander John Peabody one of your
group?" the Praefect asked sharply.

"No, sir. He retired shortly after our old Captain did.
Until yesterday, none of us had seen him for three
years."

"Your old Captain was, I believe, the late Nicholas
Jourdan?" Sarto asked.

"Yes, sir."

"Why did you dislike Commander Peabody?" the
Praefect snapped.

Jamieson's face became suddenly pinker. "No particular reason, sir. I didn't like him, true, but it was just
one of those things. Some people rub each other the
wrong way."

"You hated him enough to kill him," Praefect Cesare
said flatly.

It was as though Jamieson were prepared for that. He
didn't turn a hair. "No, sir. I didn't like him, that's true.
But I didn't kill him." It was as though he had rehearsed
the answer.

"Who did, then?"

"It is my belief, sir, that some unknown person got
aboard the train during the ten minutes we were at the
Italian border, came in, killed the Commander, and
left." That answer, too, sounded rehearsed.

"Very well," the Praefect said, "that's all for now. Go

to your compartment and stay there until you are called."

Jamieson obeyed.

"Well, what do you think, Father?" Cesare Sarto asked.

"The same as you. He gave us some of the truth, but he's still lying." He thought for a moment. "Let's try a different tactic. We can get—"

He stopped. A man in red-and-blue uniform was coming toward them from the passageway. It was Goodman Fred, the day man.

He stopped at the table. "Excuse me, gentlemen. I have heard about the investigation, of course. The Trainmaster told me to report to you before I went on duty." He looked a little baffled. "I'm not sure what my duties would be, in the circumstances."

Before Sarto could speak, Lord Darcy said: "What would they normally be?"

"Tend the bar, and make up the beds."

"Well, there will be no need to tend bar as yet, but you may as well make up the beds."

Fred brightened. "Thank you, Father, Praefect." He went back to the passageway.

"You were saying something about trying a different tactic," Praefect Cesare prompted.

"Ay, yes," said his lordship. And explained.

19

Maurice Zeisler did not look any the better for the time since he had had his last drink. He looked haggard and old.

Sidney Charpentier was in better shape, but even he looked tired.

The two men sat in the remaining empty chairs at the rear table, facing the three inquisitors.

Master Sean said: "Goodman Sidney Charpentier, I believe you told me you were a licensed Lay Healer.

May I see your license, please." It was an order, not a question. It was a Master of the Guild speaking to an apprentice.

There was reluctance, but no hesitation. "Certainly, Master." Charpentier produced the card.

Master Sean looked it over carefully. "I see. Endorsed by My Lord Bishop of Wexford. I know his lordship well. Chaplain Admiral of the Imperial Navy. What is your rank, sir?"

Zeisler's baggy eyes looked suddenly alert, but he said nothing. Charpentier said: "Senior Lieutenant, Master Seamus."

The sorcerer looked at Zeisler. "And yours?"

Zeisler looked at Charpentier with a wry grin. "Not to worry, Sharpy. Young Jamie must've told 'em. Not your fault." Then he looked at Master Sean. "Lieutenant Commander Maurice Edwy Zeisler at your service, Master Seamus."

"And I at yours, Commander. Now, we might as well get all these ranks straight. Let's begin with Sir Stanley."

The list was impressive:

Captain Sir Stanley Galbraith
Commander Gwiliam Hauser
Lt. Commander Martyn Boothroyd
Lt. Commander Gavin Tailleur
Lt. Commander Maurice Zeisler
Sr. Lieutenant Sidney Charpentier
Sr. Lieutenant Simon Lamar
Sr. Lieutenant Arthur Mac Kay
Sr. Lieutenant Jason Quinte
Lieutenant Lyman Vanderpole
Lieutenant Valentine Herrick
Lieutenant Charles Jamieson

"I presume," Lord Darcy said carefully, "that if the *Helgoland Bay* were not in drydock at present, it would have been inconvenient to allow all you gentlemen to leave at one time, eh?"

Zeisler made a noise that was a blend of a cough and a laugh. "Inconvenient, Father? *Impossible.*"

"Even so," Lord Darcy continued quietly, "is it not unusual for so many of you to be away from your ship at one time? What occasioned it?"

"Captain Jourdan died," Zeisler said in a cold voice.

"Many men die," Lord Darcy said. "What made *his* death so special?" His voice was as cold as Zeisler's.

Charpentier opened his mouth to say something, but Zeisler cut him off. "Because Captain Nicholas Jourdan was one of the finest Naval officers who ever lived."

Praefect Cesare said: "So all of you were going to the Jourdan funeral—including the late Commander Peabody?"

"That's right, Praefect," Charpentier said. "But Peabody wasn't one of the original group. There were sixteen of us going; we wanted the car to ourselves, you see. But the other four couldn't make it; their leaves were suddenly cancelled. That's how Peabody, the good father, here, and the master sorcerer got their berths."

"You had no idea Peabody was coming, then?"

"None. We'd none of us seen him for nearly three years," Charpentier said.

"Almost didn't recognize him," Zeisler put in. "That beard, you know. He'd grown that since we saw him last. But I recognized that sword-stick of his, and that made me look closer at the face. I recognized him. So did Commander Hauser." He chuckled. "Of course, old Hauser would."

"Why he more than anyone else?" the Praefect asked.

"He's head of Ship's Security. He used to be Peabody's immediate superior."

"Let's get back to that sword-stick," Lord Darcy said. "You say you recognized it. Did anyone else?"

Zeisler looked at Charpentier. "Did you?"

"I really didn't pay any attention until you pointed it out, Maury. Of course, we all knew he had it. Bought in Lisbon four, five years ago. But I hadn't thought of it, or him, for three years."

"Tell us more about Peabody," Lord Darcy said. "What sort of man was he?"

Charpentier rubbed his big nose with a thick forefinger. "Decent sort. Reliable. Good officer. Wouldn't you say, Maury?"

"Oh, yes," Zeisler agreed. "Good chap to go partying with, too. I remember one time in a little Greek bar in Alexandria, we managed to put away more than a quart of *ouzo* in a couple of hours, and when a couple of Egyptian footpads tried to take us in the street, he mopped up on both of them while I was still trying to get up from their first rush. He could really hold his liquor in those days. I wonder what happened?"

"What do you mean?" Lord Darcy asked.

"Well, he only had a few drinks yesterday, but he was pretty well under the weather last night. Passed out while I was talking to him."

The Roman Praefect jumped on that. "Then you *were* the last to see him?"

Zeisler blinked. "I don't know. I think somebody else went in to see if he was all right. I don't remember who."

Praefect Cesare sighed. "Very well, gentlemen. Thank you. Go to your compartment. I will call for you later."

"Just one more question, if I may," Lord Darcy said mildly. "Commander Zeisler, you said that the late Peabody worked with Ship's Security. He was, I believe, the officer who reported Captain Jourdan's—er—liaison with a certain unsavory young woman from Messina, thereby ruining the Captain's career?" It was a shot in the dark, and Darcy knew it, but his intuition told him he was right.

Zeisler's lips firmed. He said nothing.

"Come, come, Commander; we can always check the records, you know."

"Yes," Zeisler said after a moment. "That's true."

"Thank you. That's all for now."

When they had gone, Praefect Cesare slumped down in his seat. "Well, It looks as though Praefect Angelo Ratti will have the honor of making the arrest, after all."

"You despair of solving the case already?" Lord Darcy asked.

"Oh, not at all. The case is already solved, Reverend Sir. But I cannot make an arrest."

"I'm afraid I don't follow you, my dear Praefect."

A rather sardonic twinkle came into the Italian's eyes. "Ah, then you have not seen the solution to our problem, yet? You do not see how Commander Peabody came to be the *late* Commander Peabody?"

"I'm not the investigating officer here," Lord Darcy pointed out. "You are. What happened, in your view?"

"Well," Cesare said seriously, "what do we have here? We have twelve Naval officers going to the funeral of a beloved late Captain. Also, a thirteenth—the man who betrayed that same Captain and brought him to disgrace. A Judas.

"We know they are lying when they tell us that their conversations with him last night were just casual. They could have spoken to him at any time during the day, yet none of them did. They waited until night. Then each of them, one at a time, goes to see him. Why? No reason is given. They claim it was for a casual chat. At that hour of night? After every one of them had been up since early morning? A casual chat! Do you believe that, Reverend Sir?"

Lord Darcy shook his head slowly. "No. We both know better. Every one of them was—and still is—lying."

"Very well, then. What are they lying about? What are they trying to cover up? Murder, of course."

"But, by which one of 'em?" Master Sean asked.

"Don't you see?" The Praefect's voice was low and tense. "Don't you see? It was *all* of them!"

"What?" Master Sean stared. "But—"

"Hold, Master Sean," Lord Darcy said. "I think I see where he's going. Pray continue, Praefect Cesare."

"Certainly you see it, Father," the Praefect said. "Those men probably don't consider it murder. It was, to them, an execution after a drumhead court-martial. One of them—we don't know who—talked his way into Peabody's compartment. Then, when the opportunity presented itself, he struck. Peabody was knocked unconscious. Then, one at a time, each of the others went in and struck again. A dozen men, a dozen blows. The deed is done, and no single one of them did it. It was execution by a committee—or rather, by a jury.

"They claim they did not know Peabody was coming along. But does that hold water? Was he on this train, in this car, by coincidence? That stretches coincidence too far, I think."

"I agree," Lord Darcy said quietly. "It was no coincidence that put him on this train with the others. It was very carefully managed."

"Ah! You see, Master Sean?" Then a frown came over Sarto's face. "It is obvious what happened, but we have no solid proof. They stick to their story too well. We need *proof*—and we have none."

"I don't think you'll get any of them to confess," Lord Darcy said. "Do you, Master Sean?"

"No," said the sorcerer. "Not a chance."

"What we need," Lord Darcy said, "is *physical* proof. And the only place we'll find that is in Compartment Number One."

"We've searched that," Praefect Cesare said.

"Then let us search it again."

20

Lord Darcy went over the body very carefully this time, his lean, strong fingers probing, feeling. He checked the lining of the jacket, his fingertips squeezing everywhere, searching for lumps or the crackle of paper. Nothing. He took off the wide belt, looking for hidden pockets. Nothing. He checked the boot heels. Nothing.

Finally he pulled off the calf-length boots themselves. And, with a murmur of satisfaction, he withdrew an object from a flat interior pocket of the right one.

It was a flat, slightly curved silver badge engraved with the double-headed eagle of the Imperium. Set in it was what looked like a dull, translucent, grayish, cabochon-cut piece of glass. But all three men knew that if Peabody's living flesh had touched that gem, it would have glowed like a fire-ruby.

"A King's Messenger," the Praefect said softly.

No one else's touch would make that gem glow. The spell, invented by Master Sorcerer Sir Edward Elmer back in the Thirties, had never been solved, and no one knew what sorcerer at present had charge of that secret and made these badges for the King.

This particular badge would never glow again.

"Indeed," Lord Darcy said. "Now we know what Commander Peabody has been doing since he retired from the Navy, and how he managed to retire honorably at such an early age."

"I wonder if his shipmates know," Sarto said.

"Probably not," Lord Darcy said. "King's Messengers don't advertise the fact."

"No. But I don't see that identifying him as such gets us any further along."

"We haven't searched the rest of the room thoroughly yet."

Twenty minutes later, Praefect Cesare said: "Nothing. Absolutely nothing. And we've searched everywhere. What are you looking for, anyway?"

"I'm not sure," Lord Darcy admitted, "but I know it exists. Still, it might have ended up on the track with the compartment key. Hmmm." With his keen eyes, he surveyed the room carefully. Then he stopped, looking at the area just above the bed where the body lay. "Of course," he said very softly. "The upper berth."

The upper berth was folded up against the wall and locked firmly in place, making a large compartment that held mattress and bedclothes safely out of the way.

"Get Fred," Lord Darcy said. "He has a key."

Fred, indeed, had a key, and he had been using it. The beds were all made in the other compartments, the lowers changed to sofas and the uppers folded up and locked.

He couldn't understand why the gentlemen wanted that upper berth unlocked, but he didn't argue. He reached up, inserted the key, turned, and lowered the shelf until it was horizontal, all the time doing his best to keep his eyes off the thing that lay in the lower berth.

"Ahh! What have we here?" There was pleasure in Lord Darcy's voice as he picked up the large leather case from where it lay in the upper berth. Then he looked at Fred. "That'll be all for now, Fred; we'll call you when it's time to lock up again."

"Certainly, Father." He went on about his business.

Not until then did his lordship turn the seventeen-by-twelve-by-three leather envelope over. It bore the Royal Emblem, stamped in gold, just beneath the latch.

"*Uh*-oh!" said Master Sean. "More here than we thought." He looked at Lord Darcy. "Did you expect a diplomatic pouch, Father?"

"Not really. An envelope of some kind. King's Messengers usually carry messages, and this one would probably not be verbal. But this is heavy. Must weigh five or six pounds. The latch has been unlocked and not relocked. I'll wager that means *two* keys on the railroad track." He opened it and lifted out a heavy manuscript. He leafed through it.

"What is it?" Cesare Sarto asked.

"A treaty. In Greek, Latin, and Anglo-French. Between Roumeleia and the Empire." There was a jerkiness in his voice.

Master Sean opened his mouth to say something and then clamped it shut.

Lord Darcy slid the manuscript back into the big leather envelope and clicked the latch shut. "This is not for our eyes, gentlemen. But now we have our evidence. I can tell you exactly how John Peabody died and prove it. You can make your arrest very soon, Praefect."

21

There were seventeen men in the observation car of the Napoli Express as she rumbled southeast, along the coast of the Tyrrhenian Sea, toward the mouth of the Tiber.

Besides the twelve Naval officers, Praefect Cesare, Master Sean, and Lord Darcy, there were also Fred, the day attendant, and Trainmaster Edmund Norton, who had been asked to attend because it was, after all, his train, and therefore his responsibility.

Praefect Cesare Sarto stood near the closed door to the observation deck at the rear of the car, looking at sixteen pairs of eyes, all focused on him. Like an actor taking his stage, the Praefect knew, not only the plot, but his lines and blocking.

Father Armand was at his left, seated at the end of the couch. Fred was behind the bar. The Trainmaster was seated at the passageway end of the bar. Master Sean was standing at the entrance to the passageway. The Navy men were all seated. The stage was set.

"Gentlemen," he began, "we have spent many hours trying to discover and sift the facts pertaining to the death of your former shipmate, Commander John Peabody. Oh, yes, Captain Sir Stanley, I know who you all are. You and your fellow officers have consistently lied to me and evaded the truth, thus delaying our solution of this deadly puzzle. But we know, now.

"First, we know that the late Commander was an official Messenger for His Imperial Majesty, John of England. Second, we know that he was the man who reported to higher authority what he knew about the late Captain Nicholas Jourdan's inamorata, certain facts which his own investigations, as a Ship's Security officer, had brought out. These facts resulted in Captain Jourdan's forced retirement, and, possibly, in his ultimate demise."

His eyes searched their faces. They were all waiting, and there was an undercurrent of hostility in their expressions.

"Third, we know how John Peabody was killed, and we know by whom it was done. Your cover-up was futile, gentlemen. Shall I tell you what happened last night?"

They waited, looking steadily at him.

"John Peabody was a man with enormous resistance to the effects of alcohol, and yet he passed out last night. Not because of the alcohol, but because someone drugged one of his drinks. Even that, he was able to fight off longer than was expected.

"Then, when Peabody was unconscious, a man carefully let himself into Peabody's compartment. He had no intent to kill; he wasn't even armed. He wanted to steal some very important papers which, as a King's Messenger, Peabody was carrying.

"But something went wrong. Peabody came out of his drugged stupor enough to realize what was going on. He made a grab for his silver-headed stick. The intruder got it first.

"Peabody was a strong man and a skillful fighter, even when drunk, as most of you know. In the struggle that ensued, the intruder used that stick as a club, striking Peabody again and again. Drugged and battered, that tough, brave man kept fighting.

"Neither of them yelled or screamed: Peabody because it was not in his nature to call for help; the intruder because he wanted no alarm.

"At last, the blows took their final toll. Peabody collapsed, his head smashed in. He was dying.

"The intruder listened. No alarm had been given. He still had time. He found the heavy diplomatic pouch in which those important documents were carried. But what could he do with them? He couldn't stop to read them there, for Tonio, the night man, might be back very soon. Also, he could not carry them away, because the pouch was far too large to conceal on his person, and if Tonio saw it, he would report it when the body was found.

"So he concealed it in the upper berth of Peabody's compartment, thinking to retrieve it later. Then he took Peabody's key, locked the compartment, tossed the key off the train, and went on about his business. He hoped he would have plenty of time, because the body should not have been found until about an hour ago.

"But Peabody, though dying, was not dead yet. Scalp wounds have a tendency to bleed profusely, and in this case, they certainly did. The blood pooled on the floor and ran out under the door.

"Tonio found the blood—and the rest you know.

"No, gentlemen, this was not a vengeance killing as we thought at first. This was done by a man whom we believe to be an agent of, or in the pay of the *Serka*—the Polish Secret Service."

They were no longer looking at Cesare Sarto, they were looking at each other.

Sarto shook his head. "No; wrong again, gentlemen. *Only one man had the key to that upper berth last night!*" He lifted his eyes and looked at the bar.

"Trainmaster Edmund Norton," he said coldly, "you are under arrest!"

The Trainmaster was already on his feet, and he turned to run up the passageway. If he could get to the door and lock these men in—

But stout little Master Sean O Lochlainn was blocking his way.

Norton was bigger and heavier than the sorcerer, but Norton had only seconds, no time for a fight. From somewhere, he produced a six-inch knife and made an underhand thrust.

Master Sean's right hand made a single complex gesture.

Norton froze, immobile for a long second.

Then, like a large red-and-blue sack of wet oatmeal, he collapsed to the deck. Master Sean took the knife from his nerveless fingers as he fell.

"I didn't want him to fall on the knife and hurt himself," he explained, almost apologetically. "He'll come around all right when I take that spell off."

The Navy men were all on their feet, facing Master Sean.

Commander Hauser fingered his streaked beard. "I didn't know a sorcerer could do anything like that," he said in a hushed, almost frightened voice.

"It can't be done at all unless a sorcerer is attacked," Master Sean explained. "All my spell did was turn his own psychic energy back on itself. Gave his nervous system a devil of a shock when the flow was forcibly reversed. It's similar to certain forms of unarmed combat, where the opponent's own force is used against him. If he doesn't attack you, there's not much you can do."

The Roman Praefect walked over to where the Trainmaster lay, took out a pair of handcuffs, and locked Norton's wrists behind his back. "Fred, you had best go get the Assistant Trainmaster; he'll have to take over now. And tell the Master-at-Arms who is waiting at the far end of the passageway to come on in. I want him to take charge of the prisoner now. Captain Sir Stanley, Commander Hauser, do you mind if I borrow Compartment Eight until we get to Rome? Good. Help me get him in there."

The Assistant Trainmaster came back with Fred, and the Praefect explained things to him. He looked rather dazed, but he took charge competently enough.

Behind the bar, Fred still looked shocked. "Here, Fred," the Praefect said, "you need some work to do. Give a drink to anyone who wants one, and have a good stiff one, yourself."

"How did you know it wasn't *me* who unlocked that upper berth last night?" Fred whispered.

"For the same reason I knew no one in the other cars on this train did it," Cesare whispered back. "The dining car was locked, and you do not have a key. Tonio did, but he had no key to the berth. Only the Trainmaster has *all* the keys to this train. Now make those drinks."

There were sixteen drinks to serve; Fred went about his work.

Boothroyd smoothed down his white hair. "Just when did the Trainmaster drug Peabody's drink, anyway?"

Master Sean took the question. "Last night, after we left Marsaille, when Norton sent Tonio off on an errand. He told Tonio to get some towels, but those towels wouldn't be needed until this morning. Tonio would have had plenty of time to get them after we retired. But Peabody was drinking, and Norton wanted to have the chance to drug him. I've seen how easy it is for a barman to slip something into a drink unnoticed." He did not look at Zeisler.

Sir Stanley cleared his throat. "You said we were all lying, Praefect, that our cover-up was futile. What did you mean by that?"

Lord Darcy had already told Sarto to take credit for everything because "it would be unseemly for a man of the cloth to be involved in such things." So Cesare Sarto wisely did not mention *whose* deductions he was expounding.

"You know perfectly well what I mean, Captain. You and your men did *not* go into Peabody's compartment, one at a time, for a 'friendly chat.' You each had something specific to say to the man who turned in Captain Jourdan. Want to tell me what it was?"

"Might as well, eh? Very well. We were pretty certain he'd been avoiding us because he thought we hated him. We didn't. Not his fault, you see. He did his duty when he reported what he knew about that Sicilian woman. Any one of us would have done the same. Right, Commander?"

"Damn right," said Commander Hauser. "Wouldn've done it myself. Some of us older officers told the Captain she was no good for him from the start, but he wouldn't listen. If he was brokenhearted, it was mostly because she'd made a proper fool of him, and no mistake."

Captain Sir Stanley took up the story again. "So that's what we went in there for, one at a time. To tell him we didn't hold it against him. Even Lieutenant Jamieson, eh, my boy?"

"Aye, sir. I didn't like him, but it wasn't for that reason."

The Praefect nodded. "I believe you. But that's where the cover-up came in. *Each and every one of you was afraid that one of your group had killed Peabody!*"

There was silence. The silence of tacit assent.

"I watched you, listened to you," the Praefect went on. "Each of you considered the other eleven one by one, and came up with a verdict of 'Innocent' every time. But that doubt remained. And you were afraid that I would find a motive in what Peabody did three years ago. So you told me nothing. I must confess that, because of that evasion, that lying, I was suspicious at one time of all of you."

"By S'n George! Then what made you begin to suspect that Norton was guilty, sir?" asked Lieutenant Valentine Herrick.

"When it was reported to me that the Trainmaster showed up within half a minute after he had been sent for, right after Tonio found the blood. Norton had been awake since three o'clock yesterday morning: what was he still doing up, in full uniform at nearly one o'clock this morning? Why hadn't he turned things over to the Assistant Trainmaster, as usual, and gone to sleep long before? That's when I began to wonder."

Lieutenant Lyman Vanderpole ran a finger over his hairline mustache. "But until you found that pouch, you couldn't be sure, could you, sir?"

"Not certain, no. But if one of you had gone in there with deliberate murder on his mind, he'd most likely have brought his own weapon. Or, if he intended to use that sword-stick, he would have used the blade, since every one of you knew it was a sword-stick. But Norton didn't, you see."

Senior Lieutenant Simon Lamar looked at "Father Armand." "With all that fighting going on next door, I'm surprised it didn't wake you up, Reverend Sir."

"I'm sure it would have," Lord Darcy said. "That is how we were able to pinpoint *when* it happened. Tonio left the car to go forward about midnight. At that time, Master Seamus and I were out on the rear platform. I was having a smoke, and he was keeping me company. We went back to our compartment at twenty after twelve. Norton didn't know we were out there, of course, but the killing must have taken place during that twenty minutes. Which means that the murder took place *before* we reached the Italian border, and Norton will have to be extradited to Provence."

Fred began serving the drinks he had mixed, but before anyone could taste his, Captain Sir Stanley Galbraith said: "A moment, gentlemen, if you please. I would like to propose a toast. Remember, we will have another funeral to attend after the one in Napoli."

When Fred had finished serving, he stood respectfully to one side, his own drink in his hand. The others rose.

"Gentlemen," said the Captain, "I give you Commander John Wycliffe Peabody, who did his duty as he saw it and died honorably in the service of his King."

They drank in silence.

22

By twenty minutes after one that afternoon, the Napoli Express was twelve miles out of Rome, moving on the last leg of her journey to Napoli.

Lord Darcy and Master Sean were in their compartment, quietly relaxing after an excellent lunch.

"Me lord," said the sorcerer, "are you sure it was right to turn those copies of the treaty over to the

Praefecture of Police for delivery to Imperial Naval Intelligence?"

"It was perfectly safe."

"Well, what's the use of our carrying our copies all the way to Athens, then?"

"My dear Sean, the stuff Peabody was carrying was a sham. I looked it over carefully. One of the provisions, for instance, is that a joint Anglo-French-Greek Naval base shall be established at 29° 51′ North, 12° 10′ East."

"What's wrong with that, me lord?"

"Nothing, except that it is in the middle of the Sahara Desert."

"Oh."

"Kyril's signature was a forgery. It was signed in Latin characters, and the Basileus reads and writes only Greek. The Greek and Latin texts do not agree with each other, nor with the Anglo-French. In one place in the Greek text, the city of Constantinople is referred to as the capital of England, while Paris is given as the capital of Greece. I could go on. The whole thing is a farrago of nonsense.

"But—*Why?*"

"One can only conjecture, of course. I believe he was a decoy. Think about it. Sixteen men all about to go to a funeral, and, at the last minute, four of them have their leaves canceled. Why? I feel the Royal touch of His Majesty's hand in there. I think it was to make certain Peabody got aboard that train with his fellow officers. It would look like a cover, as though he, too, were going to Jourdan's funeral.

"I think what happened was this: His Majesty found that the *Serka* had somehow gotten wind of our Naval treaty with Roumaleia. But they didn't know it was being signed by Prince Richard as proxy in Rouen, so they started tracing it in London. So His Majesty had this utterly nonsensical pseudo-treaty drawn up and sent it with Peabody. He was a decoy."

"Did Peabody know that?" Master Sean asked.

"Highly unlikely. If a man knows he is a decoy, he tends to *act* like a decoy, which ruins the illusion. No, he didn't know. Would he have fought to the death to preserve a phony document? Of course, being an honorable officer, once that pouch was locked, he would not have opened it, so he did not know its contents."

"But, me lord! If he was supposed to be a decoy, if he was supposed to lead *Serka* agents off on a wild goose chase somewhere else while you and I got the real thing safely to Athens—*why was the decoy dumped practically in our laps?*"

"I think," said his lordship with care, "that we missed connections somewhere. Other transportation may have —*must* have—been provided for us. But something must have gone awry.

"Nonetheless, my dear Sean, all will work out for the best. A murder aboard the Napoli Express will certainly hit the news services, but the story will be so confused that *Serka* won't be able to figure out what happened until too late."

"It would have been even worse confused if Cesare had come out with his conspiracy theory," the magician said. "He's a good man at his job, but he don't know people."

"His problem," Lord Darcy said, "is that he happens to be a master at paper work. On paper, he can spot a conspiracy two leagues away. But sentences on paper do not convey the nuances of thought that spoken words do. A conspiracy is easy to concoct if it involves only paper work, and it takes an expert to find it. But you, as a sorcerer, and I, as a criminal investigator, know that a group of human beings simply can't hold a conspiracy together that long."

"Aye, me lord," the stout little Irishman agreed. "I'm glad you stopped me. I almost told Cesare to his face that his theory was all foolishness. Why, that bunch would have given it away before they finished the job.

Can you imagine Zeisler tryin' to keep his mouth shut about somethin' like that? Or young Jamieson not breaking down?"

Lord Darcy shook his head. "The whole group couldn't even hide the fact that they were doing something perfectly innocent like assuring an old comrade that they did not think ill of him. Even more ridiculous than that is the notion that any such group would pick a train to commit their murder on, a place where, to all intents and purposes, they would be trapped for hours. Those men are not stupid; they're trained Naval officers. They'd either have killed Peabody in Paris or waited until they got to Napoli. They still couldn't have held their conspiracy together, but they would have thought they had a better chance."

"Still and all," Master Sean said staunchly, "Cesare Sarto is a good investigator."

"I must agree with you there," said Lord Darcy. "He has the knack of finding answers even when you don't want him to."

"How do you mean, me lord?"

"As he and Præfect Angelo were taking Norton away, he offered his hand and thanked me. I said the usual things. I said I hoped I'd see him again. He shook his head. 'I am afraid, he said, 'that I shall never see Father Armand Brun again. But I hope to meet Lord Darcy some day.' "

Master Sean nodded silently.

The train moved on toward Napoli.

H. BEAM PIPER

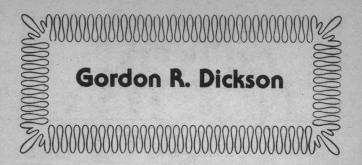

Gordon R. Dickson

☐ 16015	Dorsai!	1.95
☐ 34256	Home From The Shore	2.25
☐ 56010	Naked To The Stars	1.95
☐ 63160	On The Run	1.95
☐ 68023	Pro	1.95
☐ 77417	Soldier, Ask Not	1.95
☐ 77765	The Space Swimmers	1.95
☐ 77749	Spacial Deliver	1.95
☐ 77803	The Spirit Of Dorsai	2.50

Available wherever paperbacks are sold or use this coupon.

Fred Saberhagen

☐ 05404	**Berserker**	$1.75
☐ 05407	**Berserker Man**	1.95
☐ 05408	**Berserker's Planet**	2.25
☐ 08215	**Brother Assassin**	1.95
☐ 16600	**The Dracula Tape**	1.95
☐ 49548	**Love Conquers All**	1.95
☐ 84315	**The Ultimate Enemy**	1.95
☐ 52077	**The Mask Of The Sun**	1.95
☐ 62160	**An Old Friend Of The Family**	1.95
☐ 86064	**The Veils of Azlaroc**	1.95

145